Olympian Confessions

HADES

and

PERSEPHONE

ERIN KINSELLA

Published by Tychis Media

inquiry@tychismedia.com

Book design by Joseph Langdon

Set in FF Scala by Martin Majoor (1990)

Cover art by Renee Robyn, reneerobynphotography.com

For everyone who believed I could do this.

PART I

LIFE AND DEATH

1

HADES

"Hades, stop them!" Hera's voice rips through the chaos, sharp and piercing as an arrow through flesh. The earth heaves as I wrench my power upwards, a roaring wall of stone and soil barrelling towards those who have come to destroy us. Having grown paranoid beyond reason, our father, Cronus, has summoned together his siblings, the primordial Titans. Cronus swallowed my siblings and myself the moment we were born; afraid that we would threaten his authority and only Zeus was spared. Zeus is the youngest of us and was protected by our mother, Rhea. He is the one who freed us and consequently created the very circumstance our father feared. We follow him in honor of our liberation from that dark prison and we have agreed to make him our King if we are successful in this war. Now we battle the Titans to gain our sovereignty, fighting for the very right to exist. Zeus rains lightning from the heavens and I struggle against the blinding light to see my opponents, who only appear in alternating flashes of light and dark. The seas crash around us, raging to boiling point as Poseidon thrashes against his foes.

Shrapnel bursts around me as a boulder collides with the ground, crushing a Titan about to bring down his fists upon my spine. I plunge my power into the Earth, spiraling it up and around, snatching up Titans close by and hurling them into the roiling oceans. The waves conspire, dragging them beneath the water; caging them where they might languish in torment, their immortality forbidding their demise. Some of the Titans have sided with us, fighting by our side against the tyranny of Cronus, but most follow my father, struggling viciously against us.

Demeter forges vines from the ground, using them to strangle any who come within reach of her, subduing them so they cannot move or breathe. A few lose their heads from the force of the constriction. I rub my own throat, conscious that if I surprised her I could be the recipient of such actions. There is no death among us, but there are worse things in this world than death. Every injury that occurs will slow someone down, forcing them to fall back and heal. Our only hope is that we can deal out enough damage to weaken them sufficiently to contain them before they rise up again.

My siblings and those fighting with us all wear gold sashes, to help distinguish us from the Titans in my father's battalions. The years of battle have left our distinctive color stained by dirt and blood, barely visible in the chaos. The shrieks of fury and sound of thunder are overwhelming and I battle on, hoping that soon the end will come. Ensnared in this ritual of slaughter, I focus on breathing, in and out, not allowing myself to become distracted by the hot spatter of blood or the raging limbs that aim to remove my head from my body.

A torrent of fire races towards me and I am knocked breathless to the ground by the small, fierce body of my sister, Hestia. The eldest of us all, she is sweet and quiet by nature, but even she must tap into her skills as a warrior if she ever is to find peace. The heat makes my eyes water and I feel the flesh down my arm and back begin to bubble. Her eyes flash with power and flames erupt from her fingertips, scouring the very flesh off the one who had attacked us. I know none of their names for we flew almost immediately into battle when we were freed from the darkness of my father's belly. The scent of ash and smoke fills my nose, clouding my lungs. I press down the urge to cough knowing that any wasted moment could mean the defeat of my family. I scramble across the heaving ground, fighting on, forging ever forward into the landscape of war. Hands close around my head from behind and a sick twist leaves me limp and unseeing, the agony of separated bone searing through my spine.

I BURST AWAKE. SWEAT COATS MY SKIN and the air scrapes against my lungs. I suck in deep breaths despite the acute discomfort, using the sensation to bring myself back to reality. The silk fabric enclosing my body feels too tight and I untangle myself from the bed. The icy feel of the marble floors against my feet a welcome relief. I am safe. The Titanomache, the Great War that nearly destroyed us all, is over. My father and those who stood with him have been locked in Tartarus, the darkest and deepest part of the Underworld, for millennia. Now we are the rulers of the known world, the Olympians, Gods of immense power. Yet, even now I cannot look upon the flames of Phlegethon, that which contains the dark realm Tartarus, without remembering the flames of that battle.

I run a hand over my arm where the physical scar of the flame has long since healed, but in my dreams the vicious burning still remains. I splash water from an urn onto my face, hoping the freshness will drive away the last of the dream. The nightmare, I correct. Even now, thousands of years after we succeeded in taking power from the Titans, I cannot escape the dreams. I take a moment to survey my room. It is stark and black, composed of marble floors and walls with a bed too large for a single person. I am alone and have been so for many thousands of years, but I have created my home in the guise of a place that has a large family. The last time I shared proper companionship was when I dwelt within the belly of my father amongst my siblings. Since the end of the Titanomache, I have resided in the Underworld serving as the Guardian of Tartarus to ensure that the Titans never rise again, never challenge Olympian rule. In order to do so I have given up many things, but such things are worth the security of my family. So I tell myself, at least.

A shudder glides up my spine as I shake the images of chaos from my mind. Honestly, I am not entirely alone; not the alone that comes from lack of physical proximity to others at least. Since Prometheus created man I have become the Guardian of Souls as well. The first death brought forth Thanatos, the Collector of Souls and the Guardian of the Doors of Death. He frees the mortals from their suffering and Hermes, the Psychopompos, brings the souls to me. We three are the Keepers of Death, the Collector, the Guide and the Caretaker. They are a great comfort to me, but such intermittent companionship leaves me desiring more. Duty does not console loneliness, no matter how I might try to convince myself that it does.

2

HADES

"I am *not* dead!" The cry rings out, one that has been repeated many times before by many others. I join Thanatos and Charon, the Ferryman in Erebus, where the souls await the ferry that takes them properly into the realm. Souls sometimes do not understand that they have moved on without their bodies and require some convincing to cooperate. Thanatos guides them over the River Styx and across the outer borders of the realm, but Charon is responsible for safely transporting them across the River Acheron.

The rich scent of water and earth permeates the air, thick with moisture. I inhale slowly and prepare myself to deal with the rambunctious spirit. Charon has dealt with them in the past, but after a few thousand protests he started to tune them out and his patience runs thinner with every century.

"But you are, now get in the boat." Charon stands with thin arms crossed over a slim torso, staring down the frantic soul.

"No!" The spirit shouts. "I am not dead." Spirits, shades, souls, whatever name they go by, tend to have a profound transitional period after death. They quite easily accept leaving their body, until they arrive in the realm where they will be judged for the choices they made in life.

This spirit in particular still maintains a faded appearance of his mortal body, bearing flaxen hair and gray eyes. He is making a valiant attempt at appearing brave, chewing a trembling lip and clutching his fists firmly together in front of his belly. Fear radiates off him like the stench of a carcass left too long in the sun. He struggles to raise his eyes to meet my gaze, succeeding for only a fraction of a second before his head drops once more.

"You are in the Underworld," I reason, "so you must either be dead or an intruder to my realm."

I can see the desire to flee almost overwhelm him, a shiver rippling from his toes to the top of his head. Until souls get used to being without a body, they behave much as they would if they were still in possession of one. You can see non-existent muscles bunch in preparation to fight or flee; sweat breaks across a brow; cheeks flush red with blood.

"I am the son of Gods," he insists. "I should not be here, I should be immortal." He speaks slowly and with great deliberation.

This claim is not uncommon, given that the males of Olympus have rather prolific affairs and consequently a plethora of demigod children roaming the earth. It is far too much effort to keep track of things in the mortal world and most of the time I only become aware of individuals or events when they arrive at my own doors. Honestly, the apocalypse could occur up there and I wouldn't know until all the souls came for processing.

I request the information of his parentage and find him to be a son of Zeus and a nymph named Aegina. are vulnerable to death as their lives depend upon a single source in nature. This prevents their children from actually achieving immortality, which I convey to the spirit.

He staggers back, nearly toppling a line of waiting shades. I take a deep breath, willing myself to be calm. Immortals are not very even tempered by nature, but I have cultivated patience by necessity since my emotions are so intimately connected to the realm. If I become agitated, that energy spreads out and agitates the souls. I cannot allow the souls in my care to suffer because I lack control.

I summon two dæmons, earth spirits that have pledged their service to the Underworld, and have them escort the soul onto the boat. He struggles against Pamphilos and Aeschylus, but they restrain him easily. The other souls pile into the boat behind him and Charon ferries them all over Acheron. The rushing black water is infused with all of the misery of the mortal world. It drains away into the depths of Gaia where it is cleansed. We'd rather not have any souls topple overboard and be cleansed away along with the waters, so restraints are sometimes necessary.

I assess the situation carefully, no God has come to intervene for him, as they sometimes do for their favorites, so it seems I'm free to Judge him as I see fit. The spirit is muttering about how he needs to go home, how his family and kingdom need him. I take another deep breath and set out to root out the core of him, the part not crippled by fear.

"They will manage," I assert, "it is the nature of death and succession. If you have raised your family well they will care for your kingdom." I opt to take him straight to Judgement and have the dæmons carry him up the stairs and settle him across from me at a long stone table. I unfurl his tapestry. These tapestries are woven by the Moiræ, the Fates, and record all of the choices made by mortals during their lives. Through those choices I can determine whether they should spend their eternities in the realms of Elysium, Asphodel or Tartarus. These three realms are the holders of Paradise, Peace and Punishment, respectively.

Aeacus' most notable moment on the tapestry is when he had been selected as an adjudicator for the Olympians. Only mortals considered to be just and fair above all others are generally selected for such a role. An idea kindles and I give it a moment to flare to life. I pour Aeacus a cup of wine, the crimson liquid enchanted so that he can taste it. The fizzy texture of the enchantment tickles my throat, but it stokes the little fire. After a few sips of the drink I can see Aeacus' cheeks flush and his shoulders relax.

"I'm often running behind on Judgements, due to the vast number of souls and only myself to decide their eternities. If my kin saw fit to use you as an adjudicator, I wonder if you might be willing to do the same for me. If you, and others like you, would consent to forestall Elysium then I would employ you as a Judge of the Underworld."

Aeacus chokes briefly on the wine as he takes a large gulp. It fortifies him, allowing fear to clear so his choice can be made without extraneous emotions clouding his judgement. "It would be an honor to be of service to the Gods once more."

"Then we are agreed?" He nods and I bind the last threads of his tapestry in gold to claim him for myself. "I will have the dæmons set you up with your own quarters in the Palace and while I search for others to assist, you may begin your study of Judgement."

3

HADES

Hermes lets out a low chuckle, swirling a cup of nectar in a pewter goblet. We are on a rare break, lounging in the Great Hall of the Palace. The expansive room is detailed in black marble with a cavernous ceiling that holds glowing crystals for light. It can comfortably hold about three hundred people, but on most occasions it holds no more than two or three of us. Upon this occasion, it is only Hermes and I sitting at the long table that fills the center of the room.

"They've started on your temple, but they tremble as they work. I suspect they fear you might rise out of the Earth and punish them for laying the stonework improperly." Hermes' mischievous eyes glitter with humor against a pale face and black curls.

I cannot help the sigh that releases in a huff of breath. "They wouldn't need to fear me if they were just decent people." I mutter into my drink, swirling the sweet, fruity liquid over my tongue before setting down the cup. The emptiness of the room amplifies the clacking sound of pewter against stone.

"They look to us for guidance in morality," he reminds me. "It's a wonder that any of them make it to Elysium at all. They are right to fear you." He stretches his arms above his head, leaning his brow forward so his black curls bounce carelessly. Whipping his head back he sprawls out in the chair like a dog in front of a hearth. "I challenge you to name one of our kin that has not committed some travesty that would get a mortal barred from paradise."

"Well, Hestia never leaves her hearth at Olympus, so perhaps her." My eldest sister is the rightful heir to the Olympian throne, but she, like the rest of us, agreed to Zeus' ascension during the Titanomache. She's seemed content to tend the hearth of Olympus and has lived out her days in relative peace since then. "Otherwise I can think of none, unless there were some new Gods born that no one told me about."

"Actually," Hermes swallows down the last of the nectar in his cup, "there is one." Of course there would have been an Olympian born and I am not informed. Clearly I am not deemed important enough to alert when familial events such as this occurs. A spike of irritation flares in my belly and the sensation must have been obvious on my face because Hermes throws up his hands in a defensive posture. "Demeter has kept the poor girl locked up since her birth, even I have only recently discovered she exists."

It is exceptionally uncommon for any deity to go unknown. Traditionally they flaunt themselves, exposing their names and gifts to the mortal world and one another as soon as possible. I'm not particularly knowledgeable about Demeter. I took up my place in the Underworld after the Titanomache, and she tends to ignore the other Olympians with every fiber of her being so we have never had the opportunity to become close. I know only that she gifted mankind with the knowledge of Agriculture, and that she has one other child, a Horse-God named Arion, who was fathered by Poseidon, despite her protests. I would imagine that this new daughter is fathered by Zeus since it seems unlikely she ever let Poseidon get near her again.

"How are the mortals to know the name of this new Goddess if Demeter will not even expose her to her own family?" Demeter is denying the poor girl her entire purpose. The Gods must serve the mortals and the mortals must know their names and worship them.

"I highly doubt that Demeter cares, she has always kept to herself." Hermes heaves a sigh, rubbing at his ears. "Duty calls, and I mean that literally. Zeus is making my ears ring." Hermes is the Messenger of the Gods in addition to the role he plays in guiding the souls. It's a tiresome duty, but if he shirks it he finds no rest from his father's demands.

Hermes waves at me as his winged sandals whisk him away to Olympus. I take another few moments for myself, finishing the last of the nectar. My curiosity has been piqued by this new immortal. Despite her chronological age being quite young, she will be physically an adult by now in both mind and body as immortals have an expedited growth pattern in their early days. I wonder if this new Olympian will be any different than the others. I cannot bring myself to hope that she might treat me in a positive manner, or even consider meeting me for that matter. Hope allows you to be vulnerable and vulnerability allows you to be hurt. I don't want to be hurt anymore. I shall have to wait and see whether this cloistered Goddess manages to avoid the carelessness and cruelty that plagues so many of our kind.

4

PERSEPHONE

The rich green grass of the meadow cushions my body as I sprawl on the ground, swimming in self-pity. A cacophony of laughter wars against bird calls for who can draw the most attention. I draw my hands up and press them against my ears, seeking out a moment of peace. The wind tugs at my hair, teasing locks the color of hazelwood to dance in the breeze.

I breathe, slowly and deliberately, inhaling the scent of green. It is the sort of scent you can only find when you are surrounded by nature, wrapped in a cocoon of delicate leaves, petals and blades of grass. It all lends itself to enhance the feeling of being part of something much larger than yourself. I am a part of nothing else, so it is a comforting feeling. The meadow is my only solace, my only escape and even there I am under guard. My mother has assigned nearly a dozen nymphs to keep an eye on me when she is not around. Nymphs have always been the caretakers of young Gods, though some are more responsible than others. I flip over on the grass and burrow my face into it, squeezing my eyes tightly shut in a pointless effort to stop the tears that leak out between the lashes.

"Daughter of Demeter!" The epithet rings out, snapping through the chatter and startles me. I hastily wipe my eyes before the nymphs can see the tears. Daughter of Demeter. Sometimes I feel like that is all I will ever be. All of my siblings have wonderful titles; Lord of Light, Goddess of Wisdom, Smith of the Gods; but I am nothing. When I was first born I questioned the nymphs constantly about who was in my family and the purposes they fulfilled. My mother became uncomfortable with my curiosity when she found out and the nymphs have been silent on the subject since then. My days have been a waste of an existence, doing nothing but pretending to be pleased with my complete lack of freedom. I want to go to the mortal world, to help people as my mother does, but I have never been allowed there, nor even allowed to ask questions about it. For reasons she has never shared with me, my mother gets very agitated, almost angry, when I ask about things beyond the small sliver of the world she has given me to enjoy. I cannot even mention my father, Zeus, without provoking the same reaction.

"My Lady, what flowers would you like us to gather for your mother's temple?" Alexis inquires, tossing her golden brown hair over her shoulder. It is a casual movement that is characteristic of nymphs. They are prone to flaunting, twirling and prancing, anything that draws the eye. They mellow with age and become more reserved over time, but my nymphs are still young.

Flowers for mother's temples are the only reason I am generally allowed as far from her sight as the meadow. I grow them for her, the nymphs gather them and distribute them in the mortal world. The mortals think the blossoms are a gift from my mother, but they are brought into existence by myself and by Gaia. The Earth Goddess, my great-grandmother has been my teacher since I first set foot upon her, and she is the only other immortal I have ever actually met. Technically I have not physically met her, but I have heard her voice and felt her power as she reaches out to me. I mentioned hearing the primordial Goddess' voice only once to my mother, and promptly learned never to do so again. I am unsure if it is only my mother or the other Olympians as well, but mention of the Gods that ruled before them seems to be a controversial topic.

"Perhaps myrtle, I will grow both white and purple ones," I tell Alexis. I enjoy creating them and watching them grow, but I want more.

Alexis grins so widely I am almost afraid that her face might crack. "Wonderful, my Lady." I suppress a sigh and try to make myself savor the interaction. It is shallow and repetitive as is almost every other inter-action I have with them, but it is the only opportunity for conversation I have with someone who is not my mother and who I can physically see. I take a deep breath, digging my fingers into the grass.

'Gaia, be with me.' My thoughts are barely a whisper in my mind, but I can feel her energy brush against me. The energy coaxes my head to turn until I see Chloe sitting in the grass alone. She is the quietest of the nymphs that guard me and oftentimes can be found practicing her craft. She is quite talented at coaxing seedlings into life, but after that loses all influence. I crawl over the grass, ignoring the green stains forming on the pale gold fabric of my gown. I sprawl on the cushiony green next to her and she turns startled soil-brown eyes on me.

"Come help me grow the myrtle, Chloe." She looks intensely nervous, but bobs her head, swishing the silvery blond hair. I call upon Gaia and pick up the myrtle seeds that form beneath my fingers before tossing them across the field. Chloe breathes very carefully and spreads her fingers in the grass, muttering to herself as tiny leaves poke above the grass where the seeds had fallen. She goes red faced with the effort, but they do not grow any taller. I smile and pat her shoulder. "Rest now, you have done your part and I thank you for it."

A sweep of power sends the myrtles shooting into the air, glossy leaves and fragrant blossoms bursting into being. The nymphs shriek with excitement and scamper around collecting the flowers. They twirl as they do so, forming a dance and moving between the plants and one another in an intricate pattern.

"Persephone, my dear." I whip my head around as my mother materializes in the meadow. She draws me up and into a bone-crushing hug, pressing me into her ample bosom. Her golden skin glows like the midday sun and is just as warm. Her wheat gold hair tickles my cheek as I squirm.

I wiggle free and smooth down my hair. "Mother," I paste a smile onto my face, "I selected myrtle today, and I hope it pleases you." She nods her head and I immediately prepare to follow her to Olympus. She never takes the time to speak to the nymphs, but rather appears only to collect me and return me to my Olympian confinement.

I shake away the tingling sensation of traveling through the æther. Our private rooms in our Temple are alight with gold, white marble and vases of ripe wheat. There are fountains and streams of cool water in neat, straight paths in the marble that give the only sound. There's a small hearth that perpetually smells of baking bread and herbs, which fills my senses with delight.

Mother and I sit across from one another on plush cushions and she instructs me to relay the events of my day to her, though they are little different from every other day she has had me do this. Each word is a pinprick in my chest, adding to the feeling of discontent. She nods at the end of my story and leaves me to my own devices as she disappears into her own quarters. I hug my knees to my chest and push down the despair; the longing to be anywhere but here. Can't she see how unhappy I am? I want to be in the mortal world, assisting them by bringing fruitful trees and flowers touched by the sun, but unfortunately it does not seem to matter what I want.

5

HADES

Oh, tedium, thy name is Olympus. Despite not getting any of the perks of being an Olympian, I'm still expected to fulfill the obligations. The particular obligation I'm preparing for currently is the Hekatombaion; a large festival held every year by the mortals, but is only attended by the Gods every century or so. I would skip it entirely, but for the fact that it is really the only opportunity I have to see any of my family, though it's generally awkward and uncomfortable. Part of me wants to be included in their world, but at the same time, I desire only to retreat back into my own.

With a sigh I pull on my best robes of black silk, trimmed in violet and pinned with an ostentatious gold clasp, that Evaristus picked out for the event. He's in charge of my general care, since I tend to neglect myself when I fall into patterns of work. He makes sure I'm fed, cleaned and dressed and that I take enough breaks to ensure my continued sanity.

"You look splendid, my Lord." Evaristus grins at me, dark blue eyes glittering with excitement. "I will retrieve the matching cloak and your gold sandals." He skitters around procuring the various items he deems necessary and lays them out across my bed. Most of the time I dress for comfort with simple chiton and lambskin sandals, but I do have an impressive supply of formalwear that Evaristus keeps in perfect condition just on the off chance it might be required. He enjoys designing and I'm more than happy to allow him the freedom to do so.

I stand patiently while he straps on a belt of gold with square cut black sapphires; pins on the black and violet cloak; and arranges my hair around a crown of small gold leaves. The pomp and ceremony make me uncomfortable and no amount of finery has ever been able to undo this fact, but Evaristus insists that I must dress to fit my station when I leave the Underworld. I have little doubt that he would dress me up like this every day should I ever give him the opportunity.

"Would you like Eustathios to prepare your horses or will you be arriving on your own?" Evaristus asks as he surveys his work proudly, chest puffing out with glee. He picks and prods, tucking fabric and hair until it falls just the way he desires.

"That will not be necessary, but please tell him to exercise the horses." The last thing I want is to draw more attention to myself.

Evaristus bows and backs out of the room, giving me a few much needed moments to breathe and mentally prepare myself. The slow inrush and outpouring of air helps calm my thumping heart and soothe nerves I can already feel fraying.

My breaths grow longer and deeper, slowly releasing my physical form to the æther. I float upwards through the Earth and catch a breeze that carries me to the dizzying heights of Olympus. There I return to my body and the blazing light makes me squint. Everything here is white marble and gold, designed to reflect as much light as possible. Without fanfare to announce my arrival I, thankfully, am barely noticed.

Hera and Hebe, the Olympian Queen and her youngest daughter, are mingling and when they catch sight of me Hebe waves frantically. The exuberant girl drags her mother over to meet me and gives me a brief, friendly hug. Hebe has only met me once before by chance, but she is overtly friendly and tries to greet everyone in every situation. They are made up nearly the same, with auburn curls spiraled neatly, mother's up and daughter's down, and both are gowned in sunset pink. They both have sun-touched skin, a shimmering golden tone that makes them radiant. Hera nods politely to me, but when Hebe extends a tray of goblets towards me I can see the flare of indignity in her mother's gaze. Hebe is a Princess of the Gods, but Zeus chose to make her their Cup Bearer, a fact that constantly galls her mother. I cannot blame her for being upset. Zeus has a cruel streak and it is expressed often against his children born by Hera.

It is not my place to intervene, nor would I be able to affect any positive change should I decide to do so on Hebe's behalf. The affairs of Olympus are beyond me and I have not the time nor the inclination to get involved in their issues. Hebe is easily distracted and when she catches sight of her brother, Hephæstus, she bows her head at me and then pulls her mother along to greet him. My nephew is rarely on Olympus either. He has a tense relationship with his father and spends much of his time in his workshop among his creations. He is the Smith of the Gods and fabricates anything from furniture to weaponry to jewelry out of metal and stone. His skill is unparalleled. In fact, he is the one that made every bit of metal finery I own, including the belt and crown I'm wearing. I do my own stone crafting when the mood strikes me, but I've done little since the construction of the Palace.

"Having fun yet?" Hermes asks, swinging his arm over my shoulder as he grins at me.

"Of course," I comment dryly, "it is a wonder I can contain my excitement."

He snorts with laughter. "Go and make your rounds and then I'll see about introducing you to the newest Olympian." My jaw drops open, which prompts another burst of laughter from the Messenger God. "Come now, I know you. I saw the spark in your eye when I mentioned her. You're dying to meet her, are you not? And yes, pun was completely intended."

I do want to meet her, but I hardly desire that to be common knowledge. "Please try not to mention that to anyone."

"Of course not, I have more tact than that." He smacks my shoulder and then leaves me to weave his way through the crowd. A small part of me wants to beg him not to leave, but the prideful part of me would never condone such an action.

I greet many of my kin and my expectation of drama is not unfulfilled. Hephæstus is planning a marriage the intended bride knows nothing about, Poseidon and his wife, Amphitrite, are not on speaking terms due to his latest infidelity, Athena and Ares are shouting at one another about their armies, and the lovely Aphrodite is making a beeline for me.

"Hades, you arrive alone again." Her sharp blue eyes take in the absence of any partner accompanying me. "This has been a pattern for too long, I'm taking it upon myself to find someone for you. How would you like a pretty mortal to warm your bed?"

It takes me a moment to formulate a response beyond staring blankly at her. "Do tell me what mortal would be so willing to join with one so intimate with her death?"

She looks vaguely thoughtful for a moment. Vague is a good description of the striking Goddess as she often has the emotional depth of a puddle. She is beautiful though, her form morphs to the preferences of the viewer so she is always exquisite. "I could find someone desperate, there are mortals who are barren and lonely, or I could find someone old, they get less picky with age."

Her flippancy is appalling, but I cannot bring myself to begin an argument with her about it. "I would truly prefer to have them come to me out of love and not desperation, and love coerced by a Goddess does not qualify."

"You are too righteous for your own good. You'll never find anyone at this rate." She toys with the long golden waves of hair, nibbling at her plump pink lips. Her aura of power is magnificent, an energy that draws people to her, but centuries of controlling myself have allowed me to resist her. Mortals and immortals flock to her, even Hermes was once held firmly in her sway, but lately it is Ares, the God of War who she keeps as her paramour.

"You will have to forgive me my morals, my Lady." If there was any immortal who would understand, you would think it might be the Goddess of Love, but even she is confused by my choices. Love is the only way I will bring a woman into my life. I have no desire to take one who is desperate, coerced or afraid. No matter how pleasing a form might be, lust does not overcome fear.

"I could look for a Goddess instead," she offers, still insistent. "There must be a pantheon somewhere with a Goddess willing to have you." When I decline her offer again the softness leaves her features and her eyes become diamond-sharp. "Fine, be lonely and miserable. I have better things to do anyway." Aphrodite can be flighty and mercurial. If you don't give a favorable response she immediately seeks to coerce or she gets frustrated and bored with you and leaves.

I watch her go without any feeling of regret. She upsets easily, but recovers just as quickly. The swarm of Olympus is slowly crowding me, suffocating me under the press of foreign bodies and flaring powers. All of us together presses clashing personalities close. It's enough to start my head aching and make me long for the cool darkness of my realm. I take a deep breath and wipe the sweat which has accumulated on my brow.

"There you are." Relief pours over me, hot and potent and I sigh with pleasure when Hermes holds out a fresh cup of wine for me. "Sorry I took so long, Zeus decided he needed a message sent right in the middle of the party."

Hermes beckons me to follow him, to where I can only assume is the hiding place of Demeter and her daughter. Cloistered away from everyone they sit at a low stone table, sipping at cups of wine. Demeter's wheat gold hair is styled in a variety of braids and her daughter's hazel brown hair is similarly fashioned. Beyond their hairstyles and skin tone they bear little similarity. Demeter is in gold and green and her daughter is gowned in a rich red, the color of wine in sunlight. She shares the same radiant golden skin as Hera and Hebe, but is not quite as tanned as her mother who spends her days under Apollo's orb.

"Lovely Lady of Wheat." Hermes slides smoothly next to Demeter, making her jump slightly. "Are you enjoying the party?" She eyes him suspiciously, but Hermes has a talent for putting people at ease through effortless conversation. He has no ulterior motive to speak with her beyond keeping her engaged so I might speak with her daughter and he somehow manages to find just about everything interesting. The sincerity in his speech and face have Demeter relaxing little by little until she is speaking with him like an old friend.

As I move closer, preparing to take a seat, the daughter turns to look at me and my heart thumps in my chest. Her eyes are the most remarkable green, vibrant as new leaves. Heat floods my cheeks. She bows her head down, but I can see her watching me shyly through her lashes.

"Hades," Demeter's voice catches my attention and with surprising effort I pull my eyes away from her daughter.

"*Adelphi.*" I smile at her warmly, using the epithet for sister. I have not seen Demeter for a long time, but for the most part I do actually like her.

"This is my daughter, Persephone." She gestures casually towards the girl across from her, but her tone very clearly tells me to abandon any hope of familiarity with her daughter. Physically she is an adult, but in terms of experience she is still just a child. She seems to be handling the masses quite well, even if she does look nervous enough to jump out of her skin. She fidgets restlessly and I can sense a profound discomfort from her, but I do not know her well enough to judge what it is precisely the cause might be. She keeps glancing past us all and it makes me wonder if she wants to join the rest of the world out there, but cannot.

"I am Hades, Lord of the Underworld." I settle myself next to her.

"I am Persephone," she pauses as though unsure of herself, "Daughter of Demeter."

There is a twinge of disappointment in her words and it piques my curiosity. She has a slight tremble to her, like a filly not yet used to her legs. She picks at a pomegranate in her lap, plucking out the fleshy bits and popping them into her mouth.

"Persephone, stop that." Distracted from her conversation with Hermes, Demeter snaps at her daughter. The voice is piercing, sharply popping the girl's reverie. Persephone hastily sets down the fruit, wiping her hands on her gown. Thankfully the color of the fabric matches the juice or I suspect she would have been scolded yet again.

Persephone leans a bit closer to me and whispers, her voice hidden under Hermes' overtly loud speaking voice. "My Lord, do you not visit Olympus often?"

"I rarely come here," I say, keeping my voice low. "Olympus is not my home and I have a realm to care for."

"Oh." She reaches for the pomegranate again, but stops herself and draws her hands back into the folds of her gown. "I wish I could see your realm."

"You do?" Intrigued I lean closer. Her eyes widen in surprise and I very consciously lean back.

"Yes, but then I should love to see any realm. Mother does not let me out much." I watch her fidget with her gown and I am struck again by the brilliance of her eyes when she finally raises her head to look at me. I swallow past the lump in my throat with considerable difficulty. "Mother almost forbade me from coming today, but I am glad she changed her mind."

"I'm glad too." Persephone seems sweet, if a bit insecure, a most uncommon quality in a Goddess. "You would certainly be welcome to visit my realm if you wish." With a quick glance at Demeter I add, "I am sure your mother would show you hers as well if you asked." I stumble over the words, realizing I just invited her home. I have never invited anyone home before, not even for a casual visit to see the realm. Rein it in, Hades, this is not the girl to pursue, and Demeter will skewer you alive for even thinking about it.

Persephone shakes her head. "No, I have asked before. She said the only way to keep me safe is to keep me close, though I am not exactly sure what I am being protected from." Her eyes make me dizzy and I can feel tendrils of her soul reaching out, yearning to experience life. "If I am ever to see this world I would have to disobey her." She wants to, I can hear it in her voice and see the longing in her eyes. She wants to see everything, but fears hurting her mother by doing so. As a God I have an excellent memory, but I cannot recall ever having encountered a Goddess like her. I want to reach out and offer her these things she desires, but then it occurs to me that I am exactly what her mother is trying to protect her from. Demeter hates the Olympians, even ones so far removed as I am.

There is an odd pulsing beat inside of me, a clutching in my belly, the recognition of something in Persephone that is also inside of me.

The desire to be a part of something, yet still always being kept apart. It takes a great effort to not reach for her in that moment. Demeter would likely slice off my hands if I did so in her presence, and while they would certainly heal, that is not a pain I am eager to experience.

Suddenly, as if sensing a shift in the energy, Demeter snaps to attention and announces that she and her daughter are leaving. My heart sinks and I fear I will never see Persephone again. A moment later I feel it too, the crackle of lightning in the air and Zeus appears, clapping me hard on the shoulder. His touch sends a buzz of power zipping painfully over my skin.

"Hades, join us, we are going to the mortal world." His words are not a request. He is a man very used to getting what he wants, even if he has to resort to unsavory methods to get it.

I manage to twist a grimace into a smile and nod my head. "I will accompany you for a short while, but I should not leave the Underworld for too long."

"Nonsense, you will stay with us until the festival is over." His eyes grow dark and the color shifts, reminiscent of a thunderstorm. Zeus will not be denied.

Hera appears beside him and slips her hand over his, drawing him away from me. "My love, Hades has many responsibilities. Do not press him to give more of his time than he is able." She turns and gives me a wry smile, her brown deer-eyes radiant with suppressed power. "You will have to forgive us, Hades, the importance of your position is not always properly acknowledged."

I have always thought Hera to be a very suitable Queen for Olympus. Sometimes her temper gets the better of her, usually after extensive provocation from Zeus, but she is regal and she is wise. She knows Zeus and I have seen eye to eye on very little and spares me his presence when she is able. She elbows her husband in the ribs and he responds by swinging his massive arm around her as he crushes her to him in what looks like a rather uncomfortable hug. His bulk dwarfs her, nearly drowning her in his bushy black beard and muscular form. The intoxicating effect of too much nectar is clearly evident in his exuberance.

"Fine, you may leave, but only after you attend the party in the mortal world." Taking advantage of mortals is not my idea of a good time and spending more time with my family in the rowdier stages of the festivities is the last thing I want to do, but I cannot deny such a simple request without triggering Zeus' formidable anger.

When dawn arrives and I return to my own bed, I lie awake and think back on the night. The pulsing in my chest is still there and my head swims when I recall Persephone's magnificent eyes, but it is more than the nectar and wine that brings on those sensations. There is something there, maybe not something I can ever hope to have, but there is nothing I can do now to stop the hoping. I drift into sleep, allowing Morpheus, the God of Sleep, to cast his power over me. I fall into nightmares and unfulfilled dreams, convinced that this is my reality and only a miracle beyond the power of any God can change it.

6

PERSEPHONE

The rich earthy scent of the meadow surrounds me as I squeeze my knees to my chest in glee. My nymphs are gathered around me as the sun sets, painting the sky with soft pink, orange and lavender. They sprawl and curl on the thick grass, eyes watching me expectantly.

"It was so wonderful." I gush, heat rushing into my cheeks. "There were so many people, it was absolute, beautiful chaos."

"You must tell us everything," Zoe squeals, bouncing happily in place, red hair flailing wildly, "the sights, the sounds, the guests!"

I close my eyes, calling it to mind. "It was very loud, hundreds of voices mixed together and the air was so clear. I remember the scent of nectar, sweet and pungent and the sharper smell of the wine that everyone walked around carrying in goblets. I did not meet many guests, but Lord Hermes spoke with my mother and I got to meet Lord Hades."

The squeals are deafening as they all clamor closer. A few shoot questions at me, but most dissolve into chatter among themselves about how handsome Lord Hades is and his apparent and rather confusing aversion to nymphs.

I settle against my pomegranate tree as their conversation diverts into past conquests and the favorites they have taken to bed. Considering my confinement there is no way for me to engage in the same discussion unless I was to get involved with the nymphs themselves, but it is certainly interesting to listen to. I have no desire to follow their example though, for though they all speak of pleasure, not one of them has spoken of love. Gaia has whispered to me of love and one day I hope to know it for myself.

I have almost nodded off to sleep when suddenly the nymphs are all around me. "My Lady," Ambrosia speaks to me, her brown eyes shining with laughter, "we have been conversing and have decided that if you wanted one of us to send a message to Lord Hades, we would convey it for you."

I stare at them with wide eyes, the very idea making my heart race. "Why would I want to do that?"

"Hades is beautiful," she explains. "You are a Goddess and while your mother might not approve, if you desired to make a conquest of the Lord of the Dead, then we could distract her if she comes looking for you here." Ambrosia twists her ebony hair as she speaks, catching the sun in tiny flares of light.

Heat rushes up my chest and flares over my cheeks. "I have no desire to make a conquest of anyone." Part of me is terrified of the whole concept. Lord Hades is like a piece of a dream and it could all fall away if I pursued such a thing.

Eumelia tucks her legs under her rump and settles in front of me. "Would it surprise you to know that we wish you had more freedom? We do not agree with the restrictions your mother has placed upon you and while we cannot oppose her openly, we may still offer to assist you without her direct knowledge."

Myrrine snuggles herself up against Eumelia, matching heads of brown curls blending together. "Is there truly no one? No God or mortal that has captured your fancy?"

"I have met no mortals and barely any Gods, and I am young yet, must there be someone?" Images of dark eyes fill my thoughts, and with some effort I push the visage of Lord Hades from my mind. Tears prick the back of my eyes as I do so, but I squash down the feeling of loss. Lord Hades is the first God I've met; the first to take even a minuscule interest in me.

"No, but you would be a minority among the Gods if there truly is no one," Tryphosa answers.

My words freeze in my throat. I want there to be someone, not necessarily a lover, but someone who will reach out to me and share experiences I am so consistently denied. When I think of asking Mother to show me the world beyond here I think only of her eyes snapping with fury as they had done last time I asked. She questions me about why I want to leave, who told me there was even anything beyond what she has shown me already and why I do not love her enough to simply be content with what she has offered to me. I want a companion who will show me something of the world outside of this meadow, outside of Olympus.

"I love my mother and whatever our differences may be, I do still want her to be happy." Part of me wonders if she feels the same, if she wants me to be happy as well. Every request I have made beyond coming to this meadow has been denied and further requests are met with quick and decisive anger. "I am not so selfish that I would put my whims above her happiness, not when I know it would cause her pain."

"Freedom and happiness are not whims, my Lady," Chloe whispers. "They are your rights and you should be free to seek them out."

I sniff back my tears. They do not understand, they may go where they wish, see whomever they desire. They do not understand that

Mother will not let me do that and they have not felt the fear and confusion to see my usually sweet mother turn on me with rage in her eyes and shut me down. The concept seems so foreign, but maybe Chloe is right. I deserve the same freedom as all of my Godly kin and perhaps one day I will be brave enough to take it.

7

HADES

"My Lord," Anaxagoras, one of the dæmons that monitor Erebus, approaches me as I survey a tapestry for Judgement. "We have found another soul that might suit the position of Judge for you."

It takes me a moment to shift my focus. My mind rarely wanders, but I have been struggling to keep it focused on work as it's developed a distracting habit of returning to the Hekatombaion. "Of course, I will be there in a moment."

I complete the judgement, sending another soul for Asphodel's peace, and head over to our proverbial waiting room, Erebus. Thanatos is speaking to a plump soul that looks to have died at a rather advanced age. Thanatos nods to me when I come into his line of sight and the soul bows deeply.

"Hades, this is Minos, previously the King of Crete." Thanatos ushers the spirit towards me. "I do believe that he is a brother to your current Judge."

The aforementioned being appears on the opposite shore of Acheron, excitedly calling out. "Minos, oh brother, I've missed you."

Aeacus has adjusted well to his station, taking on a corporeal form of a fit youth with curling blond hair and arresting gray eyes. I bring Aeacus across the rushing black waters and the two brothers embrace. Souls retain the form they were most comfortable with, which means Minos was very attached to his aged body, but his brother was more comfortable in the body of his youth. They look more like grandfather and grandson, but Aeacus must remember what Minos looked like in life.

"Come, we will take Minos through Judgement and determine whether or not he will be suitable for my purposes."

We bid Thanatos farewell and I bring Minos and Aeacus to the Towers where I unfurl the exceptionally long tapestry of Minos' life. I read over the points; son of Zeus and Europa, King of Crete, creator of their navy and an all-around exceptional ruler. He somehow managed to gather the esteem of both Gods and mortals, which is rather rare. Often the personality types that impress the Gods are big, bold and insensitive to the needs of others; and they are generally glory hounds who focus on power and prestige. Men like Aeacus and Minos were born to power, yet rather than reaching for more they focused on care and justice, dedicating their lives to the service of others.

As I reach the end of his tapestry, I relay a question that had popped into my head when I first saw him. "Why were you not afraid of Thanatos?"

Minos shrugs. "I was quite old when he came for me. My bones ached and it was becoming harder to breathe properly. My children were grown and I know my son will be a good ruler. I had no fear of death and am pleased to be released from my withering body."

Minos had the luxury of a long life to reconcile himself to his death, but not all mortals do. It is still admirable that he was able to do so. Too often mortals fear the beyond, fear their eternity, but Minos has the confidence of a man with a life well lived behind him. I explain the concept of the Judges to him and offer him the position.

"I would be honored to be of service to you, Lord Hades." Minos clasps his hands over his belly and watches me intently.

I bind the end of his tapestry in gold and roll it up to be archived with the others. "Evaristus," the dæmon appears immediately, "please show Minos to his new quarters."

"Of course, my Lord." He bows politely and holds out his hand to Minos. "Follow me, please."

After they are out of sight Aeacus turns to me. "When will we take over Judgement, my Lord?"

"Soon, I hope. I would prefer there be three of you so you may take counsel from one another. You are both capable based on your mortal lives, but I still wish you to all be completely comfortable with your duties before you take on the task without my direct supervision. For now you will both sit with me while I continue my duties and observe. "

Aeacus nods. "You are right to be cautious with the care of your realm, my Lord, as we would have been with our own kingdoms."

8

HADES

The barrenness of the Great Hall overwhelms me sometimes. Every sound echoes off the stone and the glowing crystals in the ceiling never seem to reach the edges of the darkness. I reach up and pull more crystals through the Earth and give them a punch of power so they shine like stars against the black. Light makes all the difference considering my realm dwells in the depths of Gaia.

Hermes has his face in hands, elbows resting on the black stone table. I brought Hermes and Thanatos in here so we might speak. I pour them each wine and set the cups before them.

"Hera is in an uproar." He sighs, his shoulders slumping even further. "Zeus has fathered three new bastards and made a great show of it. He knew the pregnancy would have the girl cast out of her family and that the birth of triplets would kill her. He made the selective choice to father three on her at once just to see if he could."

I cannot stop the sigh that escapes me. Her soul must be awaiting us now. She is not the first mother of a demigod to find herself here much sooner than anticipated. As dangerous as mortal births are, divine ones are even worse for the mothers. The children grow faster and their bodies have a difficult time keeping up, not to mention that they are carrying around Olympian power in their bellies and too much divine energy in a mortal body tends to make their minds unstable. She is only one of many that suffer for the choices of the Gods and Zeus has a long list of women who have experienced destruction by his hand. Hera and Apollo have done what they could to help, from what the souls have relayed, but they're not able to keep up with the demand.

"Does Zeus care so little for the well-being of these women?" Thanatos asks, "His children will grow up without a mother, without any family to speak of. What sort of life is that for children?"

Hermes raises his head, dragging his fingers through his hair. "Hera is furious with him for being so callous. I know many immortals take less care than they should, but he goes beyond general carelessness and moves into cruelty. It is terrible to watch. Hera is hurting, it is not only the mortals and his children that face his brutality. He flaunts those other women in front of her and it's nothing but a plot to get a reaction out of her. He uses the mortals as toys to see how far he can push her."

I take a gulp of wine as though the liquid might help make sense of his actions. Was he born cruel or did something happen in his early days none of us know about that caused his compassion to desert him? "Hera is a devoted and beautiful companion, one that he fought very hard to get. He does them all a disservice to behave as he does."

"Perhaps the intrigue was gone for him after she agreed to be his wife," Hermes suggests.

"She never agreed, not willingly, but perhaps he does not tell his children that story. Zeus cares only for his own pleasure." Thanatos slams down his cup, the clacking sound echoing in the chamber. Thanatos is rarely angry, but some things strike a chord in him and he cannot stay silent. He shoves at the chair and begins to pace, black robes and wings flaring out behind him as he ghosts from one end of the hall to the other. "There are too many mortal men who treat their women as Zeus does Hera and the mothers of his children. He should think more on his actions when he knows how the men idolize and worship him. I am tired of collecting the souls of women who take their own lives or suffer their last days in misery because of his games."

I nod in agreement. "Many tapestries of those women show that they were imprisoned much of their lives due to prophecies of their children rising up and destroying their grandfathers. Zeus still manages to get to them and then they birth demigods, are treated poorly through much of their remaining days and are generally immediately forgotten by the Gods. I wonder if he seeks them out specifically to fulfill the prophecies. He should be more mindful of them considering the Titanomache was caused by one. He knows fathers and grandfathers of divine children are fearful of being overthrown."

Hermes looks uneasily at the ceiling. He grips his cup so hard his knuckles turn white. "I am grateful to him for my life, but sometimes I hate him." He shakes his head and snatches up the wine Thanatos had set down, draining the contents. Hermes is usually so upbeat and I find it disconcerting when he slides down this slope of outrage. He shivers head to toe and his expression softens. "Distract me, give me something more pleasant to think of." His bright eyes find mine. "Persephone, you never told me what you thought of her."

Thanatos stops short and raises his eyebrow in question. "Persephone?"

"Demeter's new daughter." Hermes turns to him briefly before refocusing his attention on me.

I take a few moments to consider a proper adjective to describe her. "She was intriguing."

Hermes laughs. "Intriguing? She is beautiful and the sweetest thing I have seen on Olympus in a millennia. Are you going to see her again?"

"Why would she want to see me again?" As a general rule no Olympian wants to see me unless there is something I can do for them. I am not eager to find out what favor Persephone will request of me before disappearing again. There is no reason for me to believe she is any different from the rest of them.

"Well," Hermes considers, "unless Demeter has been feeding her false stories, she will not have formed any prejudices against you. You both spoke pleasantly as far as I could tell so that must mean she found the experience at least minimally agreeable. So, tell me, why would she not want to see you again?"

"Hermes does have a point," Thanatos smirks at me. "Stop looking like a startled cat," Thanatos chides. I imagine that his words only make me look all the more startled. "You have as much right to companionship as any, why should it not be with someone as lovely as this Goddess you are speaking of?"

"Talk to her," Hermes insists, "she will not be under Demeter's power forever."

9

PERSEPHONE

A sharp pain in my foot makes me gasp as I collapse to the ground. Half the nymphs are napping and the others are playing some sort of game with a string so they take no notice of me. The dense meadow grass cushions my fall, but there is still an ache from the impact. I stare petulantly at the stone that tripped me. The dappled sunlight through the leaves makes the stone glimmer and I realize belatedly that it's faceted. Curious, I crawl over to it and rest my fingers on the smooth surface.

I've never seen such a thing before and it seems so at odds with the rugged nature of the meadow. I'm profoundly fascinated by the skill that has gone into creating something so delicate and complex out of stone. It's a deep purple color, shot through with white and gold. A gentle pulse, like a heartbeat, emanates from the rock, rebounding against my palms and fingers pressed to the surface. I scoot closer, and gaze into the center, marveling at the pulsing energy. It thrums stronger with each second I keep my skin to it. I press a cheek to the stone, enjoying the sensation of the energy rippling through me, trailing down through my arms and legs to my feet. It feels similar to the power Gaia emanates, but distinctly different.

"Persephone." I catapult away from the stone and topple myself backwards. I glance around, but see no one. A quick walk through the surrounding woods reveals no other source of the voice either. Could it have come from the stone itself? Curiosity overwhelms me, and, with a quick glance to ensure that my nymphs are still not paying attention, I let my fingers drift back to the stone.

"Yes?" My heart pounds in my chest, propelled by a thrill of anticipation.

"Are you still interested in seeing my realm?"

I stare for a moment before realization dawns on me. My hands grip the stone like a lifeline. I can feel my heart rapping ever harder in my chest. There is a stab of glee in my belly at the thought that someone who'd met me wants to pursue further contact. Mother always told me that the Olympians would never be interested in speaking to me even if I were allowed to do so. I never tried, fearing those words to be true, but maybe she is wrong. "Lord Hades?"

The stone shivers, almost like a laugh. "Yes, I am afraid I must apologize, I should have mentioned that first."

A little flame of hope kindles to life in my chest as whispers of freedom and adventure fill my mind. Then I feel guilty; I don't want to use Lord Hades to fulfill my selfish desires.

"That's perfectly all right. I figured it out. I would love to see your realm." I bite my lip, knowing what my mother will say. She will never let me go. I need help with this and the nymphs offered before. "One moment, please."

I fly away from the stone and nearly trip over Chloe, who was napping in the grass, in my haste to get to the nymphs. Excitement and panic are vying for control and both quickly overwhelm me with their combined force. "Tryphosa!"

"My Lady?" She and the others turn to look at me, faces creased with concern.

"I've changed my mind about Lord Hades." The look of glee that instantly fills their faces almost makes me want to retract the statement. I swallow down my nervousness. "I do *not* mean to make a conquest of him, I'm merely accepting his offer to visit."

"Shall we send a message?" Tryphosa asks, bouncing with joy among the throng of nymphs.

I chew my lip and fidget a few moments before working up the nerve to speak. "There is no need, he's sent me one himself." They all clamor over one another to hug me, squealing in my ear.

"Girls!" Chloe snaps in a rare display of aggression. "We have to think about this clearly. Lady Demeter will flay us if she finds out about this. It cannot be done now, we will have to organize another time for Lady Persephone to sojourn in the Underworld." She turns to me. "Will he wait for you?"

I had not thought to ask and tell them so. They immediately start to shove me back in the direction from which I had come, asking where he is. "He's not physically here, he is speaking through a stone."

"Why is he talking through a rock?" Eumelia asks, quirking her head to the side, hands on her hips.

"Lord Hades is the Lord of the Underworld and sovereign of all precious stones found in the earth," Chloe states, "it makes sense that he would also be able to use them to communicate if he so desired."

I let them shove at me until we reach the stone and I settle myself before it, placing my hands upon it. The energy ripples up like a cool breeze on my skin, a gentle and pleasant hum to let me know there is still a connection.

"I've spoken with my companions," I start to speak, but he interrupts me to ask who I told. His voice sounds panicked. "Just my nymph companions. They won't say anything to anyone, I promise." Does he not want anyone to know about us speaking? Is he ashamed of it? Questions bounce around in my mind, but I push them away. I'll give him the benefit of the doubt for now. I forge on ahead, though my tongue feels thick with nervousness. "We can coordinate a visit in the future when my mother is less likely to notice my absence." I have to admit that talking to a stone while surrounded by a dozen nymphs is the oddest experience in my life thus far. They crowd close to listen, pressing against my back and sides.

"My Lord Hades," Eumelia calls out, "wouldn't you rather one of us visit you?" She lets out a squeal as she is literally thrown out of the group.

"Don't be so rude, Eumelia," Melissa chides. "If Lord Hades wanted a nymph in his bed he would have asked one."

A cough rises discretely from the stone. "Actually, I only meant to speak with her, I had no plans on bedding her."

"Lord Hades," Eutychia calls out, "why must you be so cruel?"

I stare at them uncomprehending and make shushing motions, but they are not even paying attention to me anymore. "What cruelty have I committed?" The stone asks.

The nymphs titter and another voice mutters, "So like a male." A number of heads nod in agreement.

"Do you not find her attractive?" Charis inquires.

"Well, she is beautiful." Lord Hades begins and I feel my cheeks flush.

"Why then would you not want to take her to bed?" Alexis interrupts him.

I wonder if Lord Hades is as wildly uncomfortable as I am right now. I wave a hand to shush them again, but they are already moving away from me, talking among themselves, buzzing like a hive of bees in their flurry of conversation.

I scoot close and whisper to the stone, my face barely an inch away. "Lord Hades, I believe it would be better if we spoke another time."

"Yes, I would say so. Take this." I watch in fascination as a red stone on a gold chain burrows itself out of the ground next to my knee. I snatch it up and tuck it into my gown before the nymphs can see. He bids them all farewell.

"Goodbye Lord Hades!" They chorus excitedly.

Aspasia giggles and grabs my hand as she forcefully twirls me in a circle. "My Lady, you are so lucky to have caught the eye of Lord Hades. He is so handsome, truly a King among Gods."

"Hush, Aspasia, or your words may reach my father's ears." I correct her automatically, having been told that Gods, my father most of all, can be temperamental about potential insult.

Her eyes grow wide, a bone-deep terror reflecting there as she drops my hand, pressing her fingers to her lips. "Hail Lord Zeus, King of the Gods, Ruler of Olympus."

Her words are whispered in reverence, but I feel a tightening in my stomach at seeing her fear. I've never met my father before, only seen him at a distance and he had a fearsome energy about him then. I have heard whispered rumors on the wind. The tales of him are that he is both volatile and amorous. It is a terrible combination if you are the one he wants or happen to be standing in the way of what he desires. Some might imagine it to be an honor to be chosen by the King of Gods, but I imagine many more hope that his stormy eyes never fall upon them.

10

HADES

I rub at my cheeks, unaccustomed to the sensation of blushing. Alone in my chambers I was able to hide the conversation from the others, but discomfort still permeates me. I'm unsure if that interaction could have been any more embarrassing. I should have assumed that she would be under some sort of guard with how Demeter hovered over her. I would love to contact her when she's away from the nymphs, but I have no way of knowing when that might be. The ruby pendant I had sent to her should help matters as it is a smaller version of the speaking stone, assuming she figures out how to use it. In my haste to avoid the nymphs I had neglected to provide any instruction, but mayhap she will determine it on her own. I do not want to risk using it to contact her myself when she might be next to her mother.

"So, how did it go?" Evaristus pokes his head in the door, sleek black hair sweeping across his brow. His eyes sparkle with anticipation, eager for a story.

"I spoke to her for less than two minutes and was propositioned in that time."

His eyes widen as he bursts into laughter. "I was not aware Lady

Persephone was so bold. The way you spoke of her I expected her to run at the mere mention of relations."

"Not her," I correct, "the nymphs were there."

"Oh my, they are not known for their discretion," he nods sagely.

Overcome for a moment, I sink to the floor. "I don't think this is a good idea. I worry she will be bored or repulsed by our home after the brightness and grandeur of Olympus. What could we possibly have in common?"

Evaristus settles himself next to me, unusually calm. "You know," he says slowly, "one day you are going to have to accept that you are a genuinely good person and that someone is going to see that in you. Obviously you're not as bad as you think or you would not have instilled the loyalty of the dæmons. We follow you by choice, because you treat us well and listen to us when we have something to say to you."

"Thank you," I sigh. "I cannot shake the feeling that something unpleasant is going to happen if I pursue Persephone, but I feel equally unable to stop myself from doing it anyway. I'm not sure what I even hope to gain from seeing her."

All I know is there is a long buried need for acceptance and deep companionship that is churning inside of my belly, demanding I move forward. I had shoved it down for so long that I had almost forgotten it was there. Almost.

Evaristus shrugs. "What we all hope to gain, I suppose. I think you've guarded yourself for a long time and you see Lady Persephone as a potential source of love and acceptance, but also see it, and her as something unattainable for yourself. Try not to paint her with the same brush as the rest of your kin. Let her surprise you."

"What right do I have to pursue someone like her?"

"The same right as any," Evaristus insists. "If she liked you enough to accept your invitation then I would suggest that you simply relax and go with the flow. Lady Persephone is young and I can hope that she has not adopted the guile that so many wear as a second skin. If she is speaking with you then I must assume it is because she enjoys doing so."

I take a deep breath and rub my hands over my face. "When did you get so wise?"

"With age, comes wisdom," he shrugs, "or so I am told."

The unpleasant possibilities and realities of Olympian relationships swarm in my head. "The marriages of Olympus do not exactly inspire optimism." I comment dryly.

"Who said anything about marriage?" Evaristus asks, a smirk twitching up the corner of his mouth. He pats my arm, hopefully out of comfort and not pity. "You have already worked yourself up into a state over simply talking to the girl. I would sincerely fear how you would react if there was a marriage involved. Remember, my Lord, you are not your brothers."

11

HADES

Hermes plummets to the ground in front of me. I jump sharply and nearly yank the tapestry off the table to steady myself. He grins at me and the souls stare curiously up at the Tower of Judgement, wondering at his sudden appearance. They mill about in a sea of muted colors, waiting for their allotted time for Judgement to come.

"Mail time, someone is getting married." He passes over a golden scroll, which I accept and unfurl.

I stifle my automatic response of annoyance. "Who?"

"Thetis and Peleus." He answers flatly, clearly not pleased by the situation. Seeing my blank expression, Hermes explains further. "She's one of the daughters of Nereus and Peleus was an Argonaut on the voyage for the Golden Fleece."

"Please explain to me why the wedding of a sea nymph and a mortal is an Olympian event."

"You are so out of the loop," Hermes chides me. "You need to hang out on Olympus more."

"I have you so I can avoid that." I remind him and he huffs out a breath that whips the jet colored locks out of his eyes.

"Zeus learned of a prophecy that said the son of Thetis would become greater than his father. You know how paranoid Zeus is about being dethroned." I nod as I listen to Hermes explain. Our family has a history of sons deposing fathers with Cronus ousting Uranus and Zeus ousting Cronus. Logically he is next in line to be dethroned, but he's terrified of the prospect. "Anyway, Zeus was planning on just having his way with Thetis, but he seems to be afraid of fathering a child with her. Poseidon wants Thetis as well, but he too fears the prophecy. It would appear they figure the best way to avoid the prophetic issues would be to marry her to a mortal and then when she is good and pregnant they can do as they please with her. As you can imagine, Thetis is not overly impressed by this whole ordeal."

"Nor should she be. It is unacceptable on every level." Being a target of Zeus is bad enough, but Poseidon being involved makes things doubly miserable for her. If the stories are to be believed he is no kinder with his women than Zeus is with his. Still, Thetis is a sea nymph, she is subject to both Poseidon and Zeus as Poseidon rules the Seas in which she lives and Zeus is Poseidon's King. There's no way for her to get out of it, nowhere to run.

"Peleus is not so bad," Hermes explains, "he is son to your Judge, Aeacus."

"Her father must be furious over this arrangement," I point out.

"Oh, he is, but there's nothing he can do about it. He's not so stupid as to confront Zeus and Poseidon over this. He cannot shelter his daughter in Poseidon's realm. She needs the sea to live and there's nowhere there she can hide. Honestly, short of someone staging an uprising, no one can do anything to help her."

"Do the men in our family not grasp the concept of simply asking a woman to bed with them? There are plenty out there, if they are denied there will be another somewhere that will have them. Why force someone who is unwilling? It baffles me that they feel this need to resort to trickery and abuse when they could simply be kind and show love."

"You and I both know they will never be convinced that their actions are wrong. Now, are you going to come to the wedding or not?"

The truth of his statement angers me. Gods are so blind to their own faults, yet so quick to judge them in others. Manipulating the life and free will of another being is wrong, but Zeus and Poseidon are blinder than most and refuse to see that. "Would they notice if I did not?"

Hermes gives me a dubious look. "You know they would. They could hardly care less most of the time, but if you try to shirk your duties attending Olympian events you will certainly find someone beating down your door over it."

"Very well, I will attend." I accept with a feeling of deep unease.

"Thetis may grow to love Peleus in time," Hermes offers. It's only words to bury the unease of the situation, but I can understand why he needs them.

I shoot him a look of incredulity. "I very much doubt that Thetis will do anything but loathe Peleus for the rest of his days."

Hermes only shrugs. "I'll see you at the wedding, but I must be off now."

This wedding is going to be a disaster. I can only imagine the misery it will create.

12

PERSEPHONE

I've been beyond joy since we received an invitation to the wedding of Thetis and Peleus. My cheeks are exhausted from smiling, but I can't stop. I pour over the invitation again, sitting nestled in my own chambers on Olympus. A thick cushion props my back while I trail my toes in the stream that bisects my room.

I have never been to a wedding before, but the idea seems so lovely. A celebration of love between two people, supported by their families and expressed to the world. In the mortal world I have heard that weddings are more a transaction of goods, but since the Gods do not require food or things of monetary value they are free to pursue love matches.

I tuck the scroll away and fidget while I wait for Chloe to arrive to style my hair for the wedding. On a lark I pull out the ruby pendant, the stone that had burrowed out the earth at my last interaction with Lord Hades, and examine it. When I had washed away the dirt clinging to it I realized it is made of bright rubies set in gold and it forms the shape of a half peeled pomegranate, with the flesh made of crushed ruby and enamel. I slip the gold chain attached to it over my head and settle it against my chest below the hollow of my throat.

The chiton mother chose for me is golden fabric, shot through with gold fibers to make it glimmer in the light. It makes my skin look even warmer and is a beautiful combination with the pendant.

Chloe arrives and sets immediately to work, plaiting my hair in sections and spiraling them around to be speared with flowers the color of sunshine. My mother arrives while Chloe is at work and her eyes are immediately drawn to the necklace.

"Where did you get this?" She asks, and I cobble a lie about having had Chloe commission it from Lord Hephæstus for me for the wedding. Chloe glances at me from the corner of her eye while she combs the length of my hair. I smile brightly to hide my discomfort over using her as my cover and in lying to my mother. I don't want her to know where it came from or that it was a gift for fear that she might take it or become angry with Lord Hades. Mother runs her finger over it and gives me a small smile. "It suits you."

Seeking to distract myself from the guilt weighing me down, I inquire as to the gift we're bringing to the wedding. "I don't want to give them anything, under the circumstances, but I will be providing the wedding feast."

"Given what circumstances?" Curiosity fills me to bursting, but I bite my tongue when my mother narrows her eyes and tells me it's none of my concern. I should have known not to ask. If she hasn't told me by now, she doesn't want me to know. Perhaps I will learn at the wedding what unfavorable circumstances plague what should be a happy day. Before I can ask if I should provide a gift as well, she snatches up my hand and we vanish into the æther, reappearing on Mount Pelion.

A lush forest coats the mountainside and I can see the wide sweep of the blue sea from our vantage point. The heat bakes the juniper and cypress trees, permeating the air with the scent of sun-drenched sap.

There is a light tang of salt in the air, but Mount Pelion is not quite close enough to the ocean to bring the scent of fish and seaweed with it.

A creature with the body of a horse and the torso of a man greets everyone. I tug at my mother's sleeve and ask who and what he is. She sighs as if I should already know, though no one has ever bothered to mention to me that creatures like him exist. "That is Chiron, he is a centaur and he has trained many demigods, including the groom of today's wedding."

Thetis is nowhere to be seen, not that I've ever seen her before, but I'm certain I'm capable of picking out a bride. I scan the crowd, searching for familiar faces. My heart trips a little in my chest when I see Lord Hades; dark and brooding in dusky gray fabric, with an unquestionably uncomfortable expression on his face. The color makes him look all the more pale, but the shimmer of the cloth makes his skin slightly luminous, like a moonbeam. His dark curls are pinned loosely with a silver circlet and he's speaking with Lord Hermes. The discomfort in his face is almost a reflection of my own. I feel a little lost since I don't know anyone and the commonality brings a smile to my lips.

I bump into my mother's back when she stops suddenly. A beautiful Goddess with vibrant red hair and sparkling blue eyes stands before her. They both squeal, clutching at each other like young girls. Mother introduces the woman as Harmonia, the Goddess of Harmony and daughter of Lady Aphrodite and Lord Ares. Her voice is smooth and lyrical, lifting my spirits as the sound reaches me. Her presence is soothing and I feel relaxed just being near her.

"Would you mind if I borrowed your mother until the festivities begin?" Lady Harmonia asks. My mother's brow furrows at this, but I assure them both I'm pleased to let them enjoy their time together. Whatever concerns my mother has seem to be dispersed by Harmonia's power as she tugs mother away

Suddenly free of my guardian an overwhelming giddiness fills me. I try to mould my expression into one of calm joy, but the suppressed grin repeatedly escapes. I mill about, weaving through the crowd, accepting half-hearted greetings and smiles. Most of them give me odd looks and I realize it is probably because they have no idea who I am. I nod politely and smile and continue on, searching for anyone I recognize. Mother had instructed me before we arrived to not give anyone too much information, not even my name unless she approved of them first, so I at least follow that rule and avoid standing next to anyone long enough for them to ask.

I nearly jump out of my skin when Lord Hermes appears out of nowhere and bows in front of me, his body moving with fluid grace. I had been so intent on not making eye contact with anyone that I hadn't realized I'd wandered right over to Lords Hades and Hermes. "Lady Persephone, it's so lovely to see you again."

Lord Hades appears to choke on his wine and Lord Hermes thumps him hard on the back.

"The pleasure is mine, Lord Hermes." I clasp my hands before me to calm the nervousness that's working itself into my limbs.

"Oh, I do believe I see my mother, if you will both excuse me." His winged sandals lift him up and over the crowd, leaving Lord Hades and I alone together. I follow Lord Hermes with my gaze and see him speaking joyfully to a statuesque woman with waving brown hair and the same lovely gray eyes as her son. I search my mind for who she is, but come up short. I am sadly lacking in knowledge of the Olympian family tree.

I glance back towards Lord Hades, unsure of what to say. Thankfully, he speaks first. "I see you like the necklace I made you."

"Yes, it's lovely. Thank you." I slide the pads of my fingers over the stones, using the texture to settle my mind. "I have never met Lord Hermes' mother before, what is she like?"

"Maia? She is kind, but not very open to anyone, save her son of course. She raised another of Zeus' bastards." He looks absolutely aghast for a moment. "I'm sorry, Persephone, I certainly did not mean you when I used that term. I hope you're not offended."

He continues to babble charmingly to cover up the flub. "Why should I be offended? I am not a child of the King and Queen of Olympus, but being a bastard does not negate the love my mother has for me, nor my worth as a person. Besides, a child could never have control over the circumstances into which they are born."

He stops short and stares at me openly. I feel as though he wants to say more, but a steadily increasing rumbling from the crowd distracts us. People begin to shift and gravitate towards the mouth of a cave at one end of the clearing and I assume this means the ceremony is about to begin. I reluctantly leave Lord Hades and seek out my mother and Lady Harmonia, praying silently to Great Mother Gaia that she has not seen me with him. He heads to the back row of the crowd and I try to be subtle so no one notices that I'm watching his dark hair weave through the crowd.

I have a good view of the bride and groom from the spot my mother chose. Thetis is gowned beautifully in ocean blue, accented with opalescent shells that reflect the sun. She has a very sour expression though and twists the bracelets on her wrist with such force that her knuckles are white. She looks far too angry to account for nervousness, but I had forgotten to see if Lord Hades knew anything and it's too late to do so now. Peleus smiles tentatively at his bride. He has a reasonably handsome face and his decorative armor seems to be made of polished gold. This is hardly the heart-warming spectacle I had been expecting, but at least everyone still looks exquisite.

After the ceremony finishes and the gifts are exchanged, everyone drifts back to their own conversations, I work up the daring to approach

Thetis. She is temporarily alone and looks relieved to be so. "I wish you many blessings on your wedding day, Thetis." She presses her lips together and nods her head sharply. "I would like to give you a gift myself, but I don't know you well enough to know what you might like. Is there any plant or fruit that you favor?"

Her mouth twitches at the corners and she whispers that she is fond of apricots. I clap in delight and conspire with Great Mother Gaia to draw up the fragrant tree from the earth. The tender sprouts reach up, twisting together to form a solid wood trunk, bursting outwards in branches laden with leaves. Blossoms erupt into being before being caught on the wind, petals dancing in a gentle rain around the unhappy bride. Plump, golden fruit droops from the branches, bowing down to tap Thetis on the head. It's the first time I have seen her smile.

13

HADES

Thetis' smile makes her as radiant as a moonlit sea. Persephone's gift is a stroke of brilliance, the only gift anyone had thought to provide exclusively to Thetis herself. I watch Persephone beams as Thetis reaches out and snatches a plump fruit off the tree to take a bite. The juice runs down her chin and she grins like a girl-child at Persephone.

I'm glad that at least for a few moments Thetis can be happy and remove the threat of the future from her mind. I watch Persephone, finding myself unable to move my eyes from her. Her joy radiates from her like ripples in water, but drawing others to her, rather than pushing ever outwards. In truth, I hardly noticed I made my way to her until both she and Thetis are looking at me curiously.

I cough to give myself a moment to think and recall that my own gift to the bride had yet to be presented. I had also prepared a gift for Thetis, allowing the others to shower Peleus with their own. I remove a pendant from a silk pouch at my hip and hold it out to Thetis. "I wish you a bright future filled with happiness."

She reaches out and takes the pendant, a faceted sapphire nearly the size of her two fists, set in gold. "Thank you, Lord Hades. Your words are appreciated, but I am not putting much faith in them coming true."

"What is going on here?" A voice dripping with bitterness fills the air and everyone turns to look at the source. I try and fail to suppress a sigh. Standing there with poker straight blonde hair whipping around a stick thin frame is Eris, the Goddess of Discord and Strife. She is a dangerous Goddess, especially since there is naturally discord between others, so it takes very little to whip it up into a frenzy.

"Dear me, a party and no one invited me? You are all so very rude." She strides up to us and gives Thetis a mocking bow, a cruel grin twisting her features. "Your wedding? How fortunate that I have come prepared with a wonderful gift."

She reaches into the bodice of her gown and retrieves a chunk of gold in the shape of an apple. She sneers at the Gods present as she sets it down on the main banquet table. The apple shimmers with a violent spell, dark magic that is even now reaching out.

"Eris, you are not welcome here," Zeus speaks up. "Leave now."

She skips over to him and slides her bony hands over his arms and chest, purring. "Now, now, are you sure you're not glad to see me?"

"Leave, Eris." Hera stands up sharply, her voice ripe with venom. "You have caused your discord, now be content with that and be on your way."

Eris shrugs and slides like water through the crowd. "Very well, I was ready to leave anyway." She vanishes, but true to her name, she's managed to stir up everyone in the brief moments she was here.

"Oh!" Aphrodite lets out a coo and snatches the apple off the table, cradling it to her bosom. I nearly blanch at the words that are engraved into the side. *For the Fairest.* Dark strands of discord wrap around the Goddess of Love, the spell plunging into her heart. "Obviously this was meant for me."

"Why would it be for you?" Athena snaps, reaching for the cursed object. Her light gray eyes turn dark as a storm as Aphrodite dances away.

"Of course it's for me. I am the fairest, after all."

"Is that so?" Hera strides towards her, hand extended. "I do believe that as your Queen, I would qualify as the fairest."

Tempers snap immediately under the pressure of the discordant magic. Vicious words are hurled back and forth and within moments they are tearing at each other like wild dogs over a scrap of flesh. We respond on instinct, my brothers and I snatching up one Goddess each, while they scream and flail, trying to launch themselves back at one another. Their eyes are unseeing, blinded by the power of Eris fueling the tensions between them.

Harmonia floods us with power, but it is not enough to fully overcome Eris' spell. Aphrodite clutches the apple firmly in her hands, Athena and Hera eyeing it.

"A true man is impressed with a woman's wit, not her body. Why should Aphrodite get the apple over me?" Athena struggles in Poseidon's grasp. Hera would have added to the protests, but Zeus has a hand firmly clasped over her mouth, silencing her despite her efforts to free herself. Lightning crackles around him and small flashes of it sear Hera's skin where he's pressed against it.

With a frustrated cry Zeus shoves Hera behind him and shouts at everyone. "Enough! This will be decided, but not here and not now. We are at a wedding and it is not the time for your petty squabbles."

The Goddesses direct such a look of fury at him it's a wonder he does not simply melt from existence. I hold my tongue and don't point out that the entire wedding is only occurring because of petty squabbles.

Aphrodite begins to sob in my arms when Zeus snatches the apple out of her grasp. I turn her over immediately to Ares, the God of War and her current lover. Harmonia's gentle power continues to pour out to the three Goddesses, but unfortunately it's no match for the discordant magic that burrows deep into the heart where it plants the seeds of misfortune. They have all latched onto the magic and integrated it into their being.

I shiver, brushing away the energy of the conflict and retreat to the comforting shade of Persephone's apricot tree. I run a hand through my hair, a gesture of exasperation, and select a plump fruit to consume. Conflicts like these are far from uncommon and yet somehow people still wonder why I have no love for family events.

"Well, that was rather eventful." Persephone settles next to me with a lap full of apricots.

I stare at her for a moment. "Why didn't you fight for the apple?"

She shrugs, sucking at the tender fruit. "How could I even begin to compete with them? They are all far more beautiful than I."

I have never before heard any immortal state that someone else possesses more beauty than they do. "Beauty is in the eye of the beholder." She looks at me curiously, but I do not elaborate.

I force my eyes to the fruit in my hand when Demeter rushes up to collect her daughter. The apricots she carried tumble to the ground as she is snatched away. The wedding is all but ruined and those who had only reluctantly attended begin to filter out. Those who remain are distracted by the tension between the Goddesses. All three are muttering to Zeus, and I can just make out what sounds like demands for him to judge between them himself. He refuses, as any intelligent male would, given that he would be judging between his wife, his daughter and the literal embodiment of beauty.

"Dismissed, everyone." Zeus' voice rolls over us like a ripple of thunder. He turns to the bride and groom, a disturbing leer upon his face. "Peleus, take your bride and celebrate your marriage."

The look of hot fury Thetis gives him could have melted iron. The calculation in her eyes tells me that she is seriously contemplating murdering her bridegroom, but she must also know that they will only match her up again. I am certain it is a humiliation she is unwilling to face again. There is nowhere for her to run and my heart goes out to her.

Chiron, the great trainer of heroes, steps aside to let Peleus drag an unhappy Thetis into the cave. As much as I want to speak for her, I cannot hold my own against both of my brothers at once. They are both adamant that this marriage happens and I can only hope that one day the consequences of their choices will create as much misery in their lives as they have created for Thetis.

14

PERSEPHONE

The energy of Olympus has felt different since the wedding. Tensions remain unresolved and I have hidden away in my chambers, safe as I can be from their conflicts. I've lost track of how long I've been confined here. Time is rather irrelevant when one will live forever, and consequently many of the Gods don't notice the passing of time. I have slipped back into my days and nights of tedium, moments blurring together into one long expanse of dissatisfaction. I have been restricted to Olympus since the wedding, the conflicts between our kin making my mother exceptionally paranoid.

The only relief to my boredom is my silent studies with Great Mother Gaia and the pomegranate pendant that Lord Hades had crafted for me. I discovered after a time that it works much the same as the speaking stone he had used to communicate with me in the meadow. We speak on occasion, but the times when he was available to speak rarely coincide with times where I am alone. I still long to visit his realm, but I am so fearful of discovery that I haven't ventured from Olympus to the meadow where we might meet.

I stroke the rubies and focus my thoughts, but Lord Hades is not available to speak. Frustration swirls in my belly, not at him, but at my lack of courage to defy my mother and seek him out. I resolve to petition my mother again to release me from my captivity for a visit with the nymphs. Only Chloe has been allowed to visit and even then her appearances have been infrequent and short. Mother's temperament has been unstable lately. Sometimes she is pleasant and I almost gather enough fortitude to request my freedom, but just as quickly her mood takes a downturn and she grows sullen and angry. I try to speak as little as possible and simply agree with anything she says so I don't trigger a decline in her emotional condition.

The stones hum in my hands and a rush of delight washes over me. "Hello, Persephone." Lord Hades' voice reminds me of night; a calm, cool presence that envelops you into a state of peace.

"Good evening, Lord Hades." I curl onto my bed, tucking up my knees to my chest while I cradle the pendant. "I'm going to petition my mother again to let me visit the meadow."

"If she agrees I could meet you and bring you to visit my realm. Perhaps she will be more lenient this time than your previous requests."

"I hope so." I sigh deeply, wishing that I didn't have to get permission to begin with and that I were free to make my own choices. "Tell me about your world?"

"You will see it one day, but I shall do my best to describe it to you until then." He pauses, as though taking a moment to collect his thoughts. "The air is very rich, the scent of deep earth is the most prominent, but there are touches of cool water and salt. When you enter you will see the great rivers that divide my realm, rushing waters, ebony and azure, racing into the depths of Gaia."

"Are there flowers?"

"In Asphodel, the Realm of Peace, there are millions of them. It is like a sea of white blossoms, tinged with pink and the wavering silver of the resting souls. Beyond Asphodel there are very few, save those conjured in Elysium."

I take a moment to breathe, filling my find with the world he describes and alter my perceptions to breathe in the same scents. Curls of anticipation fill my belly. "Tell me of Elysium."

"It's the Realm of Paradise. It responds to thoughts, altering itself to the viewer's perceptions of paradise. Elysium can show anything or anyone, allowing each who resides in it to live an eternity suited to everything they have ever wanted."

I roll over onto my stomach, stretching out across the bed. "What does it show when you enter it?" He's quiet for a long time and I begin to fear that I've offended him with my question.

"I can make it show anything, but as for its natural state when I let it craft my own paradise... I'm not yet comfortable enough to share that information."

A flash of power alerts me to my mother's arrival and I bid a hasty goodbye to Lord Hades before shoving the pendant into the bodice of my gown.

I peek out of my room and study her features and body language before deciding that her mood is most likely pleasant. I set about uncoiling her braids while she seats herself on a cushion and pours herself a cup of nectar.

I comb the golden locks until they lay smooth and shining. "Mother, I've been meaning to ask you about visiting the meadow. I haven't seen the nymphs for such a long time."

She eyes me speculatively, but I keep my expression neutral and she slowly nods her head. "I suppose you're right, it has been quite some time, but you know how I worry for you."

"I know the rules and I will be careful. I simply wanted a change of scenery."

She sighs and pulls me around so we are facing each other. "The nymphs have been requesting your presence as well. I suppose I cannot keep you to myself forever. One visit, and if you feel threatened or afraid at any time you are to return immediately."

I nod my head mechanically. The teasing concept of seeing paradise and the wonders of the Underworld delight my mind and I decide that yes, I am willing to accept any risk to experience that freedom. If she discovers what happens and I am locked up again then at least I will have my memories to sustain me until my mother sees fit to release me once more.

15

HADES

I pace the Great Hall in a futile attempt to keep myself calm. Guests to the Underworld are so uncommon that when Persephone informed me she would arrive with the sunrise, I found myself thoroughly unprepared for her. Years have passed since I last saw her face and I wonder at what she will be like.

I express my fears to Thanatos who is watching me with crossed arms. "You're distressing the souls, please calm down. You have no reason to fear, you have spoken to Lady Persephone many times in these past years and you said yourself she seems to be unchanged. Worrying now will not change the reality of the situation when she arrives."

"How about you go and find a nice girl and invite her back here and then we'll see how bloody calm you are about it." I wring my hands and continue to pace.

Hermes watches me with a look of clear amusement over my situation. "It's not as if you're marrying the girl, you're simply inviting her for a chat and tour. Take a deep breath." He grins at me, swinging one leg like a pendulum from his perch on the edge of the table. "You spend too much time down here and you've forgotten how to enjoy female company. When was the last time you spent time with a woman?"

"You know the answer to that." I answer more sharply than intended.

"Has there truly been no one? I have never heard tell of you with anyone, but that doesn't mean that it never happened." His head quirks to the side, a physical expression of his confusion.

"Can we please not have this discussion right now?" It takes considerable effort to keep the begging tone out of my voice. Waves of panic and nerves wash over me like a raging tide and it's all I can do to avoid being pulled under. I've never dealt well with new people or situations. The Titanomache was the exception since it was literally adapt or perish, but since then I've tried to avoid stressful situations wherever I can.

Hermes only shrugs. "As you will it."

"She's there." I can feel the ripples of her presence, detected by the speaking stone still nestled in the soil of her meadow. I turn plaintive eyes upon them both. "What should I do?"

"Go get her, perhaps?" I resist the sudden urge to punch Thanatos for his obvious enjoyment of my circumstances. With a deep breath I use my power to part the earth so I can ascend to the meadow.

Deafening squeals assure me that I'm in the right location. Blazing sunlight bursts through the earth and I have to blink a few times before I can see anything more than shadowy figures through the brightness. Persephone stands front and center, her gaggle of nymphs huddled behind her.

The nymphs rush towards me and I'm instantly surrounded. They press at me from all sides, shouting questions until my head begins to spin from the cacophony of voices. A sharp clap reverberates through the air and the nymphs immediately fall silent.

"Step back, you are all being terribly rude." Persephone has her hands on her hips and a firm stare leveled at the nymphs. Grumbles and squeaks follow her order as they all reluctantly retreat to stand behind her once more. I unclench my fists, not having realized they had formed, and extend a hand to Persephone as my breathing calms.

With a slow, tentative smile she steps forward and places her hand in mine. Her expression still has the same gentleness I remember and it does a great deal to soothe my frazzled nerves. She follows me onto the stone steps that descend into my kingdom and she glances at me with wide eyes when we turn down the spiraling path. It seems as if the earth swallows us up, the sun disappearing behind us. I place my free hand onto the dirt walls and golden crystals press out of the soil at regular intervals, each giving a gentle glow, akin to the light of sunrise.

She pauses and traces her fingers over the rough cut of the natural crystal. It sparks at her touch and she gasps with pleasure. "These are lovely. Until I met you I had never thought of stones as being beautiful."

Her joy in the crystals buoys a budding confidence that perhaps she will find my realm as beautiful as I do. The walk is slow, but soon it comes to an end and the earth opens once more to the stretch of land before the Towers of Judgement. Hermes and Thanatos are waiting for us when we emerge and Persephone's fingers clench mine almost painfully. I rub my thumb over the back of her hand in what I hope is a soothing motion. Her grip slowly relaxes, but the feeling of crippling awkwardness does not fade with the release. Hermes grins and Thanatos watches us expectantly.

"Everything is ready, my Lord, as you requested." Thanatos smiles softly, holding out a basket, the contents hidden by a tucked piece of silver fabric. Not having a clue what he means, I settle for staring blankly at him until he is urged to explain. "I have packed everything for your picnic in Elysium."

Thanatos deserves to be both cuffed upside the head and hugged. I can't quite decide which I would rather do. He had this all planned out, but never bothered to tell me, opting to watch me squirm for his own amusement. I babble my acceptance, pretending I had known of this plan the entire time and offer a brief introduction of my colleagues to Persephone. She's met Hermes before, but she stares in awe at Thanatos and his halo of ebony wings. Her fingers squeeze my hands as she gives a small bow to each, a controlled trembling in her limbs betraying her nervousness. To save us both from further discomfort I usher her past the crowd and lead her to my Palace.

She looks around constantly, like a blind man suddenly gifted with sight. Her jaw drops open with awe as we pass through the Palace gates and into the expansive courtyard. The ground is flat black marble, reflective as a still pool in moonlight. The walls are the same vibrant stone, rising up like a raven's wings to enclose the courtyard. She kicks off her sandals and runs her toes over the cool stone. Rather like a child she sinks to her knees and runs her hands over the surface. Her reflection gazes back at her, grinning features as beautiful in stone as in person.

"You have no flowers to adorn your Palace, Lord Hades. It would be a shame for only Elysium and Asphodel to have their beauty. May I grow some for you?"

I survey the stark stone. The question may be simple, but the weight of the words is heavy. We two have so little outwardly in common, but I feel as though this is her attempt to bridge the gap between our worlds. She is reaching across the chasm of awkwardness and unfamiliarity, offering me a foothold into the world she knows. I reason with myself that if things turn sour between us I can always easily remove flowers, but part of me shies away from letting anyone else leave their mark on my realm.

The imploring hope in her eyes makes my decision for me and I nod my head. I curl my fingers into a fist, coaxing the stone to retract around the border of the courtyard. It slides away revealing the dense, dark, fertile earth. The scent of freshly turned soil invades my nose and I breathe deeply of it. She gently caresses the soil before digging her fingers in happily. A gentle ripple of energy flows outwards. Small bursts of color pop into being and she gasps, reaching out to touch the sweet smelling blossoms.

"My flowers have never looked like this before, they're so beautiful." I kneel down next to her and inspect the blooms. Some are darkly colored, rich as sumptuous velvet in shades of indigo, garnet and mulberry with pine dark stems. Others are akin to alabaster with delicate pale mint stems.

She plucks a dark violet blossom and offers it to me. When I don't immediately reach for it, she begins to retreat, but I snatch at her wrist. Her eyes widen briefly, but she doesn't struggle from my grasp. "Forgive my hesitation, Persephone. I'm used to others giving with the expectation of reciprocity, not simply giving because they desire another to have something."

Her lips purse and she holds out the flower again, my hand still gripping her wrist. "Then you had best adjust."

I tuck the vibrant petals under the clasp at my shoulder. She smiles, shyly at first, but as I lead her from the courtyard and into the realm of Paradise her smile becomes a grin that overwhelms her features with joy.

Elysium is filled with more magic than any place in existence. It is bursting with the hopes, love and dreams of all the souls who have entered it and the dreams of the Earth itself. Most of the souls in residence have simple pleasures and Elysium initially shows us the azure waters of the Mediterranean Sea accented by white and black sand beaches with a backdrop of rolling verdant hills dotted with flowers.

"It can show you anything, choose anywhere in the world and Elysium will create it for you," I explain and she looks contemplative.

"I could not even begin to imagine the wonders of this world. All I have ever seen is my meadow and Olympus." Her expression is sad, but she gives her head a shake and looks back at me with brighter features. "Show me a place that you love." I oblige and send my thoughts out to coax forth a land I hope will intrigue Persephone.

She gasps as the world ripples around us, wonder painting her features so profoundly that my heart thumps in my chest. She drops to her knees and gingerly peers over the edge of a stone precipice, gazing in awe at the ocean of trees that spread before her. The forest undulates across the towering mountains that reach so far into the heavens their peaks are obscured by clouds. The Elysian moon hangs like a giant pearl in the sky, faded with the low light of a sleepy sun as it descends into the horizon. The scent of chilled pine and fresh snow are intoxicating, a fresh and vibrant combination that clears the lungs and draws one into a feeling of peace. A long howl breaks the silence, a chorus following it to create an enchanting echo.

"Where are we?" Persephone breaths deeply, eyes closed as she savors the crisp mountain air.

"In a land far beyond the sea, it is where Boreas grows his frigid north winds." The echoing howl fills the twilight. "The wolves are restless. We have them around Olympus, but the wolves of the Boreal Forests are larger and travel in packs of much greater numbers. They're free to roam through nearly unlimited space and some may never encounter a human in their lives."

"Can I see one?" She stands and clasps my hand in hers imploringly. "Please?"

I nod, wrapping an arm around her waist and plunge us both over the cliff edge. She clings to me as we descend and despite landing soft as a butterfly, she flings herself away from me when we touch down. Her eyes are wild and startled as she presses a hand to what I assume is a racing heart.

I step towards her, but she retreats unsteadily. "What on Earth would possess you to do something like that?" She's shouting, but I can detect a tremble in her voice. "I know we cannot die, but we can certainly be injured."

Her whole body shivers, making her look very young and frightened. "Persephone, I'm so sorry. I should have explained, there is no danger in Elysium." Granted Persephone has likely never flung herself off a cliff before, but it should be common knowledge among immortals that an application of power could slow any fall enough to avoid injury. In Elysium no such power is required, anyone could do as we had just done and the realm would protect them from harm.

"I-I didn't know." I step forward again and when she does not retreat I gather her into my arms until the trembling subsides. Even in the brief time I've spent with Persephone, these small bits of contact make me realize how starved I've been for physical affection. I shouldn't push for such things with her, but I'm drawn to her energy, to her spirit and I can't help but reach out.

"Forgive me, I will not be so foolish in the future. I will always keep you safe while you're with me."

She tilts her head to look up at me, her eyes like emerald reflecting pools set in golden flesh. "Do you promise?"

"I do. Now, come and let's seek out the wolves." I send the thought out into Paradise and Persephone exclaims, this time trembling with excitement when a female slides fluidly from the trees. Her intelligent gold eyes survey us, ears twitching to take in Persephone's excited breathing and rapid heartbeat.

One by one more wolves emerge, standing guard behind their alpha. I usher Persephone forward and she progresses hesitantly. She reaches out tentatively, but pauses before touching the female. I slide my hand over hers and press her palm down into the sleek, mottled gray fur.

A grin bursts over Persephone's features immediately and she glides around the wolf to stroke the silky fur. Her attention to the adults is quickly abandoned when bundles of squirming gray fur scamper between the legs of their parents. She snatches one up and giggles gleefully as the tiny creature squirms and assaults her face with licks. As she continues playing with the pups, I unpack our basket and settle myself to watch her while the other wolves gradually move closer and lay down in a protective circle around us.

As the novelty begins to wear down Persephone settles next to me with a sleeping pup in her lap and the head of the alpha female resting on her knee. She feeds the more rambunctious pups bits of roasted meat from the basket before gorging herself on pomegranate seeds.

After some time she turns to me. "As much as I hate to leave, I have no concept of how much time has passed and I don't want my mother to come looking for me and find me gone."

My thoughts tumble out my mouth before I can stop them, hopefully without the edge of desperation I suddenly feel. "Will you come back?"

A smile brightens her features. "Do you honestly think you can keep me away?"

16

PERSEPHONE

I find that memories don't sustain me quite as well as I'd hoped they would. I've supplemented them by coaxing a young pine tree to life in my quarters. The sweet, sticky smell of the sap and the fragrant greenery reminding me with every breath of the wonders I had seen in Elysium.

Presumably my mother has not yet discovered my temporary defection to the Underworld. Thus far her behavior towards me has remained unchanged and my minuscule freedom has not been rescinded. I wear the pomegranate pendant openly now, the time for suspicion over its origins long since passed. I need only run my fingers over the stones to initiate contact with Lord Hades, though he is only available to speak during half of my attempts.

My mother glides through my open doors and breathes in the rich fragrance of the pine tree, humming in pleasure. "There has been a considerable crop failure in the northern territories that I must attend to. I will be gone some time as it runs quite close to the Eleusinian festivals and I will be attending this year." Every few years she attends the mortal festival dedicated to her, just to remind them that she is listening. They never see her, but she gifts them with exceptional crops and blesses a few choice mortals with visions to boost the overall worship in the area.

I wonder aloud whether or not she would like my assistance in rejuvenating the fields. She cups my cheeks and gives me an indulgent smile. "My sweet baby girl, you have no idea what the world is like. It's far too dangerous out there for you."

"Can it possibly be so dangerous for me to just watch you mend crops?" My attempt at reason proves futile as she begins to laugh.

"Oh, my dear, you have no concept of the anger of mortals. They fear the day that Thanatos comes for them and when the crops fail they are faced with that occurring far sooner than they might desire. There will be warfare soon as they plunder one another for scarce resources and you could be wounded if you're not paying attention." She strokes my hair as though soothing a small child. "They worship me because I tamed the grains and taught them how to grow and care for them. You would be of no help to them, the trees that you grow can take years before they bear fruit and the mortals would starve long before they provided any sustenance."

"Athena gave the olive tree to Athens and they take years, sometimes half a generation before they produce fruit. How are my gifts so different?" I argue feebly, watching any foothold I might have had in this discussion crumble in the breeze as she begins to shut down.

Her face becomes impassive and my mother only shrugs. "Olives are a luxury compared to grains. You have nothing to offer the mortals, Persephone." She gives me a hard look. "You are not to leave Olympus while I am away, the nymphs may visit, but the meadow is off limits until I return."

My body feels numb as she embraces me and I do nothing but stare into space for several moments after she vanishes to fulfill her duties. I realize belatedly that tears are slipping down my cheeks and the hurt over her words finally spills free. My fingers fly to the pendant, the warm vibrations of power a soothing balm on my bruised spirit.

Her words make me hate the only home I have ever known. I want to go somewhere I feel truly free. I slide my fingers over the stones, praying to Great Mother Gaia that Lord Hades is prepared for an unexpected guest.

17

HADES

"Hades, I apologize for the interruption, I know you're on your way to meet Hermes," Thanatos appears composed, but his wings tremble, "but there is someone at the Gates that you must attend to."

He does not reveal anything more, so I follow him immediately to the outermost borders of my realm. There, in the radiant sunshine stands Persephone surrounded by several of her nymphs. Her eyes are glassy and the remnants of tears reflect upon her cheeks.

"Persephone, what are you doing here?"

"It's silly, I shouldn't have come. I got very upset with my mother and then she left and I didn't want to remain on Olympus, but I wasn't sure where else to go."

"Of course you should have come, you are always welcome here." I pass through the barrier of the realm and the nymphs usher her towards me. I wrap an arm around her shoulder and several tears slip down her golden cheeks. She leans into me, the warmth of the sun still on her skin as she wraps lean arms around my waist.

"Lord Hades, we leave our Lady in your care, if you have need of us, please do not hesitate to summon us." A silver haired nymph with dark brown eyes gives me a gentle smile before bowing and ushering the nymphs to take their leave.

With Persephone tucked against my side I swiftly escort her to the Palace where I summon Evaristus to prepare a room for Persephone. "Evaristus will take good care of you. I will return shortly." I hesitate to leave her, but I must.

In the Great Hall I find Hermes pacing restlessly. He throws his hands into the air, his countenance riddled with exasperation. "He let a mortal pass judgement!"

"What on Earth is going on?" I'm used to seeing Hermes happy and care-free, it takes a lot to upset him and it rarely bodes well when something has gone so wrong as to agitate the Messenger God.

"Zeus picked out an idiot shepherd boy to judge which of the Goddesses is the fairest." I immediately recall the golden apple from the wedding of Peleus and Thetis. "Aphrodite won the apple by promising him the love of the most beautiful mortal woman in the world. She just failed to mention that this woman is already married and to the King of Sparta, no less. Zeus was too much of a coward to choose himself."

Still not entirely clear as to the extent of the problem, I inquire further, for besides angering two Goddesses, I can see no other misfortune here. "How is this our problem?"

Hermes lets out a sound that is almost part animal and drags his hands over his face. "Please at least try to pay attention to what happens in the mortal world. When Helen grew to marriageable age all of the kings wanted to marry her. There would have been a war then but for the quick thinking of Odysseus who orchestrated the Oath of Tyndareus." Before I can inquire as to what that might be, Hermes elaborates. "They all swore a blood oath that they would protect Helen and the husband she chose. Now every king on the Aegean is bound for war because Helen has been taken. Whether by accident or design, the shepherd Zeus picked out is Paris, son of the King of Troy, who was cast out as a child for a prophecy that said he would bring destruction to his city. His acceptance of Helen from Aphrodite is a declaration of war between Troy and Sparta."

"So the mortals are all going to war?"

Hermes looks grim. "The Gods are going to war, Hades. This conflict has split them, Hera and Athena against the Trojans, Aphrodite against the Greeks. Others are choosing based on which side their children or favorites fight for."

Panic begins to bubble to the surface, flashes of the Titanomache filling my thoughts. Torrents of fire, water and earth cloud my mind and I rub at the arm that I had once almost lost to the flames. A war among the Gods could destroy us. The mortals would be left Godless or with a crippled Pantheon to worship as the Olympians tear themselves apart from within. Hermes wasn't around for the Titanomache, but he has heard the stories and he has a keen mind. He knows from myself and his mother, who fought by our side, the sort of destruction another War of the Gods could bring.

"What do we do, Hades? I've never witnessed a war like this before. There are so many more lives at stake now, the mortals never existed during the Titanomache. I fear the worst." Hermes words echo in the cavernous hall. I only hope Hermes' fears do not come to pass.

18

PERSEPHONE

I followed the petit dæmon, standing just higher than my waist, as he leads me through the labyrinthine halls to the quarters designated for me for the duration of my stay. The doors along the extensive hallways are all unique, each hewn from a different type or color of stone, with intricate patterns carved into their faces.

Evaristus brings us to a stop in front of delicate pink crystal doors that arch up and form a point where they meet. A design of roses and assorted blossoms covers them, accented here and there with fragments of yellow and green stones to simulate leaves and pollen rich centers. The doors swing open without touch and reveal a suite lit by rose quartz crystals that give the whole room a blush pink tinge. A large bed cloaked in shimmering gold fabric fills the center of the space and the walls are lined with crystal shelving filled with delicate glass bottles of so many colors it resembles a rainbow. Cool white marble, shot through with gold, covers the floor and slopes into a pool at the far side of the room. Steam mists upwards in graceful tendrils while water pours out of gold spouts into the waiting basin. An exquisitely embroidered screen in a mahogany frame partitions a portion of the room next to the bath. The air is moist and fragrant with a delightful heat.

"Lady Persephone, if you would like to step behind the screen to bathe, I will prepare an outfit for you. I apologize that there is only myself to assist you, Lord Hades does not keep female dæmons in his employ."

I slip off my gown and hang it over the edge of the screen. I've bathed in the stream near the meadow with the nymphs before so the screen seems unnecessary to me. I've never had an issue with nudity around others when it comes to bathing, but I will follow the customs here, guided by Evaristus. I slip a tentative foot into the water. A hiss escapes my lips, followed by a groan as I sink in up to the knees.

"Is there a problem, my Lady?" I slip all the way into the water, never having felt something quite so wonderful before.

"No problem. It feels as though I am swimming in sunshine. I have never bathed in hot water before."

Evaristus pushes the screen aside a little. Following his apparent preference for modesty I clap my arms across my chest as he chuckles. "There is no need to be shy, my Lady, you are quite beautiful, but I prefer the company of men so you need fear nothing from me. I'm also a fan of hot baths," he smiles softly. "They are one of the few luxuries we are all afforded here."

"Oh, I'm not shy about my body. I was raised by nymphs and they have no shame in their forms, so I have no shame in my own." He chuckles again and I change the subject. "Who are the we you speak of?" I inquire, slowly relaxing into the warmth.

"There are hundreds of dæmons that serve the Underworld and Lord Hades has provided all of us with our own chambers. The other immortals have rooms as well, but they go largely unused as many of them do not enjoy being within walls." He perches on the edge of the baths and gently nudges me so my head tilts back into the water and the strands swirl out around me. A blue bottle from the shelf snaps into his hand and he douses my hair with a concoction that saturates the air with the scent of spiced fruit. His fingers make my scalp feel incredible, a wave of relaxation moving through my limbs as I surrender to his expertise.

"I have decided I no longer require nymphs, you just need to come to Olympus and stay with me forever."

Evaristus laughs. "I appreciate the offer, my Lady, but I am afraid my heart remains here with Lord Hades."

"He must be a wonderful ruler to inspire such loyalty." I comment, hoping Evaristus will elaborate and satiate my curiosity.

"He is a kind soul, even to those who I know he finds frustrating. He tries to remain calm, otherwise the souls get agitated. If you have not already noticed, I shall inform you that his emotions are deeply connected to the realm, as he built much of it himself to house the souls. His power permeates everything here and it is why he tries so hard to be neutral. Any negative feelings could be absorbed by the souls."

I cannot imagine how difficult that must be. To always subdue how you feel would be exhausting. "He is certainly different than the rest of the Olympians."

Evaristus nods, his smile turning grave as he works the bubbles from my hair. "The Gods of Olympus tend to care only for those that worship them. When those people die and their souls come here they are all but forgotten by the Gods above."

A stab of anger twists in my gut. "That's hardly fair. How can they forget about mortals who serve them faithfully?"

"I agree with you, as does Lord Hades. That is why he works so hard to care for the souls. They rarely worship him in life, but he refuses to hold that against them." Evaristus cocks his head to the side, sleek locks falling over his shoulder. "Lord Hades may appear fierce and withdrawn, but he has a good heart and will always care for and protect what he loves."

I fall silent, unsure of how to respond and simply enjoy the warmth. To break the awkward silence I latch onto a piece of information revealed earlier. "Evaristus, why does Lord Hades not employ female dæmons?"

"He did in the early years," he pauses to lather up my arm before speaking again, "but there were a few too many that thought he was lonely and refused to let the subject drop. He dismissed them and all the others, though they had done nothing wrong. It is one of the few decisions of his that I have never agreed with or even understood, but I know he found it easier to simply remove them than deal with each incident as they happened. Everyone left wisely kept any such inclinations to themselves after that. I like to believe he sees me as a friend after all this time, but that doesn't mean I am privy to his innermost thoughts on the matter."

He rinses one arm clean before applying the same ministrations to the other. "Lord Hades doesn't get out much, nor does he particularly desire to do so. For as long as I have been here, and I have been here a very long time, he has always put his duties before his personal needs. I should not speak so openly to you about him, but then no other Goddess has ever been introduced to me before so I must take that to mean you are worthy of at least a modicum of trust or Lord Hades wouldn't have allowed you this far. I would appreciate if you do not divulge any of what I have said to you, nor what I am about to say." I nod my head and swear to silence. "I was among the first dæmons who offered him our services. I watched him guard the Titans dutifully, saw how for thousands of years his family did not so much as give a thought to his existence down here. When they finally did remember he was here it was only to tell him to overturn his judgements and to put horrible people into paradise. They forget him otherwise. They think on him only for what he can do to satisfy their whims. I remember seeing his face when they first came, how it lit up, how hopeful his eyes were when he believed his family had finally remembered him and the sacrifices he had made to keep them safe. I saw his face as well when he realized why they had really come. He hides it well, but it hurts him even now, I know it does. I do believe that he wants to love them and to find someone to share his life with as well, but he cannot bear opening his heart to another only to have them do as his family has done to him for thousands of years."

My chest aches as I absorb Evaristus' words. To give myself a moment to think before responding I slide beneath the water and free myself from the suds. When I surface Evaristus applies another potion to my hair. I have no words to speak about the hardship and loneliness Lord Hades has experienced. I chew my lip and turn instead to another thought. "Do the souls not desire the care of a female? Goddesses usually have different energy than Gods. Why is there no Goddess devoted to the care of this realm alongside Lord Hades?"

The dæmon is silent for several moments and I feel the air grow thick with tension as he contemplates how to answer. His voice has a slight edge when he finally speaks. "There have been none who have expressed a desire to do so. No one has ever been assigned as Lord Hades will only allow someone who is truly passionate about the care of the souls to be dedicated to such a task." He heaves a deep breath, the tension in the air dissipating a fraction. "I cannot say I disagree. A Goddess who is unhappy could do far more harm than good."

He slips off his sandals and places them neatly to the side before dipping his feet into the water. He draws a wide-toothed comb through my hair to cure it of unruly tangles. "Lady Persephone, if I might be so bold as to ask, why are you here?"

I ponder his question, feeling suddenly insecure. "To be honest, I'm not quite sure. Something my mother said upset me and I found I could not bear to be anywhere associated with her. Lord Hades was the first person who came to mind when I thought of where I might find some solace."

Evaristus nods sagely as though he understands completely. A knocking at the door captures our attention and Evaristus excuses himself to answer it. The hair on the back of my neck prickles when I hear Lord Hades' voice pass into the room.

"How is she?" He asks, and embarrassment creeps into a blush on my cheeks as I recall the disheveled state in which I had arrived. Evaristus keeps his voice low so I cannot hear his response, but I crane my head to observe him. With a final bob of his head he closes the door and trots back over to me.

Ushered out of the bath, dried, primped and clothed in a wine colored chiton, I am again led through the labyrinthine halls. I prod at the elaborate coils he made of my hair, pinned in place with combs of gold and studded with rubies. The fabric is softer than anything I have ever worn, made of something Evaristus calls silk. Traditionally I have only ever worn clothing made from plant fibers, just as my mother has always done, or in some cases I wore nothing at all when I was with the nymphs. Silk feels marvelous on my skin and I ponder if I could wear such a fabric on Olympus without my mother noticing.

"I do hope that you are as kind as you appear, Lady Persephone." I am caught off guard by Evaristus' words. "There are many here that would not take kindly to our Lord being mistreated, even by an Olympian."

"I would never mistreat him," I protest immediately.

"You must understand my suspicion. No other Olympian, save for Lord Hermes, ever comes here without some ulterior motive. Yet here you are, and I cannot help but wonder why. You say you do not know, but you must or you would not have come here. I would dearly love to be able to trust you, Lady Persephone. I am willing to try and I truly hope that you come to earn it."

19

HADES

"She could have sated any loneliness with her nymphs," Thanatos points out while we wait for Evaristus to return Persephone, "but she came here, clearly in distress of some sort. She is risking her mother's wrath to be here."

I pace, pondering her motivations. "I know that."

"Do you think she might have developed a deeper affection for you?"

"She's practically a child." I protest, but the words die on my lips at Thanatos' expression.

"She has lived over a century now, you cannot use that excuse forever. She is likely inexperienced, but you are willing to give her opportunities, to teach her about life. Take whatever time you require, but sooner or later some other God will turn his gaze towards her and she may be lost to you if you refrain from acting due to fear."

"I'm afraid." The words thicken my tongue and I swallow down the discomfort. Thanatos' expression softens. Ice has settled in my belly as I contemplate his words. I force down the panic and simply breathe. "I will help her, give her whatever she needs, but I am still afraid. What if she's the same as the others?"

"She may be, but she may also be everything you have always hoped for. That is a risk you must be willing to take." Thanatos points out. "There is nothing wrong with fear so long as you do not allow it to hold you back. Lady Persephone likely experienced fear when she thought about coming here, but it did not stop her, do not let it stop you either."

I take my leave of Thanatos and decide to engage in Judgements, hoping to settle my mind while I await Persephone. Evaristus will know where to find me when they're finished.

Aeacus and Minos are already there and have pulled out the tapestry of Iole, a woman who has spent many years on the shores of Lake Cocytus trying to come to terms with her grief. Generally, we apply terms varying from a year to a century, depending on the depth and nature of the grief and when the term is up they come under review once more, but sometimes if a soul feels they are ready sooner they are allowed to request early Judgement.

I remember every soul that passes through the Towers, but I take the time to review her story once more for the benefit of Aeacus and Minos. Iole was one of the many victims of Heracles, a mortal princess who had nearly been wed to the demigod, but for her father's fear that she would be murdered as his first wife and children were. When he was denied Iole's hand in marriage he murdered her entire family in retaliation. She had tried to escape by casting herself off the city walls, but survived and was claimed as a concubine.

Minos calls Iole forth from the crowd and a petite spirit with violet eyes and matted gold hair emerges from the crowd. Misery hangs about her like a shroud, stooping her slender shoulders so she is hunched like a crone.

"What have you learned during your time on the shores of Cocytus?" Minos inquires, as per protocol.

"I should have died." She whispers, but her words are clear enough to be heard. "I tried so many times, but Thanatos never rescued me." Her voice escalates from whisper to hysterical screech. "I wanted to die! Why did you never take me? Why did you leave me to suffer my years at the hands of the murderer of my family?" She collapses to her knees, sobs overwhelming her.

A hush falls over the spirits, Iole included, as I catch a glimpse of Persephone at the base of the Towers. Evaristus stands beside her. He looks up at me and shrugs his shoulders. The souls stare in rapture as Persephone gingerly approaches Iole. She drops to her knees before the wailing spirit and whispers something I cannot hear from my vantage point. Iole still trembles and phantom tears pour down her cheeks, but she moves closer and closer to Persephone until the radiant Goddess has enveloped Iole in her arms.

My feet move of their own accord and soon I have left the Towers to observe Persephone's interactions up close. Persephone smiles at Iole, stroking her plump cheeks until her trembling ceases and her tears retreat.

Fascinated, I kneel next to them. Iole stares at me with wide eyes, but Persephone turns a tentative smile on me. "I'm so sorry to interrupt. Evaristus showed me where you were and I had to see what I could do to help when I heard the cries."

"There is no interruption," I assure her. "You have done very well." She smiles brightly, an expression that passes to many of the souls watching her.

I turn my attention briefly to Aeacus and Minos and request their verdict. I relay the information to Iole. "Forgive our Judgement, but we have deemed you not yet ready for Elysium. You are to remain at Cocytus until you have allowed it to free you of your pain." All a soul must do to be free is to surrender themselves to the waters. Their grief and torment will pour out of them instantly and Cocytus will hold it so they need never be weighed down by it again. If they refuse to let go it will only continue to burden them. Iole herself refused to let go, she lets her misery define her and so she must stay at the lake until she frees herself.

She lets out a sound part sob, part squeak, but does not struggle when the dæmons collect her to escort her back to the shores of Cocytus.

"You are welcome to observe from the Tower, the tapestries tend to be quite interesting." I offer and she accepts my hand and follows me up the steps. Minos and Aeacus have already set Iole's tapestry aside for archiving and unrolled a new one.

The tapestries are woven perfection that document an entire mortal lifetime, created and completed by the Moiræ. Persephone scans the tapestry quickly, fingers tracing over the name stitched in the top left corner.

"Damocles." Her brow furrows. "It seems as though he was very dissatisfied with his life. No step ahead was good enough, no success provided what he craved and he always strove for more, envious of what others had. I do not think he was a very kind person, but it does not appear as though he caused any undue harm to others."

"So, what Judgement would you render based on that?" I ask as we all watch her expectantly.

"Well, from what I have gathered, a stay at Cocytus might be advisable, to free him from his greed and envy. After that, I suppose Asphodel would suit him best."

I turn to Aeacus and Minos. "Are we in agreement with the Judgement of Persephone?" Both of them nod their heads.

"Your Goddess proves a wise and observant Judge." Aeacus smiles at her and she beams in response, temporarily stunning us with the power of her radiant joy.

"May I try another?" She looks at me expectantly.

"You may," I concede, "but first you must announce the Judgement so Damocles may be escorted to the appropriate area."

I stand slightly behind Persephone at the edge of the Towers to show my support for her announcement. Damocles has already separated himself from the waiting crowd and is watching us intently.

"Damocles, your Judgement has been rendered and you will spend your eternity in the Fields of Asphodel after you cleanse your soul of envy at the shores of Cocytus." Her voice echoes with power and two dæmons, Solon and Ariston, immediately take hold of Damocles.

Damocles' face twists into an enraged, sour expression and his shrill voice shoots hostility towards Persephone. "I demand Elysium!"

"Enough." The word is ripe with all the force I can muster and Damocles immediately falls silent. "You have no authority here and you may demand nothing. The Goddess Persephone has judged you and deemed you for Asphodel. You will obey her command and there will be no argument. If you wanted Elysium the time to fight for it was in life, there is no correcting for your mistakes now."

With my silence the spell is broken and Damocles begins to shriek and struggle against his escorts. With a sigh I leap off the edge of the Towers and bring myself to my full height in front of Damocles. He cowers, but can hardly move with the two dæmons holding him. "You will face your eternity now, before I change my mind and call upon Kamp to drag you into Tartarus. You are disrespecting us all with your display."

The dæmons drag his now listless form to the shores of Cocytus where he will remain under guard until he allows the waters to cleanse him. I have a feeling that he will be there a very long while. The waters only truly work when the soul accepts their power and it can do little for one that fights against it.

20

PERSEPHONE

Lord Hades returns to the Towers where Aeacus, Minos and I watch him with interest. I grasp one of his hands in mine and give it a squeeze. "How do you find the strength to do this?"

He shrugs. "It can be difficult, but the souls that achieve Elysium make it worth it. It's all about balance and justice. There is often no fairness in life, but there is always fairness in death. It is the equalizer of all humans, for they are rewarded or punished based on no other criteria than the choices they made in life."

"Do you think one day I might be as wise as you?"

He gently guides me back to the table where Minos has laid out another tapestry. "You are plenty wise Persephone, you need only believe in yourself."

I glance over the tapestry and note the name at the top left. Evadne. A gasp overtakes me as I reach the part where Evadne's husband is struck down by Zeus for hubris and his wife follows him to the afterlife by climbing onto his funeral pyre.

I shiver, appalled by what I see in the record of her life. Lord Hades wraps his cloak around me, securing me snugly beneath one of his arms.

"She is not the first I have seen meet such a fate and she will not be the last," he tells me. "Some mortals demand that wives sacrifice themselves when their husbands die. Should they refuse they may be cast out, left to starve or perhaps even tied to the pyre by their husband's family."

I feel compelled to speak with Evadne and summon her to the top of the Tower. She is escorted by the same two dæmons who had just removed Damocles. "Why did you choose the death you did?"

Evadne's spirit has dark spiral curls and sparkling brown eyes. "I chose the fire over being forced to wed my husband's younger brother. For as cruel as my husband was to me, his brother would have been worse."

I clasp her closely and she raises tentative arms to return the embrace. "Your life has been filled with misery. What grief might you have that would keep you from Paradise?"

"I miss my children, but that is a mother's sorrow. I do not fear for them though." She smiles softly. "They are both boys and were favorites of their grandfather."

I nod and thrust her to arm's length. "Evadne, I Judge that you will go to Cocytus, to free yourself from the sorrow of being apart from your children. When you are cleansed you will spend an eternity in Elysium." I should have gathered permission from Lord Hades first, but a glance towards him tells me that he approves of my choice, despite my lack of manners in getting his approval.

Evadne accepts my judgement with grace and is escorted to Cocytus. I turn and look to Lord Hades. "What of her husband?"

Minos fishes through the pile of tapestries and extracts the one for Evadne's husband. "Capaneus is bound for Tartarus, by orders of Lord Zeus."

Lord Hades runs his thumb over the stitching at the end of the tapestry that pictures a lightning bolt wreathed in flames. Zeus is fond of burning people and the Moiræ always record diligently the punishment he has decided for those he sends to me. "So he is." He mutters, almost to himself and then there is a shift in his energy so profound it sends a thrill up my spine. A chill settles in my belly as he turns stony eyes upon the waiting souls. "Capaneus, come forward."

A short man with a paunchy belly and tightly wound black curls slides through the crowd. His face looks as though he has not quite decided whether to be fearful or defiant and so it flickers between the two.

"Capaneus," Lord Hades' voice flows with power, the volume producing an eerie echo, "for your cruelty and your hubris, you are sentenced to Tartarus. By order of Zeus, King of Olympus, you will spend your eternity burning."

Capaneus screams, the terrifying sound of an animal faced with its last moments. A snarling sound fills the air and licks of flame and darkness erupt from the base of the Towers, through the Gate of Tartarus. The licks turn to tendrils that wrap around Capaneus' panicked form and drag him, literally kicking, screaming and clawing at the ground. A bone-deep terror fills me up to bursting and it suddenly becomes difficult to breathe. Lord Hades opens his arms to me and I quickly retreat into them, grateful for a solid base against the fear that threatens to drown me. Unholy shrieks fill my senses and the choking smell of smoke invades my nostrils. My head swims and I cling to Lord Hades. Capaneus disappears through the Gate in a roar of fire and as that primal light goes out, so too does the terror drain from my body.

Shivering and incoherent, I can only look imploringly at Lord Hades, hoping he will explain what just occurred. He strokes my hair until the trembling subsides. Never in my life have I ever experienced fear such as that. The influence of Tartarus, even for those brief moments had been almost enough to undo me.

"That was Kamp. She is the Jailer of Tartarus, a primordial creature born of fire, darkness and fear. Souls never go willingly into Tartarus, so Kamp snares them and brings them to their fate." I shudder at his words. "Do not worry over them. Only the blackest of souls finds themselves in Tartarus so it actually has the fewest occupants of all the realms."

When he asks me if I want to continue with the Judgements, I can only shake my head. Though I enjoy the trust he has given me, I am still shaken by my brief encounter with Tartarus. As an alternative activity, Lord Hades guides me to the shores of Acheron where we are ferried across. I eye the Ferryman speculatively. He's extremely emaciated, all lean muscle wrapped snugly around bone. His limbs are almost disproportionately long and his black hair has thick streaks of white and gray mixed through. His bottomless dark eyes sit in sunken hollows and they avoid me as he presses the long pole into the riverbed to move us forward.

When we land he politely offers me his hand to assist me to stand. When our skin touches I feel a spark, a shooting of electricity between us and he grips my hand like a lifeline before casting it aside like a hot coal as he stumbles from the boat and onto the waiting ground of Erebus.

Lord Hades shuffles us both quickly off the boat and goes to Charon. He stares at me with wide, unfocused eyes and it takes me a few moments to realize why he looks so odd. His hair is all black now and his body has filled out, looking more like the recipient of many good meals rather than a victim of starvation.

Lord Hades flutters about Charon like a frantic mother hen, clearly at a loss of what to do. The Ferryman brushes him off and steadies himself. "I think your girl here is a Goddess of Life."

I have no idea what he means, so Lord Hades explains that some deities have the power of creation and healing and that I am apparently one of them. He apologizes profusely to Charon for not having noticed how badly Acheron had affected him.

Charon shrugs. "I accepted the position and all that goes with it." He stretches and flexes his arms, testing his renewed strength. "Whatever power you possess, my Lady, I am certainly grateful for it."

21

HADES

Cerberus comes to investigate Persephone and even he falls sway to her power. His three heads vie for her attention and his claws click joyfully against the ground as he scampers around her. She happily obliges his desire for attention with ear scratches and belly rubs. He behaves like a normal dog only with those he genuinely likes, otherwise he behaves very much like the beast he is. Cerberus is the guardian who keeps watch over Erebus, monitoring the souls that have entered the realm, but have not yet been ferried across Acheron.

While she plays I contemplate her power. I've never possessed the gifts that she does, the energy of life and light. My own powers stem from stillness and death. I am more annoyed than I have a right to be over the fact that she has spent more than a century in existence and is only just now discovering the actual root of her power. Someone should have shown her, yet even Gaia held back this knowledge. Was it because Persephone was not meant to know or because I was meant to be the one to show her?

"Cerberus, your post has been abandoned long enough." The hell-hound gives a few thumps of his tail and all three heads swivel to look at me with an expression that suggests a profound hope I'll change my mind. I raise one eyebrow and he huffs and sighs and scrambles to his feet before trotting back to properly guard Erebus.

Persephone laughs, the sound of bells rippling out. "He's wonderful, I wasn't expecting him to be so friendly."

"He's not usually, but I'm glad he seems to adore you. I have horses as well if you are fond of animals." Her vibrant grin answers my question and we return to the Palace and divert to the stables where Eustathios is covered head to toe in horse hair as he carts over a bucket of oats for one of the horses. He sets down his load and gives us each a quick bow.

"My Lord, Lady Persephone, please forgive my appearance, I've only just finished with their grooming and had not anticipated your arrival." He grins at me while he tries to brush off the worst of the hair. "Word of your presence has spread quickly, I was hoping to have the chance to meet you."

I introduce Persephone to Eustathios, the dæmon in charge of the care of my horses. He ushers us into the stables so Persephone can meet my herd of two stallions and two mares named Archihippos, Hippolytos, Alcippe and Xanthippe, respectively.

She gazes at them with starry-eyed adoration. Having Persephone here allows me to see my realm with a fresh perspective as I wonder what exactly she sees when she looks around. I inhale deeply. The scent of horse, oats and fresh grass is almost overpowering in the confines of the stable, but it's oddly comforting nonetheless. Usually they would be allowed to run free, but for the sake of expedient grooming and feeding they are confined every so often to the stables so Eustathios may care for them. Each horse is Stygian black with hair so thoroughly groomed that they appear to shimmer in even the lowest light. Easily double the size of the average horse, they towering over Persephone as she moves tentatively towards them.

Archihippos is unused to strangers and snorts as he paws at the ground. The others have a more mild temperament, but it is Archihippos that Persephone seems most intent on. Perhaps the little Goddess has more daring in her than she realizes. She kneels a moment and taps the ground, causing a tree to twist up from the earth. Brilliant red apples pop into being and hang off the branches. She picks one and holds it before her. The stallion eyes it speculatively before tossing his head, ebony mane cascading around him. My lips quirk into an amused smirk at his display.

Alcippe reaches her head out her stall and cranes it to lip Persephone's hair into her mouth. The little Goddess gives a squeak in surprise and I tap Alcippe on the nose. The pretty mare turns her gaze on me, imploring me to fetch her the apple just out of her reach.

"I imagine the others would be glad of your affection, Archihippos will come around when he sees the others rewarded for their pleasant behavior." She gathers an armful of apples for each of the other three horses and while the others gorge themselves on the sweet fruit, Archihippos dances between desire to be included and profound annoyance at having to be pleasant in order to get what he wants.

With the others appeased, she returns her focus onto the ill-tempered stallion. She plucks another apple and holds it away from him.

"Give me a kiss and I will give you the apple," Persephone requests. He snorts at this, doing his best to stare her down, willing her to just give him the treat. He tries to reach around her, but she only scoots further away. He cuffs her cheek with his nose and rears his head up, baring his teeth. I move on instinct to separate her from him, but she holds out a hand to stop me.

I glare at the horse, subtly shaking my head. Persephone reaches up and presses her palm to his nose. He snaps at her hand and she just narrowly avoids losing a few fingers. I release a sharp breath and try to stifle the urge to pull her away. She gives me a reassuring smile, but it does little to tame the thundering heart in my chest. The last thing I want to do is to have to return her to Olympus missing body parts. They would heal with time, but her mother would most definitely notice and then Persephone would never see me again.

Broadcasting my displeasure to Archihippos, he reluctantly lowers his head under my careful watch and lips Persephone on the cheek. She squeals with delight and immediately gives him the apple he desires. He ignores her while he chews, but she is not dissuaded from stroking his neck. Relieved he refrained from biting her, I feel safe enough offering up the experience of riding.

22

PERSEPHONE

Xanthippe is a huge animal and it's just not possible for her gentle personality to detract from that fact. She's tall enough I'm not even able to see over her back when I stand on tiptoe. Momentary ecstasy at the opportunity to ride these beautiful creatures had made me agree without comprehending the logistics involved, but as I stand before this magnificent animal my courage begins to wane.

Lord Hades stands silently behind me, the heat of his body ghosting through the air between us. He grasps my hips and lifts me easily into the air, instructing me to swing my leg over Xanthippe's back. I shift and wiggle atop her back in an attempt to find a comfortable position, but quickly find that there isn't one. She dances in place and I cling desperately to her mane.

Lord Hades swings onto Alcippe with an ease that makes me instantly jealous. He guides Alcippe over and pats my knee. "She can feel how tense you are, you need to relax. She won't let you fall."

Accepting his assurance with a grain of salt, I struggle to loosen my grip on her mane and relax my legs. Xanthippe's massive head swings around and lips at my calf, her own attempt at comfort. Xanthippe follows Alcippe as Lord Hades guides her into the depths of Elysium. Around us a desert of red stretches into the horizon, punctuated by massive stones that jut out of the sky to the heavens. Silvery scrub brush breaks the pattern of red at random intervals and strange laughter echoes on the wind as small, golden, wolf-like creatures dart around the russet dunes. The Elysian sun is hot on my skin, punctuated by the scent of dust and sage.

Alcippe starts to run and Xanthippe immediately follows, charging over the packed sand. A cloud of red follows in our wake and it seems as though they run forever. I let out a whoop of joy as the wind whips my hair and Lord Hades frees his own laugh to the breeze. My blood pumps wildly in exhilaration as the thunder of hooves blends with the sound of rushing air, the view around me no more than a blur of sand and sky. Xanthippe's smooth gait slows into a walk and when she stops I slide off of her and collapse to the ground, my legs jelly. Lord Hades springs down with no effort at all and bends a smiling face over me.

In a moment of child-like joy he grabs a handful of the brilliant red sand and tosses it into the air, covering me head to toe in a fine dust coating. I shiver like a dog shaking off water and look down at my filthy garment.

"Evaristus is going to roast you like a pig when he sees this." The dæmon never would, but I can just imagine his face when he sees the outfit he picked out with such care being in such a state. Lord Hades only laughs and tugs me towards the cliff edge not far from where we stopped. The view is breathtaking. A crevasse plunges into the Earth, carved out by a river that glitters like a diamond-dusted serpent at the bottom of the canyon.

We rest companionably for a while, just enjoying the sun, breeze and views. Unfortunately, the horses are less patient and Xanthippe lips at my ear until I finally give in and pay attention to her. She lowers her head so I can grab two fistfuls of her mane and then she tosses her head to lift me up as though I weigh nothing. Xanthippe whips me up and over so I have to scramble to not slide right off the other side of her broad back.

"I can't remember the last time I've felt so relaxed," he says wistfully. I'm charmed both by Lord Hades' words and his smile. I am honestly surprised to see a smile come so easily to his face. He turns to me and another, more hesitant smile blossoms on his face. He leaps atop Alcippe and strokes her flank. "I confess that there are many times in our conversations over the years when I wished it was as easy to see you in person as it was to speak through the stones. Somehow it's easy to forget the looming shadow of duty and obligation when we correspond and I know in the times between speaking I have all but drowned in my work."

Xanthippe sidles up to Alcippe so that our knees bang together. Unsure of how to verbally respond I simply reach out and take his hand. I ponder the difference between Lord Hades and my mother. Lord Hades is willing to spend quality time with me, to ask questions about my life and actually appears to be interested in the answers. I feel safe here, free to express my thoughts and opinions without fear I will trigger some volatile emotional response. I can't pinpoint what it is, but his energy just feels comforting and I like being around him.

Not yet brave enough to voice those thoughts, I present a question I have been careful not to ask many others. "Do you ever hear Gaia speak?"

He appears surprised by the question, but not angry as my mother had been when I once asked her. "Long ago I heard her quite frequently. She guided me in the construction of my realm and was a most appreciated companion in those early days. I have not heard the Great Mother for millennia now. I think perhaps I might have drowned out her voice in the chaos of the everyday."

"Gaia has been my teacher since I was born," I tell him. "My entire craft has been learned under her guidance."

"She can be a magnificent teacher," he agrees, "if you can think of the proper questions to ask her."

Before I know it the horses have reached the boundaries of Elysium and are trotting happily back to the stables, presumably expecting a well-deserved meal and brush down.

A dæmon informs Lord Hades that he is requested in the Great Hall. He excuses himself and I am led away by Evaristus to freshen up before I am to join them.

23

HADES

I wash up hastily before making my way to the Great Hall where I find Thanatos and Hermes already seated. Though we have no need to eat there are platters of honeyed fruit and ambrosia sitting alongside jugs of nectar and wine, which Hermes picks at absently.

Persephone joins us shortly, gowned freshly in pink silk, her damp hair curling wildly. Hermes nods politely to her, but wastes no time in relaying the reason he has requested my presence.

"The war has progressed," he announces. "A thousand ships have launched and sail for Troy and countless others are prepared to sail at a moment's notice." For Persephone's benefit he explains the circumstances that brought the war to pass; how the prince of Troy stole away the Spartan Queen, Helen, and how her husband and his brother, Agamemnon are taking all the kings to war against Troy. "The pretense is to return the stolen Spartan Queen to her husband, but Agamemnon has a darker purpose in mind and seems to care for very little in his quest for power. The Mycenæan King has interests in Troy and the surrounding ports, eager to gain control of the tolls and taxes that have made the city wealthy. So far as I have gleaned, he has plans to destroy the city regardless of their success in returning his brother's wife."

"Would not the value of the city be destroyed in that case?" Persephone asks and I can see the fascination playing on her features as she absorbs the information presented.

Hermes scribbles a map across the table with a piece of chalk, complete with all the ships and the positions of the armies in the mortal world. Persephone's eyes light up with interest. "It's possible that Agamemnon wants to keep the structural integrity of the city intact, but remove the people. Such action would leave it easy for his soldiers to move in and claim the port as their own. Alternatively, he could rebuild over the ruins," Hermes comments. "It is not the first time such a thing has happened there."

Hermes points out Mycenæ on the map. "As soon as Agamemnon had sailed out of sight his wife took over the rulership of Mycenæ. Agamemnon slaughtered his daughter, Iphigenia, in return for favorable winds and destroyed what little loyalty his family had for him. If he does not conquer Troy he will have no kingdom to return to."

We end the evening watching chaos sail towards Troy, discussing the potential ramifications and how best to deal with the coming tides.

In the morning Persephone returns home, but there is much to be done and I cannot allow my mind to dwell upon her noticeable absence. Before the deaths from the war come, there are those who died on the way; those who have already succumbed to starvation; and assault by looters who have taken advantage of the lack of warriors to protect their homes.

I catch information in snippets, either from Hermes, when he has a moment to spare, or through the souls who were part of the War. Protesilaus is the first Achæan to die on Trojan soil and he relays what he knows.

"Fifty thousand soldiers line the beaches of Troy, their walls seem impregnable and their archers are fierce, but we stay out of range of their arrows. Kings from each city-state have joined Agamemnon, and the Trojan allies are no match for the might of the Achæan armies. It is only a matter of time before the city is starved out."

A low wailing sound fills my ears, and soon it becomes an all-out shriek of despair. The sound begins to fill the chamber and the waiting souls look around frantically for the source.

"That must be my wife, Laodamia. I did not live far from Troy, a messenger will have reached her with news of my death by now."

"Hades?" The voice is familiar, but it takes me a moment to realize that it's Aphrodite. "I know I have sided with the Trojans in this quarrel, but I cannot bear the sound of this woman. I need you to fix it."

"Fix it? What am I supposed to do? Her husband is dead."

She appears before me, splendid as always, with her usually golden curls now several shades darker and her blue eyes now green. "I know that, or else she would not be going on in such a manner. Just bring him back to life." Her fists rest impatiently on her hips and she huffs at me.

"That is not how it works," I tell her, crossing my arms over my chest. "Mortals die and then they stay here."

Her faces twists into a sour expression. "Well, make an exception. Honestly, do I have to think of everything?"

When I don't respond immediately I can feel her power reaching out to me, a gentle coaxing as she attempts to pour into my mind and influence me towards her desired outcome. I shake off the energy, my annoyance overriding her attempts, and snap at her. "You have no authority in this realm, Aphrodite. You will make no demands."

Her eyes harden and her bottom lip plumps into a delicate pout. "Fine, but this will never cease." She waves her hand and the volume of the wailing intensifies so loudly that the walls tremble and the shades join in the desperate sound.

"Enough!" The sound is cut off and Aphrodite's energy flares with simmering anger. "Protesilaus may speak to his wife to assure her of his reception and care in the Underworld, but he will not remain in the mortal world, nor will he be provided with a corporeal body for the journey."

"Oh, very well. Hermes, be a dear and handle that for me?" She sidles up close to him, but he tenses and does not respond when she presses her lips to his cheek. She and Hermes have a complicated past, one that includes a son and a lot of bruised feelings. She does not seem to dwell on the negatives of their involvement, but he cannot help himself and ultimately stews sporadically over how it all went wrong. I never understood the attraction myself, for although Aphrodite can be painfully beautiful, she is also about as deep as a puddle. She is pushy and demanding and any conversation would likely leave you bored to tears without her appearance as a distraction.

When she vanishes, it is eerily silent and Hermes is still visibly uncomfortable. I think sometimes Hermes uses the Underworld as a refuge from Olympus, much as I do, and now our sanctuary has been violated by Aphrodite's presence. I have no desire to send Protesilaus to his wife and even less desire to make Hermes be his escort, but he is the Psychopompos, the Soul Guide, and the only one free to go and ensure the safe return of the soul.

Hermes shrugs when I give him the instructions. "You're the boss, if you want me to take him I will. I'll have to ask you to pass along the message to Thanatos, Charon and Cerberus as I do *not* have the patience for an argument right now."

I accompany Hermes and Protesilaus to the borders of my realm and see them off into the mortal world. They should be gone only a short time as Protesilaus is only to inform his wife that he is safe, at peace, and she needn't worry for him. Barely minutes later Hermes returns again bearing not one, but two souls. He looks beyond weary as he deposits them both on the realm side of Styx. "Laodamia did not take the news very well."

I don't need to see her tapestry to know she will require extensive time at Cocytus to recover from this. Suicides are treated as any other death, and though I know Laodamia likely took her own life with the expectation that she would be spending her eternity with her husband, it will be a long while before, and if, such a thing occurs. It might be easier in the short term to just allow them to be together, but the whole point of the afterlife is to let go of your mortal life. Laodamia will still find peace or paradise without her mortal husband by her side. Besides, if word got out that committing suicide allowed you to bypass judgement and the cleansing of the soul then everyone would start doing it. Some may call such a practice unkind, but death has never been about kindness. I immediately summon two dæmons to escort her to Cocytus so she may begin to cleanse her sorrow.

When Protesilaus is also escorted away, Hermes spares a moment to look down at himself. His clothing and legs are spattered with blood, presumably Laodamia's. He sighs. "Poor thing took a knife to her own throat when she saw him as a shade. Her children saw, there was so much crying." His eyes look unnervingly empty. "I need to wash up; there is too much blood ..."

24

PERSEPHONE

I n the chaos of the war I am left mostly to my own devices. Olympus
is deserted much of the time and Mother is gone far more than she's
at home. The happenings in the war between Troy and Agamemnon's
armies are quite fascinating, but I'm mostly interested in Helen. She's
my mortal half-sister and she is surrounded by a plethora of fascinating ladies that have become the focus of my attention. I try to split my
free time between the mortal world and the Underworld, but I stay in
neither for long as I have no way of knowing when my mother might
return to Olympus and find me gone.

Every time I visit Helen in the Palace of Troy she's sitting at her window, staring out at the sea where the Achæan army waits. Aphrodite's
magic is like a stifling cloak around her. There is nothing about her, not
her thoughts, emotions or speech that is not influenced by the magic
of the Goddess of Love. I have tried to tap into her thoughts, but there
is only the rose-colored world that Aphrodite has given her. Still, there
is turmoil beneath it and as strong as the magic is, it cannot bind away
all of Helen's fear and guilt, nor disguise the fact that she didn't choose
Paris of her own accord. It makes me wonder if she cares for him and if

she ever would have gone with the Trojan prince of her own free will. I wonder whether Menelaus truly loves her, or if he wants her back only to assuage his damaged pride. If that is the case, I do not believehis bruised ego is worth the lives of the thousands it will cost to retrieve her.

"Lady Helen, come eat." One of Helen's serving maids tries to break her from her reverie at the window, but she is ignored.

One of the Trojan princesses glides into the room. "I will take her." Cassandra's mind is constantly turbulent. Her thoughts blend chaotically with prophetic visions to the point I'm not even certain she knows what is real anymore. When I first came here her thoughts were calmer, but with each visit they have been worsening. I touched her mind once, but the flashes of death, destruction and violence pushed me out instantly. Cassandra hooks an arm through Helen's and tugs until she finally stands. "Come, sister, you must eat for the child if not for yourself." She rubs a hand over Helen's swelling stomach and leads her out of the room.

Cassandra is tainted by Apollo's magic. Not to the extent that Helen is affected by Aphrodite's, but there is a band of Apollonian power that covers Cassandra's mouth, altering her prophecies whenever she tries to speak them. Beneath the power of the Sun God I can also feel Gaia's touch. It was not Apollo who had gifted Cassandra with her powers, but the Earth Mother. He cannot undo Gaia's gift, so he simply changes how others perceive it. Hearing her prophecies through that veil of magic turns them false in their minds.

The two women move slowly down the hall, their frames thin due to the rationing that has been enforced in the city. Cassandra's eyes flicker between alertness and emptiness as she slips in and out of her visions. It's a wonder she has not been driven mad by what her visions show her. Apollo's magic renders her helpless, knowing what is to come, but unable to prevent any of it.

A man with brilliant auburn hair and flashing blue eyes greets the women in the hall. He smiles at Cassandra, his eyes soft with affection. He takes her free hand and tucks her arm through his, walking at a sedate pace with them. In the dining hall he settles them both at a long table where much of the nobility sits before plates holding only sparse morsels of food. Helen gets extra food to accommodate her pregnancy, but the others get only enough to keep their bellies calm.

"Thank you, Aeneas." Cassandra offers him a gentle smile and his loving eyes drink it up. "How is my sister feeling?" I have seen him before, but he has always kept his distance when I have been around in the past. I tap his mind and find him to be a demigod, a son of Aphrodite.

"Creusa is well, the babe has not made her ill at all this week." Aeneas reaches out to Cassandra unconsciously, but draws his hand back when she focuses her soulful eyes upon him. There is love there, but Cassandra has more control over it than Aeneas obviously does. It is a good thing too, because that he is married to her sister and it is doubtful the King of Troy would take kindly to his son-in-law sharing the bed of two of his daughters. "Go to her, she must be hungry. I promise I will eat."

He hesitates for a moment, but does as she says. As soon as he's out of sight Cassandra pushes half of her food onto Helen's plate. Helen eats without acknowledgement, staring blankly ahead. Cassandra nibbles at her remaining food, but her eyes fill with terror as a vision overtakes her. When she returns to normal she looks queasy and pushes the food away.

The air shivers with power and I quickly disappear from Troy so whatever Olympian is making an appearance will not find me there. Forgoing returning to Olympus, I head straight to the Underworld. Thanatos welcomes me through the Gates and Charon ushers me over the River Acheron so I can locate Lord Hades atop the Towers. Each time I see him it's a fresh shock. The war above has put a lot of stress on the Lord of the Underworld and he looks exhausted, his features forming a near permanent scowl. He brightens when he sees me, but he's obviously distracted.

The crowd of souls awaiting judgement is unusually dense. I wade through them and manage to tempt Lord Hades with a brief ride through Elysium. Only when we reach the depths of Paradise atop our mounts do his shoulders finally relax. We walk the horses over white sand beaches next to a rolling ocean. We give them free-rein and he slowly opens up to me about the goings-on in his realm. He has found his third Judge and hopes to let them take over when the war is over.

"Most of the souls waiting to be processed are from the famines. There are soldiers, as is expected with a war, but most of the victims are those left behind. The soldiers are replenished every few months, leaving the situation at home ever more dire. Rations are prioritized for soldiers and so the poor and ill are left to starve. Few families have the means to support themselves while the men are so far afield and too many have succumbed to poverty and murder." He heaves a sigh. "Disease has spread through the Achæan camp as well. Hermes tells me they stole a Priestess of Apollo and the Sun God struck them with plague as punishment." He balls up his fists, knuckles white and he bares his teeth in anger. "All of this bloodshed and misery is because of Zeus and Poseidon's selfish desires."

I'm a bit surprised by the venom in his voice. "It was Eris who gave the apple and Aphrodite who influenced Helen though."

Hades turns on me with narrowed eyes. "And where do you think that apple came from? It is one of the golden apples of the Garden of the Hesperides that Hera was given at her wedding. They are guarded by a dragon and Hera has never once given one of those apples to anyone. The only way Eris would have had access to one of the apples would be if someone gave it to her. In the entire history of the Gardens only three apples have ever been stolen and the one who came into possession of them was Heracles, the son of Zeus."

"You think Zeus gave the apple to Eris? Why would he do that?" I try to follow his thoughts, but I know very little about either Zeus or Eris.

"Discord isolates people, it is much easier for him to get to whatever he wants if they are cut off from protection and family. I cannot know for sure whether he is the one that gave her the apple, but someone had to. Hera would have known if Eris had been to her Garden, she would have said something at the wedding about it." He sighs, shoving a hand through his hair. "Zeus and Poseidon laid the foundations for everything. Zeus knows Eris hates being left out; not inviting her to the wedding we were all attending was practically a challenge for her. The wedding would never have even occurred if they could control their desires. They wanted Thetis and they made it happen. I would not be surprised if they had alerted Eris to the wedding to provide a distraction so they could get to Thetis sooner. Zeus chose Paris to make a judgement he should have made himself, there was no reason for any mortals to be involved and when he chose Aphrodite, she was influenced by Eris' magic. That apple is poisonous, infecting her with discordant energy. Under that influence it is unlikely Aphrodite would have cared if her offer to Paris had resulted in the destruction of all human life on Earth."

"The Gods seem to care so little for the mortals under their care. So much destruction could have been avoided, but they disregard others like playthings." I click my tongue and the horses pause. "They mean something to you though, and *that* is what's important. When their mortal lives end the other Gods don't matter to the mortals, but you do. The wars will fade, their pain will vanish, but the magnificent world you created for their souls will remain into eternity."

He stares at me in astonishment and I grin back at him a moment before giving Hippolytos a good squeeze with my thighs that sends him into a gallop. Archihippos follows immediately, forcing Lord Hades to grab onto the beast's whipping mane. Elysium erupts around us, painting rippling fields of green and gold as far as the eye can see. We ride on and on, fierce as a storm and just as quick. We ride until I can feel nothing but the wind and the horse between my thighs. I hear nothing but the rush of air, the thunder of hooves and the whoop of joy that Lord Hades releases as we crest a hill and plunge into the waiting valley.

I will Elysium to forge a lake and as we crest the next hill, crystalline blue water fills the next valley. It sparkles like crushed diamond and when we slow to a stop I fling myself to the ground, catching myself before I tumble head over heels and career straight into the water. Diving into the welcoming coolness washes away the heat of the sun from my skin. I stand where the water is waist deep, my gown a tangle of fabric around my legs. I tug off the gown and toss the sodden ball along with my sandals onto the shore before sinking in up to my shoulders. It's so much easier to swim without being restricted. I dive under and glide through the water, popping up every so often for air. I used to swim with the nymphs a lot when the heat of the day grew unbearable, but I wonder if Lord Hades has ever gone swimming since the Underworldis not directly exposed to the sun.

Lord Hades slips off Archihippos and joins me in the water, albeit more gingerly than my entrance. I sink to my ankles into the soft, sandy bottom, enjoying the fluid squishing of the sand between my toes. He leaves his sandals with my sodden ones and plucks off the short cloak that adorns his shoulders, leaving on his knee-length chiton. He glides slowly through the cerulean liquid, a small smile ghosting his lips as it caresses his body.

Feeling exceptionally playful, I burst from the water and catch him in a hug that leaves his robes soaked through. I almost expect him to toss me away and dismiss my foolish behavior, but instead his arms lock around my waist almost automatically. He raises one hand to my cheek, smoothing away the sodden strands from my face. My breath freezes in my chest as he continues to stare at me, his expression unreadable. The heat from his chest moves easily through the fabric and warms me, more potent than the Elysian sun at my back.

Unnerved by the intimacy I draw back slightly. His fingers slide from my cheek, forming a trail of a sparkling sensation down my throat and over my arm before they drop into the water. He blinks and seems to break free from a trance. His lips curl into a delicate smile and the world around me rushes back into focus.

"Swim with me." I pull him further into the water until our feet no longer touch the bottom and we're cradled in the cerulean depths. "Close your eyes," I instruct, dropping my voice to a whisper. "I want you to keep this moment in your mind. Keep it there for when the pressures of your role and the demands of the war become too great for your spirit. Breathe." I follow my own instructions along with him, inhaling the crisp dampness of the lake. "Smell the water and the air, the fields and the flowers. Feel the sun above you and water around you. When things become difficult, I want you to think back on this, to when there was no worry in this moment, nothing but the earth and the sky, the water and the sun to concern you." It's peaceful here, in this Elysian lake with the heat of its illusory sun above us and one another for company. He opens his dark eyes and watches me speculatively. My heart flutters in my chest and I feel myself moving closer to him. The gravity of him, a beacon of heat and power in the cool water, draws me nearer. The words tumble from my lips. "I want more."

He looks at me, slightly startled. "More of what?"

Embarrassment inundates me. I want more of him, to have more of these moments and to not have to worry about time limits or discovery. Instead I deflect this desire and tell him of another. "I want to do more, to be more." A sigh heaves my shoulders. "I have been watching the War from Olympus and I am at a loss of how to help with anything."

His shoulder sag and I feel guilty for withholding my thoughts, but I couldn't speak them. What if he doesn't feel the same? It could ruin what we have if I told him. "Oh," he pauses, "I wouldn't worry. Your time will come, be patient and watch for the right opportunity. I have no doubt that something that suits you perfectly will present itself."

25

PERSEPHONE

I continue to monitor the situation at Troy. The war has been going on for nine years at this point and morale is low. I tend to keep to the Palace, but I suppose it's time to see all of what is going on in this conflict.

A city of tents line the beach and the stench of a compact human population assaults me immediately. Blood, excrement and vomit combine into a horrific scent, mingling with ocean air, sweat and roasting meat. I clamp a hand over my nose to dampen my sense of smell so I can avoid retching into the sand.

With my initial discomfort tempered I take a moment to survey my surroundings properly. I'm cloaked in power so they cannot see or hear me, but it's still disconcerting to be among so many soldiers. There are people everywhere and the tents are set as far back from the towering city walls of Troy as possible without being so close to the ocean as to be swallowed up with the tides. Presumably this setup is to avoid being turned into pincushions by the waiting archers clearly visible along the ramparts. Many of the men I can see look worn down and a substantial number of them are visibly riddled with disease. There is an astonishing number of women in the camp as well, though a quick scan of their minds tells me that they are primarily abductees from surrounding villages. I attempt to cast out my essence to gather more information, but the onslaught of misery I encounter forces me to retract into myself again.

A commotion near one of the largest tents catches my attention. Two men are shouting at one another and a woman is tucked behind the one man in the tent. There are a myriad of soldiers standing around watching the excitement. I search the thoughts of those primarily involved. The man outside the tent is Agamemnon, the King of Mycenæ who prompted all of these men into war. The man in the tent is Achilles, the son of Peleus and Thetis. It feels as though it was only yesterday that I attended the wedding of his parents and now their child is a man grown. He has a glimmer of magic around his body, shimmering with the light of immortality, all save a small spot at his heel. I weave through his memories and find the ones that explain the light. As a baby, Thetis had dipped her son into the River Styx, keeping hold of him by his heel and the waters had granted him immortality. Achilles' memories show him to be an exceptional warrior, but it is almost an odd thing for his mother to have done for him. He cannot die from wounds to most of his body, but he could still be near death if his body was unable to heal. Poison, broken bones, any number of things would leave him completely incapacitated.

I slip out of Achilles' mind, forgetting my questions and instead I focus on the dark-haired beauty tucked behind him. I search her thoughts and determine that her name is Briseis and she was once the Queen of Lyrnessus. Her kingdom lies just north of Troy and she, among many others, had been captured when the Achæan armies marched through the territory to destroy Troy's nearest allies. Flickers of terror in her thoughts show me that she was initially given to Agamemnon before she was gifted to Achilles in an attempt to curry his favor. Now Agamemnon wants her back after having to return the Apollonian priestess he stole, but neither Achilles nor Briseis want him to regain possession. I realize the reason so many of the men appear to be riddled with disease is because of the Apollonian priestess and Agamemnon's initial reluctance to return her. Like a child forced to give up his favorite toy, he immediately seeks to steal from another to assuage his own pride.

Briseis stands naked behind Achilles, her whole body trembling. Her mind is full of fear as flashes of Agamemnon's previous abuses towards her race through her thoughts. Achilles has been kind to her, shown her affection and protection, but Agamemnon terrorized her for as long as she was his prisoner. I drift inside the tent just before Agamemnon fills the opening while shouting himself hoarse. It's mostly profanity, but the few comprehensible bits he spits out make it clear he is demanding Briseis from Achilles.

The terrified girl gathers a blanket from the ground and tucks it around her. Achilles' naked body is lined with taut muscle and is baked into a dark gold by the sun. A blush floods my cheeks as I realize the situation Agamemnon must have found them in. Achilles positions himself firmly between Briseis and Agamemnon, guarding her with his body.

"You have your own woman, leave us be." Achilles hisses through his teeth and nudges Briseis further to the back of their tent.

"You know damn well I had to give Chryseis back to the temple to stop this plague." When Agamemnon moves to grab Briseis Achilles raises his sword, pointing it at the broad chest of the Mycenæan King. Agamemnon narrows his eyes at Achilles. "Hold down your sword. I am your leader and you will do as I command or my soldiers will gut you where you stand."

With these words the cluster of warriors flanking Agamemnon slip into the tent and surround Achilles and Briseis from all sides. The girl sobs, her shoulders heaving as the despair over her potential future presses down upon her. The hair on the back of my neck rises. I reach out and find that most of the men are reluctant to take Achilles on in battle, but they are Agamemnon's own men from Mycenæ and they owe him their allegiance.

"You are not my king and I am the best warrior you have. You will not touch me, swine." Achilles eyes narrow, a hawk poised to dive on its prey. Agamemnon might not be his king, but he is the leader of the Achæan armies, the orchestrator of this entire war. Achilles may not listen to him, but it is abundantly clear that the other men do. Achilles' memories tell me he's used to fighting champion battles, one on one conflicts in which he has always been triumphant. Even the best warrior will tire and he cannot face down the entire army, Agamemnon knows he has Achilles right where he wants him.

With a subtle hand gesture from their king, the soldiers converge on Achilles. He cannot fight them all at once and while he quickly dispatches three of them, another manages to tear Briseis away from him. "Perhaps not you, but I might gut her so that neither of us may enjoy the pleasures of her flesh." The soldiers pass her off to Agamemnon and he wraps a meaty hand around her throat. "Stand down, Achilles, or I will slit her belly." He slips a slender blade from his belt and presses the point into her flesh just hard enough so a few drops slip out and slide down her skin.

Briseis succumbs completely to panic. She wails Achilles' name and clutches at the hand holding the knife. She twists and squirms, catching the blade so it punctures even deeper. A hot trail of blood licks her belly, it looks worse than it is, but her hysteria convinces Achilles otherwise.

Achilles looks beyond rage and I realize that I have seen that same look of burning fury before, on his mother on the day of her wedding. His body is tense as a bowstring, but he is helpless to move. I don't have to view his thoughts to know that he feels affection for Briseis, otherwise he would take his revenge on Agamemnon, regardless of the risk to her safety. The only thing he wants more right now than to tear the Mycenæan King's head off his shoulders is to protect the woman he loves. The smirk on Agamemnon's cruel, twisted face makes me wonder if it would not be a kinder fate to let the knife ravage her body than to let her be taken to his tents.

The guards haul a naked and screaming Briseis out of the tent. Agamemnon smirks before he turns on his heel and saunters away. "Sleep well, Achilles."

The bellow of rage startles me, a furious sound more animal than human. Achilles picks up his sword and slams it into the sand until only the pommel is visible. Anger roils about him, an aura of fury, tumultuous as water boiling over. He throws himself to the ground, screaming into the bed coverings, shouting out Briseis' name and cursing Agamemnon to a fiery eternity in Tartarus.

I abandon Achilles and follow the shrieks of Briseis, a haunting echo that permeates the entire camp. Agamemnon has a firm hold of her by her hair and she sprawls on the ground, wailing out Achilles' name. He slaps her hard across the face and in a moment of panic I shove power at him, willing him to stop. He slumps forward, fully asleep with his mouth open and drool already starting to pool below his lips. Perhaps when he wakes the high of his victory will have diminished and he will not harm her just to make a point. Briseis shivers and gingerly extracts her hair from his hand. Her lip is split and bleeding, cheeks shining with tears. I stroke her hair and though she can neither see nor feel me, her trembling slowly eases. I kiss her forehead in blessing and numb her pain, physical and emotional and try to fortify her against her coming ordeal. There's the painful, quiet knowledge that if I spare her somehow, Agamemnon will only take another and Achilles would be blamed for it. I pray to Gaia that she will be returned to her love.

I stare down in disdain at the Mycenæan king. I probe at his mind and uncover the part of him that is riddled by insecurity, the level that is small and fearful and needs to tear down others to feel as though he means something. He is a bully and a fool that has drawn thousands to their doom.

I open up myself and a flood of prayers instantly overwhelms me. I can hear prayers to anyone if I concentrate on it, but prayers specifically to me, though there are none right now, would reach me even if I did not want to listen to them. Any prayers that are unaddressed or are particularly fervent I can access easily as well. The prayers I hear tell me that many of the men have lost hope in the war ever coming to an end and the women long for their own homes. They all long for loved ones and a time when they could remember peace. It is not my place to intervene here, though I wish I could. The salvation of these mortals will be Thanatos and the cleansing waters of Cocytus.

Past the towering walls of the great city, life is little different. The siege has made food scarce and what is left is diverted primarily for the royals and the soldiers. The children are still children though, happy as they can be despite their protruding ribs and twig-thin limbs.

I meander through the city until I arrive at the Palace and pass undetected through the gates. I find several of the royal princesses, Andromache, the wife of the Trojan Crown Prince, Hector, as well as Cassandra and Helen. They are gathered together in Helen's room that overlooks the entire city and offers a disconcerting view of the Achæan camp. Andromache cradles her belly that is swelling with child. Her thoughts dwell on her husband and her worry for him each time he rides out to battle.

Helen sprawls on a long couch, well away from the windows. Several golden haired children are curled up around her and her stomach heralds the addition of another in the coming months. A tiny girl, a petite replica of her mother, crawls over Helen's lap and gives her a broad smile composed of only a few teeth. Helen manages a small smile as she strokes the child's silken curls, but her eyes are dark with despair.

I tap Helen's mind and encounter a thick wall of Aphrodite's magic. I force my way though and weave through her memories, watching when she had first come to Troy. She had been completely intoxicated by Aphrodite's power when Paris had hauled her through the magnificent Gates of Troy. Priam and Hecuba, the King and Queen of Troy had accepted an audience with the then-unknown shepherd only because Helen was known as the Queen of Sparta. His age and intensely similar appearance to Priam and Hecuba's other children left little doubt as to his true identity. They had taken in their son and the Queen he had in tow. I touch Cassandra's thoughts to try and discern the history of Paris, careful to avoid the violent turns into prophecy her mind takes without warning. She was only a babe when her brother was cast out of the city, but she has faint memories of conversations heard through the years. A prophecy foretold Paris would bring ruin to Troy and so he had been exposed in the mountains outside of the city. He had returned with the Achæan army on his heels, just as the prophecy had foretold, but by the time they realized what was following their son it was too late to do anything but barricade the city against attack. I know from my own conversations in the Underworld that Agamemnon is here for far more than Helen and perhaps Priam knows that as well; knowing if he gave up Helen and his son that the war would not cease.

I wrap my arms around Helen and whisper to her. I cannot know if my words reach past the veil of power around her mind, but I still try. "No mortal can withstand the force of Aphrodite's will. Helen, you are not to blame for what has happened. You are not the reason

Agamemnon brought his men to war, you are merely the excuse. You are a figurehead, a rallying point, but you are not the root cause. Do not let yourself despair over Agamemnon's greed and lust for power."

26

HADES

Hermes paces back and forth, his restless energy pinging against me. "The mortals are on a precipice; the major players in this war are beginning to fall. Menelaus demanded a duel with Paris and while they fought, Paris was rescued before he could be killed. His eldest brother took his place and inflicted enough damage that Menelaus later died from his wounds. Agamemnon is in a fury over his brother's death and now the warriors are saying there is no reason for them to stay in Troy since Menelaus has no need for a wife in his grave."

"I suppose Agamemnon will find some way to continue the fighting," I comment. "What of Thetis' son? I would have thought he would be handling the duels since he is their most skilled warrior, is he not?"

Hermes nods absently. "He is refusing to fight. Agamemnon stole away Briseis from him and he has not raised a sword in battle since then. None of the Myrmidons under his command have fought, they are all waiting on him."

"Agamemnon cost himself his best fighter because he wanted a woman he had no right to?" I roll my eyes as Hermes nods. If Achilles is anything like his mother, he will be volatile and stubborn, so it's not altogether improbable for him to force Agamemnon to give in and return this woman for want of competent soldiers.

"The energy of the war is fading among the mortals, but Olympus still clashes. I can hope that the Achæans will give up and go home, but knowing Agamemnon he will not leave when he is so close to victory." Hermes paces, agitated. "Without the Myrmidons to buoy them up there is little will to fight, despite how Agamemnon bellows at his fighters."

Thanatos appears before us, looking a tad disheveled. "I apologize for the interruption, but I would appreciate it if you would deal with the Spartan King."

"Is he causing problems?" I inquire. It's very unlike Thanatos to request an expedited Judgement for any specific soul.

Thanatos nods. "I can hear him from Erebus and I simply do not have the patience to listen to him." When one rules over the dead one must have an endless supply of patience. While it is not a virtue particularly known for its association with the Olympians and other immortals, Thanatos is more highly versed than most. Still, I suppose even he must have his limits. We follow the God of Death to where Menelaus is wandering along the shores of Acheron. His periodic glances into the water cause his shoulders to stoop from sadness.

As soon as Menelaus catches sight of us, he races over and clings to Thanatos' robes. "Please my Lord, please will you not tell me when Helen is arriving?"

Thanatos hunches his shoulders, looking more exasperated than I've ever seen him. "Menelaus, will you kindly *shut up*?" I choke on my laughter, making a vain attempt to smother it with my hand. I've never having heard Thanatos speak to anyone in such a manner. He shakes the Spartan King off and swivels his head to catch me in his gaze, his eyes pleading with me to intervene.

"Why should I? No one pays attention to me anyway. Everyone spits on my authority, no one loves me or cares about me, I might as well be dead!" Menelaus lets out a pitiful wail and I fight the urge to roll my eyes. I take in the image of the Spartan. His arms are well muscled, but his belly is round and his beard and hair hang in neatly in oiled spirals. His height and physical strength make him ideal for combat, but he has clearly been a king who indulged in food and drink over the years.

I cross my arms and stare down the Spartan King. "I must point out that you are dead, Menelaus. Even were you not, you have no authority in this realm." His eyes shimmer with the ghostly remembrances of unshed tears. Menelaus' voice is grating, his tones coupled with self-degradation and a deeply embedded sense of entitlement. I get the feeling that Menelaus may be one of those souls who take a *very* long time to reconcile their lives. He could walk the shores of Cocytus for a millenia and learn nothing, though I sincerely hope that is not going to be the case.

Thanatos leans towards me and whispers in my ear. "All I have heard since his arrival is him whining about his brother or Helen and Paris. I know he is only just arrived, but he follows me, clings to my robes and has been bothering the dæmons and the other spirits. When I speak to him he cowers, it is as though he is compelled to speak based on his behaviors in life, but he is too frightened by his current circumstances to maintain the bravado."

Menelaus lets out another wretched wail and drops to his knees before us. "Of course you are right, my Lord, please forgive me." He grips the hem of my cloak and his lip wobbles precariously when I extract it from his grasp. "You will tell me when Helen arrives, my Lord?"

His face falls and he recoils when I make direct eye contact with him. "Helen is no longer your concern. You will come with me now for Judgement."

Thanatos leans close again. "Are you sure we cannot feed him to Kamp as a midday snack?"

"Perhaps we should keep him around, use him as a punishment for those who cross us." I whisper back in a moment of mirth.

Thanatos squeezes his lips together. "You would not be so cruel."

We shuffle the Spartan off to the Towers where Minos and the others pronounce him bound for Asphodel pending time at Cocytus to cleanse himself of his mortal woes.

Menelaus' face swirls through anger, desperation and fear multiple times before settling on righteous indignation. "I am a King, Elysium should be mine!"

Aeacus stares at him from the top of the Towers. "Being King guarantees nothing but the opportunity to commit greater good and greater evil. You chose to do neither."

I summon several dæmons to escort Menelaus to his temporary resting place at Cocytus and instruct them to post several guards until he settles. Solon and Aeschylus relieve us of Menelaus who falls into a state of temper that leaves him wailing and flailing so that it takes dæmon magic to hoist his ætheric body into the air.

27

HADES

"Hades!" Persephone's voice startles me awake, the shock of the terror in her call and the heat of the flames prompting instant panic. My eyes try to adjust, but there is only chaos and flame. My arm burns, the skin bubbled black where I had drawn it from the fire. Persephone calls out again and I search desperately for the source. Drowned out almost instantly by the roar of the inferno, I'm not able to determine the direction from which the sound had come.

"Persephone!" I shout back and feel my voice being swallowed up by the fire. Other voices shriek in the distance, a cacophony of terror. I catch sight of Persephone through the flickering walls, but when I try to wade through the churning earth towards her, a torrent of lightning rains from the sky around me.

She yells until the sound turns raw, the heat and dust ravaging her throat. I try to breathe, but the earth rippling beneath my feet churns so much into the air that I can scarcely pull anything into my lungs but dirt. I claw my way towards her, or at least towards the direction I think she might be. I drag myself over the heaving terrain, each step sucking my legs into the earth.

I gaze in horror as lightning pours from the sky directly onto Persephone. The flames part just long enough for me to see the shock on her face as the *lightning rips her apart, leaving nothing but a charred corpse with disturb-ingly untouched eyes staring at me accusingly before she is swallowed up by the earth.*

Shivers rack my body as the pain in my arm and the choking panic finally takes hold. I collapse to the ground and let the swells of earth wrap over me, pulling me down into the darkness.

"LORD HADES, ARE YOU UNWELL?" I wake with a scream that shakes the walls and kick at the sheets as I scramble off the side of the bed. I trip and curse as the fabric tangles around my ankles as I I tumble towards the unforgiving stone. Half in a dream state I push harshly away from Persephone when she drops to her knees before me and reaches out. "Please, be calm, what's the matter?"

I withdraw into myself, clutching my face in my hands in a vain attempt to banish the image of her devastated body. I try to look up, but retreat into myself once more when I find those emerald orbs watching me so intently. I figure she'll leave if I stay quiet long enough and so I allow myself to retreat even further into my own thoughts as I sit curled up on the floor.

I wait in silent distress for a few moments before I feel a hand on my shoulder. I expect it to be Evaristus, come to check on me. The hands pry at me, pulling my arms away from my body and eventually I raise my head to ask Evaristus what on earth he thinks he's doing. Persephone kneels in front of me looking very much like a floating star set against the entirely black decor. Her gentle hands clutch my face and force my eyes up. The visions of my nightmare fill my mind, panic swelling in my chest. She continues tugging at me until she is wedged up against my chest with her arms around my neck. I hold her closely and breathe in the decadent smell of nature that emanates from her. The sweet scent of blossoms and clean water radiates from her and warms me to the deepest part of my being.

I never had a moment to experience such tenderness with my mother as I was taken from her at birth, nor has anyone else ever held me in such a manner. I didn't realize how much I needed it, craved it, until now. I cling to her for what is likely an inappropriately long time, but she doesn't pull away. A tentative hand strokes my hair and cheek, alternating between twirling the strands between delicate fingers and tracing the planes of my face.

"You look like Atlas, suffering from the weight of the world," she whispers into my ear. "Tell me what happened, what did you dream?"

My throat closes up, unwilling to tell her I witnessed her demise, so instead I tell her about the dream that usually plagues me. Her forehead creases and her lips drop from a frown to an expression of pure horror as I relay the events of the Titanomache. She presses my cheek to her breast, casting the protective cage of her arms around me. Her heart beats a fierce rhythm against my cheek, but I find the pounding staccato somehow soothing. While nestled against her I tell her of the chaos and the fire and my fears, how myself and my whole family were nearly obliterated; how we ravaged the Titans and condemned many of them to be locked away for eternity. The more I speak the more I feel like I'm unable to stop and it just kept pouring out.

She nods sporadically and generally seems to simply absorb my stories. As the stream of memories dampens I turn to more practical matters. "The Olympians will not let me be. It seems as though every second mortal that dies in this war is a favorite of one or another. They want their heroes in Elysium, but they are cruel and arrogant men who deserve nothing but Tartarus. I am pressed to give the heroes paradise, but my sense of ethics cannot allow it. The longer I ignore the Olympians the more persistent they will become and I cannot have them disrupting the souls and forcing their demands in my realm. I would never seek to step into their realms, yet they feel compelled to step outside of their own jurisdiction and into mine."

"This is your realm and you are the Final Judge. You must stand your ground and do what is fair and just. No soul deserves special treatment just because they managed to curry favor with a God during their life. It doesn't negate their choices, nor exempt them from the rules of death."

"I know," I tell her. The demands of warfare have exhausted us and the constant navigation of Olympian politics has done a number on morale. I debate whether or not to tell her about another development affecting the realm and decide that she needs to be aware of it. "There are thousands of shades awaiting processing and there are a growing number of them that are waiting for you."

"For me?" She seems startled by the concept.

"There are women and children who desire you to be their Judge. I agreed to let them wait until I had spoken to you about it. If you're not interested in working with me to assist them then I must ask you to tell them, so they may join the others waiting for my Judges. If you desire to perform those duties, however infrequent they might be, then I'm willing to set aside a space for those souls to await your return and Judgement."

Her forehead drops to my shoulder and my muscles immediately tense. She raises her impossibly green eyes and my breathing catches. The bottom lashes of her eyes are decorated with a line of tears that trail off the dark tips to coast down golden cheeks. She raises her hand to her heart and pulls in a deep, but uneven breath.

"I'm so honored, Lord Hades, I don't even know what to say. I cannot convey how in awe I am that those souls have put such faith in me."

As I stare at her, soaking up her tearful visage, I feel that pull once more. Our eyes catch and the distance between us becomes almost negligible. I can feel her warm breath on my lips and I am held immobile by the power of her gaze. An overly chipper pattern of knocks at the door startles us apart as Evaristus sweeps into the room with a bright smile.

"My Lord, my Lady, apologies for the interruption," he bows with a flourish. "I wanted only to inform you that Thanatos has returned with another batch of souls. Have you spoken to Lady Persephone?" He looks back and forth between us. I nod my head and Persephone grins at him. "You have agreed?" She nods as well. "Oh, wonderful! I've already sent word for the souls awaiting her to be brought to the Great Hall."

I pull in a shaky breath and dismiss him, both annoyed and relieved that he had come in when he did. Logically I know I am letting myself become too close to Persephone, but I seem to keep doing it anyway. I keep the intimacy at bay by bringing Persephone to the Great Hall where several souls already wait along with a towering basket of rolled tapestries.

Persephone takes her time with the Judgements and though I'm eager to attend to my own duties, I force myself to relax and guide Persephone through hers. She reviews each life thoroughly and speaks to each soul, providing them with her undivided attention. She clarifies life events, examining motivations and external pressures and presents a fair Judgement to each of those waiting.

Most of the souls she deals with are victims of the war. They haven't suffered direct combat, but they experience violence and starvation as their able-bodied men and supplies were diverted to the war effort. She provides a level of care that I had once been able to administer myself before the number of souls arriving had swelled beyond my abilities. Time at Lake Cocytus produces the same result, but it's refreshing to see a soul nearly ready to proceed to their eternity rather than requiring an extensive rest at the shores of the cleansing waters.

By the time she's finished with the first batch of souls she is literally glowing. Her happiness is evident and the souls hover in her light, soaking up the vibrant energy. I'm almost at a loss for words. I had scarcely been needed, save only to nod when she looked askance of me to confirm she had made the correct choice.

She turns her radiance on me, grinning ear to ear. "That was wonderful. I've never felt so fulfilled."

"You have a gift for it." Her face lights up even more at my statement. "You are compassionate and patient and have a just view of the world. I would trust no other Goddess for the job."

The truth of my own words startles me. I have known for some time that Persephone would do well when dealing with the souls, she only needed the opportunity to prove it to herself. They adore her and if she keeps up her dedication to them it will only be a matter of time before her reputation precedes her. Soon enough they will all know her name and how she treated the women and children today. She is truly wasted on Olympus. If only she could stay here instead.

I dare not speak such a thought for fear that she will find the idea unpalatable and distance herself from us, from me. She obviously enjoys her time here, but I'm not yet sure that she enjoys it enough to contemplate making my realm her home.

Thanatos bursts into the Great Hall, a shadow of himself as majority of his essence is elsewhere. "The Achæans have breached the walls of Troy, it is slaughter unlike anything I have ever seen." His shadow whips away and I follow him without a second thought.

28

PERSEPHONE

I follow Lord Hades and Thanatos, rendered speechless by what I see when we arrive. The once proud city is wreathed in flames. Consumed by the senseless violence, I can't even begin to process the atrocities I'm seeing. Lord Hades wraps me in his arms to block out the sight, but it does not muffle the sounds of the dying. Frantic prayers for rescue and salvation invade my thoughts before I can think to block them. I shrink into his embrace before I am able to convince myself that these mortals deserve to have me available for them just as much as the souls in the Underworld did. I push free and try to steady my senses through the cacophony around me. Fires roar, swallowing up entire buildings in the outer edges of the city and the screams and moans of the dying blend into a torrent with the sounds of clashing metal and collapsing structures. The invading Achæans whoop out war cries as they forge their way through the Trojans.

Thanatos floats through different parts of the city followed by a cloud of souls. Bodies litter the streets which have become slick with blood and fat. Children lay butchered, their unseeing eyes begging me to save them; the final expression of fear etched upon their ashen faces. Everywhere I look there is more violence that churns my stomach so savagely I can barely stand. Soldiers rut into the lifeless bodies of women before slitting their torsos open and hanging their bodies up the sides of buildings to join the already dead Trojan soldiers.

I want to breathe, but all I can smell is hot blood and death. Tears blur my vision and I collapse to the ground and weep over the body of a small girl who barely resembles the child she had once been. The blood pooled around her soaks into my clothes. I know she is safe now, but the images of what happened to her are inescapable. I hear others crying out and raise myself from the ground, moving in a haze of disassociation, cut off from the world around me as snippets burst through in a roar only to be silenced again by the only defense my panic-stricken soul can manage. I want to flee, but I need to be present, to find some way to help.

I move through the streets, following the cries of the few still alive. There are grievous sins occurring in the temples. The holy places are looted mercilessly and those who serve the Gods within them are at the mercy of the Achæans. They call out to their Gods, begging for mercy, but the Olympians do nothing. Above the city a storm rages, clashes of lightning and power flare as the Olympians fight one another. In the temple of Athena I come across a priestess sprawled upon the ground, her head bashed on the stones so that blood splatters across the altar of the Goddess she served all her life. Her eyes flutter and her pulse races as her life literally drains out of her body. A shadow of Thanatos appears before us both and caresses her forehead. Her soul leaps from her body to follow the God of Death as her lungs expel a final breath.

A few select servants of the Goddess of Wisdom are kept alive and trussed up like hunted animals to be hauled away as the spoils of war. I reach out to those who remain, those who have not yet been rescued by Thanatos and blanket them with light to dull their pain as they wait for freedom. I pull the youngest of the priestesses into my arms and cannot stop the tears as I look upon her golden face and cradle her ebony curls in my hands. The Achæans take what is of value, even kicking aside the dead bodies of priests and priestesses who had fallen trying to protect the treasures of their Gods.

I surrender myself to the burning power that begins to course through my veins. My skin begins to glow like a candle in the night and my soul wails, unable to feel anything but the pain of those around me. Sobs shake my body and tears fall like drops of pearl upon the cheek of the little one I hold. Thanatos appears, trailed by thousands of souls. The spirits of those around me rise up like vapor on a cool morning. Hermes appears and gathers up bundles of souls from the cloud following Thanatos and whisks them away to the Underworld.

I set down the child in my arms and respond to the pull of prayer, letting myself drift away on the wind, floating through the vanquished city. The Palace is littered with the dead. The people who lived and worked in the grand building have fared no better than the rest. Achæans loot all around me, carrying away whatever they can lay hands on. Servants lay gutted in the halls and soldiers slip on the blood in their haste.

I feel the push of Aphrodite's magic and search out the source, seeing the Goddess of Love guiding a small group of Trojans in caverns beneath the city. Helen is with them, as are Aeneas and Paris, but the others are unknown to me. They rush through the darkness, guided only by the torchlight of the lead and the whispers Aphrodite feeds into Aeneas' thoughts. I silently bless their journey away from this Tartarus on Earth.

A shriek above ground draws me back to the surface, the familiarity of the energy propelling me closer. I come upon Cassandra and Andromache, the Trojan princesses. They are trussed up like the maids from the temples and hoisted over the shoulders of two Achæan warriors heading down to the ships through the inferno their home has become. I stand frozen for a moment, realizing that when I had first shied away from Cassandra's thoughts it had been this that she was seeing. Could I have done something more if I had not been afraid to view the prophecies that Great Mother Gaia gifted to this mortal?

Thunder cracks through the heavens, nearly drowned out by the roar of the fire that has rapidly consumed every flammable item and building in the parts of the city nearest the sea. The Gods are clashing, throwing out power at one another to get the violence out of their systems, to decide on an immortal level who is the Olympian winner of this war. The torrents of violent energy are barely hidden by the clouds, disguised as a storm that now beats through the heavens. Clouds are laden with water and sorrow, but have yet to release their burden and save what remains of Troy.

In the main square is a looming horse crafted out of broken ships and crowned with shells and seaweed in homage to Poseidon. Its great belly is split open and I realize that this is how the Achæans had broken through the barriers of Troy. It is only large enough to fit half a dozen men curled inside, but that would be enough if they were able to use stealth to open the gates and allow the remaining army to enter. Thousands of Achæans had swarmed over the sleeping city like ants erupting out of their hill.

"Persephone." I turn when I hear my name and see Lord Hades watching me. He looks weary. "Don't stay here, don't do this to yourself."

I try to speak, but the words are lost behind my tears. My heart feels broken, shattered like the lives of those scattered on the streets. I take a few breaths and work up the energy to speak. "If I don't stay, who will? The Gods have abandoned Troy."

"Hermes and Thanatos are here, come back with me." He reaches out to me, but I shake my head, only half aware of my body.

"I want to help. I must find a way to do something." With the city purged of its wealth and its people, the Achæans board their vessels in massive numbers, leaving the flames of Troy to consume the evidence of their atrocities.

I seek out those Thanatos has only recently set free, drawn to them. I release the power coiling inside me until I am nothing but light. The souls divert from Thanatos and circle around me in an orbital dance, others join them from the other people on the precipice of death. I wrap them in light and follow Great Mother Gaia's whispering voice as it leads me to the Gates of the Underworld.

Those awaiting Charon to ferry them are swept up in my light, diving towards my epicenter like moths to a flame and we blaze across the River of Woe before finally settling as my light fades. When I'm finally able to see once more I find the Lords of Death; Hades, Hermes, Thanatos and Charon, standing on the shoreline of Acheron gaping at me.

29

HADES

Seeing Persephone against the backdrop of a burning city had brought forth my nightmares. I wanted her to leave, but she remained, forsaking her own comfort in order to be there for the mortals who needed her. Amid the terror she had blossomed into a strong, determined woman, a powerful Goddess who refuses to shirk her responsibilities. Seeing her in that blaze of power, surrounded by the souls of the city, pushing through the boundaries of my world to get them to safety had been both beautiful and overwhelming.

Hermes and Thanatos had returned at the same time and we had all been mesmerized, watching as she had moved like the sun in a cloud of blissful souls. I have no explanation for her abilities and when she turns to me with questions painting her features I spill out words that have nothing at all to do with the situation at hand.

"Stay here, Persephone. Stay with us." She looks a bit like a frightened deer. I shouldn't have said anything, shouldn't have applied even more pressure while she's still reeling from what she had seen in Troy. I step closer, flushing out a sigh of relief when she doesn't back away. She stands immobile as I scoop up her hands in mine, painfully aware of our rapt audience.

I'm so afraid of losing her, of losing this magnificent Goddess who has adapted so perfectly to my realm and made herself invaluable to those within it. She is loved and adored by the souls, by the dæmons, by my own animals, by me. I can't help but want more, to know that she wants more too. I want her to keep growing by my side, to keep allowing me to be near her and teach her about my world. I want her to want to be here, to be with me, not just as a visitor, but as a permanent addition to the Underworld.

There's a chance her mind will be overwhelmed by her recent experiences and she may turn and run from me at any moment, but I desperately hope she does not. I want to gather her into my arms, but I wait for her to process what I've just said. She is luminous, still shimmering as her power surge continues to fade. She's compassionate, beautiful and glorious, shining with the intensity of a star.

I heave a breath and try to formulate my words properly when she does not respond. "Persephone, when I ask you to stay with us, that is not specifically what I mean to say."

"What is it that you mean to say?" She squeezes my hand gently, almost imperceptibly. Her voice is tentative and soft as though afraid of my answer, but driven by curiosity to inquire further.

I swallow hard and my lips feel clumsy as I speak. "I am asking you to stay with me. Never in all my existence have I met a Goddess with such devotion to the souls that reside here. I've never met anyone who approaches life with your curiosity and kindness, nor anyone who possesses your beautiful heart. When I ask you to stay with me, I am asking you to make this place your home. I am asking you to be my Queen." The desire to say those words has almost been building since I first met her, but I had buried it so deeply I wasn't able to put it into words until now. Her mouth opens and closes a few times and I can feel the tremble of her body in my hands. "Please, you have become my heart. I don't know what my existence would be without you anymore. I love you."

I feel as though I'm setting my heart on a platter for her and either she will accept it and care for it or she will devour it and I will be damaged beyond repair.

"You once encouraged me to find my own path. Should I discard the identity of my mother and take on yours instead?" Cold fingers of dread grip my heart and it feels as though water is closing over my head.

"That is not what I wish for you. You would have complete freedom, to come and go as you desire, to pursue whatever path you find brings you the most happiness. I would never suggest that you merely adopt my mantle as your own."

After what seems like an eternity she slowly nods her head and gives me a soft smile. "I can only assume that what I feel is love since I have never felt it before. Gaia has whispered to me of it, how I would feel a longing in my heart. I feel that with you," she whispers, "and I admire you more than anyone. I'm not sure I can ever repay you for the faith you've put in me." Her vibrantly green eyes shimmer with unshed tears. "I should like to try though, I would be honored to be your Queen." She slips into my arms and presses her lips to mine. For a moment I can taste happiness.

PART II

GODDESS OF SPRING

30

HADES

"I am going to Olympus to petition Zeus to bless our union." Perse-phone focuses her brilliant eyes on me and I still can't quite believe my good fortune. She has agreed to be my Queen, but our marriage will not be officially sanctioned unless I can convince Zeus to agree to it. Thus far no one outside of our realm knows about it. She has not returned to Olympus and has confessed that she's afraid to tell her mother. I cannot blame her, Demeter's reaction is not something I look forward to.

The chaos of the war has dwindled in the world above and the city of Troy has fallen to ruin. The Achæans made their way home, but precious few actually arrived. Their ships were plundered by storms, Poseidon claiming the bounty meant to fill the mortal treasuries. The Gods still quarrel or ignore one another completely. Hermes relays us the stories, though I have not yet gone to Olympus to see for myself.

"What if he doesn't agree?" Persephone vocalizes my very real fear. She is the daughter of two Olympians and until we are recognized as husband and wife I have no right to keep her here against her mother's wishes.

"Then I shall just have to convince him." I kiss her cheek and bid her wait for me in the safety of Elysium. When I first asked her to be my wife I had completely forgotten that Olympian politics would intrude. For a few blissful moments I had thought that it was only Persephone's agreeableness that mattered, but I should have known. Olympus can never stay out of anyone's business for long.

Finding Olympus devoid of the one I seek, I divert instead to the Temple of Zeus at Olympia. The aforementioned temple is neither tasteful nor subtle, a veritable "Shrine to Me" that Zeus created for himself. The mortals built it of course, but he shoved their thoughts full of everything he desired to be present within the complex. It is filled with statuary, altars, smoking braziers and tapestries depicting various events from his life, topped off with a statue of gold that reaches monstrous proportions.

"Hades?" Zeus' voice booms like thunder, echoing in an obnoxious rumble as it bounces across the ceiling. "What are you doing here?"

"I have come with a request," I tell him. His eyebrow rises high in question. I force myself to take a deep breath.

He inches closer, his curiosity like a tidal wave all but slapping me in the face. "What on Olympus would you have to ask me for? I thought you had everything you need in that hole of yours."

I force down my simmering anger, snapping at Zeus will not prompt him to agree with my request. "A wife."

My left eye twitches when he bursts into roaring laughter, literally clutching his sides and carrying on until tears roll down his cheeks. I stay silent until he's finally able to suck in a few breaths and merely chuckle to himself.

"Are you serious?" He collapses into laughter anew when I nod. When he recovers he seems able to more properly focus on what I have to say. "Since you have not just taken one, I can only assume that the one you have selected is inaccessible to you."

"She is, to a point." It takes everything in me to stay calm. Zeus is impossible when he knows he has power over someone, which is pretty well always. He thrives on being in control and knowing that I need him to consent to the match is making him positively gleeful.

"Well, tell me who it is," he demands, shoving at my shoulders with his beefy fist.

"Persephone." The name makes him freeze, face caught in an expression of surprise and awe as he gapes incomprehensibly at me.

"So, you chose a woman who is not only my daughter, but the child of the one mother who can and will tear you to pieces for even thinking about such a thing." Zeus' face is painted with an expression of pure malicious mirth at the idea.

"I am aware of that." I sigh, just wanting this to be over. "That's is why I've come here requesting you to act as intercessor. Once your permission is granted there is little Demeter can do to interfere." Please, please just agree and let me be on my way.

"What do I get out of this deal?"

The smug upturn of his lip is pushing my patience to its upper limits, but I keep my fists firmly planted at my sides to control the urge to punch him. Zeus never does anything for anyone unless there is some gain in it for him. I try to not let my voice betray its exceptional annoyance level, but I am not altogether sure I succeed. "What would you like out of it?"

The question peaks my trepidation and leaves me wondering whether or not Persephone or I will end up paying the higher price for Zeus' acquiescence. He shrugs as though such an action might alleviate the worry he knows he has created.

"I'm sure that I can come up with something. For now, if you can manage to get the girl past Styx and into your realm I will consider you both to be married by Olympian standards. We can see about something proper ceremony after your success in that endeavor and when Demeter finally calms down."

Joy eventually wins out over and trepidation. Persephone is now my wife by the Laws of Olympus. For now that is all I need. The future now stretches before us, together, into eternity. A small part of me worries that she will grow bored with me, with our life, within that time, but I whisper a prayer to Gaia that I will be able to make her happy. Please, please, let me be capable of such of a thing.

I take my leave of Zeus, grateful to be out of his presence. I and my realm are generally autonomous, but Zeus is still our King and it punctures the bubble of my existence every time I must acknowledge that fact.

When I return to the Underworld I find Persephone and just about everyone in my employ waiting for me. Persephone gives me a small, hopeful smile and when I nod the roar of cheers is deafening. My new bride flings herself into my arms and laughs, a brilliant and joyful sound that has become my world.

My realm finally has its Queen, a fixture it has been lacking since its inception. She is here now and I am blessed eternally with a magnificent partner for the rest of our immortal lives. I feel blessed anew by the outpouring of love from the residents of my realm. They crowd close, a cacophonous symphony of congratulations and excitement.

Evaristus weaves his way to us and presents a package wrapped in simple white cloth to Persephone. She peels back the layers of silk and gasps at the delicate diadem fashioned from gold to look like leaves and blossoms. Evaristus blushes as she turns it in all directions to examine the exquisite craftsmanship. "I had it commissioned by Hephæstus. It was a bit premature, but I wanted to be prepared for such an occasion as this. I was hopeful it would come."

Persephone leans down and kisses the dæmon on his cheek, showering him with thanks for the gift. I settle it atop her curls and it makes her look even more like a brilliant star, tipped with a golden glow. When I look at my bride it all seems like a dream, as though she might only be an Elysian illusion constructed from my deepest desires. I can scarcely believe that she is here, that she wants to stay with me, for all of the conceivable forever. It is beyond anything I could have ever believed was possible for me. I look at her and find reality shattering, raining upon me to dissolve into mist as she takes my hand and gazes at me with more love and reverence in her eyes than I'm able to comprehend.

31

PERSEPHONE

It takes very little time for my mother to figure out that I am no longer on Olympus. My cowardice has thus far prevented me from returning, fearing she will toss me in a cage, regardless of Zeus' decision. Hades tells me it is safer for me to be closer, a sentiment my mother often expressed, though this time I am not restricted from leaving the Underworld. Knowing my father better than I do, he has expressed concern that our King may not always support our choice. The Olympian ruler is fluid and tends to switch sides and alter bargains as it suits him. Were my mother to badger him enough or he decided that he wanted us separated then I could find myself torn from my new home. I am too eager to put down roots and so I have avoided returning to the skies.

The first sign of her displeasure is an unusual influx of souls that report their crops have failed and their villages and cities have plunged into famine. Many regions are still recovering from the war, faced with failing infrastructure, looted grain stores and not enough people to sustain industry. Many of the mortals have found themselves with nothing to sustain them in the event of a crop failure.

I move through the shades and choose one of the newly arrived to question. A young man named Elias who grew into manhood during the course of the war, he had done his best to care for his mother and sisters in the absence of his father. "We prayed and prayed to Demeter to save our harvests. They had grown so well and shriveled into dust within days. The Lady of Grain did not hear our prayers. The winds of Boreas chased us indoors to hover around our braziers as they battered our homes and froze everything in the fields beyond any possible use."

My mother is doing this because of me, going after the already disparaged mortal population who begs her so fervently for their lives. It is the only real power she has to force the hand of Olympus, but she has never done so on purpose before. If she destroys all of their worshippers, there will be no one left to offer adoration to the Olympians. I rest my head upon Hades' shoulder when I join him atop the Towers. "What am I to do? They are dying because of me. She will continue this until there is no one left, but if I return she may demand I never leave again."

Guilt claws at my insides, coiling like a small, ravenous monster intent on chewing its way free. I rub my hand over my belly, willing the monster to quiet, to stop its roiling but it does not heed my desires.

Hades wraps a comforting arm over my shoulders. "It is your mother's decision to revoke her blessings, you did not make her do so. This is not your fault," he assures me. "The Thunderer will rein her in." His words do little to soothe my guilt. Thunder rumbles and I cast my gaze upwards for it is most unusual to hear the weather that occurs above ground.

"If he does not?" I ask, despite knowing what the answer will be.

"Then more will die, but he will not let this go on for too long."

Thunder roars again and cold fear snakes around my heart and plunges a dagger into my belly. Realization crashes upon me like a wave of cold water. The mortals are leverage to try and force Zeus to retrieve me. My shortly-won freedom is over.

Lightning rips through the ground, sending a shower of sparks down upon us and causing many of the souls to shriek in terror. Hades hisses and grips my hand almost painfully. He drops my hand and raises both arms into the air, clutching them into fists to use his power to keep the earth closed above our heads. He shakes with the effort as bolt after bolt of lightning flares down upon us.

I wrap my arms around my husband's chest, willing my power into him so he will not fall to the might of Zeus. The souls are in absolute panic, running and shrieking, flailing and crying. The dæmons try in vain to calm them, but the vicious sparks and pounding thunder serves only to exacerbate their fear. Torn between my need to help Hades and my duty to the souls, I make the split second choice to help my people.

I fling myself from the top of the Towers and land softly, flaring out a wave of soothing energy. Many of the souls stop as though stunned, some even falling to the ground in a wistful sleep. I use my will to send a sense of peace to them as I try desperately to tuck away my own panic. I feel myself being torn away from this world and I am reduced at once to a child, the feeling of helplessness almost choking me.

Hades visibly struggles against the onslaught. I can feel his power wavering, his gentle and determined nature being slowly overwhelmed by the incredible fury and brute force being launched at him by my father. Zeus always gets what he wants, regardless of who he destroys in the process. That destruction is coming for us.

32

HADES

Souls gather around Persephone in a frantic cloud. Her wavering energy is struck by a staccato rhythm as her own panic pierces through it. They cry out during those points and wonder aloud if Zeus has come to banish them to Tartarus.

"He's come for me." Persephone's voice is only a whisper, but it reaches my ears with startling clarity. Somehow it makes this all more real and I feel an inexplicable desire to snatch Persephone up and flee into the depths of Elysium. The destruction Zeus would rain upon my realm would be incredible and as much as I might want to keep Persephone to myself, my duty is and always will be to the souls first. She cannot abandon the mortals that are starving due to her mother's choices any more than she can abandon the souls that came into her care when she became my Queen. I know my bride and I know how she must be struggling with what to do now that we are faced with it. I feel my heart begin to crack, knowing that she will opt to save the mortals. She knows that I will care for the realm, but there is no one to care for those above unless she goes. She is too good and I will lose her because of it.

The force of power being thrown at me makes my whole body quake and I cry out, trying to call up more energy to stop Zeus from breaking through. It's a fruitless contest, I cannot keep him out forever, cannot be locked in an unending battle like Atlas holding up the world.

The lightning breaks free in one terrifying bolt and I hear Persephone shriek my name. I turn just in time to see her body flung from the steps of the Tower. A flare of light bursts all around us as my power shatters and Zeus appears in a blaze of glory, bright as the sun. Demeter rushes in after him and immediately spots her daughter. The souls scatter quickly as the agrarian Goddess rushes towards them. Demeter wails Persephone's name over and over. The souls quiver and try to edge further away. She pulls her dazed daughter into her arms, oblivious to the discomfort she is causing everyone around her.

Zeus' initial glorious light fades and he now looks rather exhausted and extremely irritated. He crosses his arms and refuses to meet my gaze. He speaks to Demeter, despite the fact that it is clear she is not listening. "You have your daughter now, release the mortals from their famine."

A hollow cold settles over me as I stare at mother and daughter. She will leave now and likely never come back. I will lose her as surely as if she had never been born. Persephone had brought down my walls and I can already feel them beginning to rebuild, stone by stone, to protect my spirit from collapsing upon itself when she is gone. Demeter is squeezing her so hard I'm almost concerned her head might pop clean off.

Desperation prods me and I force myself into Zeus' line of sight. "You promised. We are married, she belongs here."

He turns his gaze away from me again. "She also belongs with her mother. I cannot let this famine go on and the only demand Demeter has in exchange for lifting it is the return of her daughter."

"Force her to stop." The begging in my voice is painful to my own ears, but it's a tone I am unsuccessful at reining in. "You are King of Olympus, just order her to lift the famine."

He eyes me as though I have lost my wits. "You are most welcome to try and reason with her. She is too single-minded when it comes to that girl and enough have died for your ridiculous request to have Persephone as your wife."

I want to fight for her, but I cannot see a way to do so that would not end in misery for either the souls of my realm or the mortals who have yet to join me. My brother is equal to me in power, but that knowledge does not quell my desire to stamp him into dust and feed the remains to Kamp.

Demeter is still wailing incomprehensibly, alternately crushing her daughter to her and thrusting her to arm's length to look at her before bursting into tears again. Persephone gives her mother a single smile, but it is small and it does not reach her eyes. The brightness I'm used to seeing in her has dimmed. When she is clutched to her mother she levels a glare so hot and fierce at her father it could have melted stone. Zeus raises his eyebrow when he sees it and turns to me questioningly, but I only shrug. If I tell him I love Persephone he will find a way to use it against me. I want to hoard the knowledge of our love, to keep it from him for fear of what he might do with such information. Zeus has spent too much of his existence destroying what others love for me to ever give him the satisfaction of knowing where my heart lies.

Anger over this situation is writhing in my belly. I pull it in, cloaking myself in an aura of fury so thick and potent that Zeus actually takes a step back from me. Though I fervently abhor the mortal notion that women are the property of their husbands, I find myself wishing that Zeus would adopt that mindset here and allow Persephone to remain, to override familial claims with spousal rights.

"Do not let this happen, brother. Find some way to break Demeter's claim on her daughter."

Zeus heaves a sigh and marches over to mother and daughter. "Persephone, do you wish to remain in the Underworld?"

I perk at this, though Persephone does not even get a chance to speak before her mother bursts in. "She would never!"

"Be silent!" Zeus shoves power into his words and Demeter shrinks back, clinging to her daughter all the more. "Daughter, tell me now if there is any reason for you to remain in this realm rather than return to Olympus with your mother."

Breath sucks into my lungs and I stand there, muscles taut as stone, waiting for her to answer. Her eyes focus on mine and I place my hand over my heart, slowly shaking my head. Her expression grows curious, but she subtly nods and I hope it's because she understands. She extricates herself from her mother's embrace and stands at her full height before her father.

"I am married to Hades, I am Queen of the Underworld and the souls here have accepted me as such." She steadfastly ignores her mother's horrified expression and looks at me fondly. "I have willingly accepted the role I now hold here in the Underworld and I am a caretaker of souls." She does not mention love, for which I am grateful. It might convince them to let her stay if she did tell them, but they already have so much power over her, over us both, there is no need to give them more. If you love, you can be hurt and Zeus knows too well how to hurt others.

Her mother hisses at Zeus. "I will bring the mortals to destruction if you do not take her to Olympus. She is too young to decide for herself."

Persephone has been on this earth for two centuries and while it is younger than many immortals, she is certainly old enough to form her own opinions on what happens in her life. Demeter's choice has us all trapped.

"I know I am duty bound to protect those mortals who have not yet reached my care." Persephone says as she looks at me. In her eyes I can see a heart breaking; whether it is hers shattering or my own crumbling, I cannot be sure. "I will agree to return in exchange for my mother lifting the famine."

Zeus nods and appears to consider for several moments if there is a way he can manipulate this to his advantage. "Persephone will return to Olympus as per her mother's request. She will spend one half of the mortal year with you on Olympus and the other half of the mortal year here in the Underworld as its reigning Queen. Neither of you will engage with her during her time with the other."

"No!" Demeter shrieks and flies at him, but he deflects her blows. "You said you would return her to me!"

"And I have." His voice is hard and unyielding. He does not mention that he also promised Persephone would be allowed to remain with me freely and that he supported our marriage. He is breaking his word twice over, turning Persephone into a parcel to be traded between mother and husband with none of us getting what we want. Demeter is in a state of absolute rage, Persephone is in tears and I am turning so numb I cannot even determine what I feel anymore.

Persephone looks stricken. Her freedom has been ripped away and she is now a part of an endless contract. I am relieved that she will still be able to see me, but I know such an arrangement is not what Persephone deserves. They are gone before I am able to bid her farewell and despite myself I fall to my knees and bury my face in my hands. The souls rush around me like a confused hive of bees and I cannot even bring myself to look up when I feel Thanatos' cool hand on my shoulder.

33

PERSEPHONE

I made this choice, I remind myself. I agreed to this, but there really had been no choice at all. Within moments I became an object passed between husband and mother as per a contractual agreement, my autonomy stripped, my position as Queen negated. I'm such a fool to think I could ever make my own path in this world.

"Persephone." I jump and partially uncurl on my bed when my mother sits next to me. I thought I could be strong, but I find that I miss my new home more than I thought possible and its loss has left me feeling hollow. I have not yet mustered the energy to speak on my new life to my mother. She sighs and rests a hand on my hip. "You know that I love you, right?"

I nod and repeat the sentiment back to her. I never stopped loving her, but her desire to control my every action and her denial of anything resembling a purpose for me has made it difficult for me to connect with her. I struggle with the twisting feelings inside of me. I know I hurt her, but I knew she would never have let me go even if I had told her.

She sighs. "I do not understand why you are angry with me. I did the best I could. No one would tell me where you were. It was only after I badgered the Sun that I found out what happened, then Zeus would not help me until the mortals started to die. I rescued you as quickly as I was able."

"*Rescued* me?" I don't believe I could have sounded more incredulous if I had tried. She has been interpreting my recent behavior as my having been taken from her and not from my having been stripped away from a place I had grown to love. "Let me be very clear when I say that I did not need to be rescued."

"Of course you did." She pats my head like one might pet a dog. She has been condescending to me before, but I am not the same person I was before and my patience with it grows thin. "You have been under a lot of stress and I understand that you do not desire to relive your torment. I know what you have gone through, Persephone, you don't need to hide it from me. The brothers of Olympus are beasts and Hades is no better than your father."

"Hades is nothing like my father!" I snap instantly, feeling a strange combination of panic and anger surge inside of me. I have heard of my father's brutality, it's legendary among even the mortals, and the fact that she associates Hades with such behaviors makes me feel ill.

My mother turns her wide, soil-brown eyes on me. She raises her eyebrow skeptically. "Now, my dear, it's perfectly natural to repress your ordeal."

Spurred on by my need to correct her perceptions I press more forcefully than I probably should. "I'm not repressing anything. Mother, for once in your life, please just listen to me!" She reels, completely taken aback by my outburst. I have never been anything but a quiet and obedient daughter towards her before and I've become so unlike the person she has come to expect. She stares at me, completely unsure of what to do with me. "Hades is good and kind. He has never forced me to do anything. I went to the Underworld on my own. I made the conscious choice to do so and I was not kidnapped or coerced in any way. I love him."

For a brief moment there is silence between us, a dead calm that fills me with trepidation. The confusion falls from her face almost instantly to be replaced by a seething anger. Her eyes narrow and she launches off the bed and slips into a defensive stance with feet braced and arms crossed over her chest. The anger bubbles inside of her and wisps of it lash out at me. She is angry with me, more furious than I have ever seen her. The child inside of me quakes to see my mother look at me this way.

"Do not be a fool Persephone. Hades has manipulated you from the very moment you met. It is his nature. The men of Olympus take what they want regardless of who is hurt by it."

I understand, or believe that I understand why she is refusing to believe me. If I had been taken nothing between us would have changed. We could slip back into our respective roles, albeit with some extra motherly coddling to assist a fragile girl to recovery. If she actually faces reality then she will have to confront the fact that I had abandoned her, that I chose to leave Olympus and take up with someone who she believes is unsavory.

I love Hades and I love my mother, but their treatment of me in my life has been very different. I ran away from the world my mother provided for me and fell headlong into the life of wonder Hades was offering. I'm too emotionally charged to be entirely rational and I cannot even begin to figure out how to repair what I may have irreparably broken.

"Hades is not a man of Olympus. He is different, I have seen it. Please believe me, I may be young, but I am not stupid. I am not the child you believe me to be."

She rises up, her anger twisting and propelling her appearance into something fearsome. Her features darken into shadow and she towers over me easily. "You are a child, Persephone, you are my child and you are too naive to be anything else." Her will is heavy and I struggle against its force as it tries to bend mine to hers, to force me to give in. I am so used to her aura being one of overbearing warmth that envelops me to the point of smothering, but now it glints like ice and both numbs and stabs at me. I can feel it trying to reach deep inside me, searching out bitterness, trying to stir it up so I lose my clarity, trying to make me succumb.

I clench my fists and set my jaw, preparing myself for a battle of wills. "You're right, mother. I was naive, but you are a fool twice over if you do not believe that the fault was yours that I was kept in such a state. You never let me do anything, meet anyone or go anywhere. If you wanted me to be wary of the world you should have at least let me experience it or you could have given me a proper explanation for why you kept me caged up."

I struggle against the urge to shrink away as she hisses at me. "This is exactly why I kept you at home! You wanted to be out in the world and I allowed you into that meadow and now you have been taken by Hades and forced for the rest of eternity to go to that awful place. I never should have allowed it."

Fury wells up in my belly. "The Underworld is not awful. It is wonderful, so is Hades and you would know that if you had ever bothered to experience either."

She retracts behind a proverbial wall of ice and a chill creeps over our quarters so profoundly that the hairs on my arms raise and my breath puffs out in swirling clouds before me. "You will forgive me, daughter, for not desiring to put myself in the position to become the broodmare of yet another brother when I have already borne a child for two of the three." Her voice snaps like a whip and I can feel her starting to disappear entirely.

"He would not have hurt you." The words are meaningless, she is already gone, vanished into the æther. Though her physical presence has disappeared the aura of misery left behind is so thick I feel suffocated by it. My fury drains away, replaced by a sadness that consumes me from the inside out. My quarters, once my sanctuary, seem desolate and devoid of life despite the thriving plants and rippling water therein. I retreat to my little garden anyway and curl up next to the evergreen that puts forth a sticky, sweet scent in the heat. The smell of the evergreen reminds me too much of Hades, but it evokes the feeling of home. Pressing my forehead to my knees I finally feel my strength leave me as tears pour in hot rivers down my cheeks. I had run from my isolation in such a way that might have doomed me. I release an almost hysterical laugh, knowing deep down that if I had been honest with her about my desires and intentions she would have locked me away so tightly that I would have never seen anyone ever again. Being cloistered away is a fate I detest, but it seems that is what I will experience for half of the rest of my existence.

I try to understand her views. I know she's distrustful of the Olympians, but two Gods do not represent the entire population. She has closed herself off and taken me with her, to protect us both from perceived threats. Many Olympians forget those they do not see and I know she tried to slip from their thoughts by making us both as invisible as possible. My father and Poseidon are not known for their care and compassion in regards to females, and immortality has never deterred their brutality before. I know she has been hurt by them, but I wish she had not allowed both of our lives to be governed by her fear and emotional scars.

I am the product of an unwanted coupling and both my mother and I must live with that. I have always known that my mother hated my father, she made no secret of it, but not until now did she reveal why. Somewhere out there is a brother I had never known to exist, a child of Poseidon and Demeter. She has never told me of another child, never told me why she kept me to be raised, but not her first. Perhaps she feels that I ran towards the very thing she tried so desperately to keep me from. I may never fully understand her reasoning, I can only attempt to determine the motivation behind her behaviors.

Still, regardless of her past and thoughts, it was wrong of her to keep me locked up the way she did, to keep me in total ignorance of the world. She did neither of us any favors with such actions. I can acknowledge that we both made mistakes, both chose a path out of desperation, but I cannot regret my choices. I became a new person and captured my freedom, for however brief a time, and that is something I can hold forever. I have not yet determined how to gain my freedom permanently, but I'm sure my mother will not agree with it and there will be pain for one or both of us involved. I do not relish the thought. I fear now that I may have broken something between us that might never be repaired.

34

PERSEPHONE

I stand upon grass that is a sickly brown and so crisp it stabs the soles of my feet. My mother has still not returned to Olympus after several days so I abandoned it for my meadow. She was so furious with me she couldn't even stand to look at me, so she had gone without telling me where she was going or when she would be back. There is no welcome of flowers, nor of anything green at all. Even the birds have gone silent in the trees and the animals have long since abandoned this place. I sink to my knees and clutch the dried plants in my hands, the gentle action causing the brittle leaves to shatter into dust. For so long this place had been my only sense of freedom, my only solace in my life of confinement and to see it in such a miserable state burns my soul.

"How could my mother have let this happen? Is the rest of the world as damaged as this?" I say the words aloud, guiding them towards Great Mother Gaia with my intentions. I feel the energy of the Earth Mother reaching up towards me, soothing, but with a hint of sadness. Gaia has watched many die and felt the destruction of her surface, but she has long since retreated from the world. Her spirit rests within her great body, offering whispers to those who call to her, but rarely intervening directly in anything.

She whispers to me, telling me that my mother has removed the curse she put on the land, but has not restored her blessing. Nothing is stopping anything from growing, but everything is already dead and cannot restore itself to life. Surrounded by the lifeless meadow I feel loneliness swell deep within me. Great Mother Gaia prompts me to assuage my loneliness with companionship and so I summon my nymphs. Chloe is the first to appear and she rushes towards me in a blur of silver-blonde hair and red cheeks. She smells sweet, like fresh leaves and I give myself a moment to sink into the warmth of her arms. The others appear one by one and throw themselves upon us, creating a cocoon of nymphs.

Surrounded by them I feel the dam holding back my tears give way. Soon I am sobbing so hard I can barely breathe and my whole body shakes. We sink to the ground and sit, wrapped in one another until the sun begins to dip towards the horizon. None of them speak until I regain enough composure to lift my face to the sky and draw in a few trembling breaths.

Chloe cups my cheeks and uses her palms to smooth my hair. For the first time I notice that her face has strange markings on it. There are angry red patches, following a barbed pattern. The same spots spatter her arms and chest as well, and I survey the others and see that they are marked in a similar fashion.

"What happened?" I trace my fingers over Chloe's cheek and she turns shy eyes away from me. I look to the others to explain, but they too are deliberately avoiding my gaze. "Please, tell me."

Tryphosa pushes her curls from her face and moves the shoulder of her gown to expose the red welts that pepper her flesh. "Lady Demeter was not pleased that we hid your exodus from her. She summoned each of us, one by one, to punish us for not informing her immediately that you had gone."

I have never before known my mother to be physically violent and the images presented in my mind create a disturbing picture. My thoughts fly to the gold scepter my mother sometimes uses at Olympian functions, the sharp metal crashing into tender flesh could have easily made these marks. I press my palm to Tryphosa's wound and infuse it with energy, whatever healing power I possess removing all traces of my mother's anger. I do the same for the others, working methodically until each wound on every nymph has been erased.

Zoe places a hand delicately on my knee. "Do not fear for us, Lady Persephone. We made our choice of non-disclosure and we knew the risks involved in doing so." The others nod in agreement, a sea of bobbing heads. I never knew my mother was capable of hurting so many people and to know that I am the reason my nymphs suffered is greatly unsettling. I should have thought about their safety before making such a reckless decision.

"My Lady, stop that right now." I turn my attention to Chloe, suddenly aware that my features must have been twisting with worry. "We were not obligated to support your decision to leave. It was purely voluntary and knowing that our choice allowed you to make a happy home is more than enough solace for our wounds."

I draw them back into an embrace, so grateful for their loyalty and companionship. I was selfish to have ever complained about them. "Thank you, all of you. I will never forget this kindness."

"Things will improve," Tryphosa smiles at me. "With time your mother and Lord Hades will adjust to the changes. You will make such a difference in the world. The Underworld has needed a Queen since the creation of humanity. We are so proud of you. We heard that you made the choice to return in order to save the mortals."

"Do you think Hades is mad at me for leaving?" I had not wanted to go, but perhaps he misunderstood my willingness to leave.

"He is undoubtedly upset," Alexis speaks softly as she braids the tips of her hair, "but it is very unlikely that you are the target of his displeasure. If there is any immortal who understands the importance of duty it is Lord Hades. You have saved thousands, preferring to preserve their mortal lives rather than letting them perish and come into your care; it is a very honorable decision."

35

PERSEPHONE

"Persephone, wake up." I peel open my eyes and realize with a start that I am back in my rooms on Olympus. Panic chokes me for a moment as I wonder if my mother has found some new way to bind me to this place. "Calm yourself, I didn't mean to startle you."

I must have fallen asleep and the nymphs brought me back. Mother doesn't seem to know that I was gone or that I saw them. Her expression is soft, having none of the hardness and fury I remember there. I refrain from mentioning my trip to the meadow out of desire to protect the nymphs further from her wrath.

She settles on the edge of my bed. "I have lifted the famine from the mortals, as per the agreement, but since I did not get what I want I have not restored the lands. Perhaps Zeus will undo his foolish deal and reinstate you to Olympus full time."

"What do you mean? How can you have lifted the famine if you have not restored the land?" Great Mother Gaia had explained it to me, but I want my mother to tell me herself.

"I removed the magic in place that prevented things from growing, but in that time the seeds the mortals planted have grown inert and their plants dead. Should they uncover more somewhere they will be able to grow, but I am not about to provide them with new seeds." I feel suddenly sick. My returning has not saved anyone at all. "I will not allow you to suffer in that horrid place any longer than necessary."

"Hades will not hurt me, Mother, I promise you that." I offer her these words of comfort, but find her expression twist and the words spat back in my face.

"Please do not make me believe that you are stupid. Hades *will* hurt you, if he has not done so yet it is only a matter of time. I've told you before that the Olympians have no care for who they hurt. You are merely new and convenient, and when your novelty wears off he will destroy you."

In all honesty, I am probably the least convenient choice Hades could have possibly made. "You are certainly proving that fact correct right now," I snap, "you have destroyed the mortals. You should care deeply about them yet you use them for leverage to get what you want."

She slaps me and for a few moments I'm too stunned to do anything but stare at her. "I wanted my daughter home and safe, but if you are going to be so ungrateful then perhaps I should have abandoned you there."

I would have been happy if she had, but I do not voice these words out loud. Instead, I circle back to the problem at hand. "I am going to restore the land for the mortals."

She laughs, so hard that tears form in her eyes and she clutches her sides. Annoyance wars with a building determination. I will do this. I will find a way to restore what has been damaged and finally bring this famine to an end. The despair flows out of my limbs, leaving me feeling curiously light.

"You know how to grow a single tree at a time and how to make flowers bloom, what has possessed you to believe you are capable of more than that? You have no training or notion of how to do any of what you have to in order to reverse the death of all those plants."

My mother's words are sharp, her tongue a blade she wields with acute precision. I cannot understand why she tries to hurt me like this. Does she want me to accept a life of ignorance and never try to better the world? Would she be pleased if I never wanted to better myself or my skills and simply stand in her shadow the rest of my days? "I am willing to try. I certainly cannot make things worse at any rate."

"Very well," she shrugs. "If the mortals starve due to your inadequacies, so be it."

My back is painfully straight and I forcefully demand that my lip not tremble in her presence. I will not cry in front of her. "If you don't start caring for them they will take their worship elsewhere, to a Goddess who listens to them."

She brushes my words aside, painfully flippant. "There is little worry of that. They know of no other Goddess to bring them grain."

"They will know me," I snap back. "If you will not take on your duties, I will."

Her eyes narrow and I wonder if perhaps she was expecting me to simply bow down and beg her to restore things herself, to plead with her, but I have not. "It is not so easy that a child can take over. You must understand the crops and the people, where and when to assist and when to step back. You have no experience or practice with magic of this level. You might be able to alleviate pockets, but you will not succeed without my intercession."

I steel myself further and stand toe to toe with her. "Watch me."

36

HADES

Fire roars, a terrifying scream of unbridled power galloping towards me. I collapse, my soul crying out to the Earth to shield me, but there is little to be done with a storm of flame intent upon searing the very flesh from my bones. The agony of my skin blistering black fills my vision with darkness, draining away my strength. I slog through the ground, now a sea of mud from water rushing, compelled by the power of some Titan or another to slow our progress.

It becomes hard to move, hard to breathe. I try to, to continue on to the goal of victory, to the goal of survival. My limbs are so heavy, my throat closed off and choking. Breathe. Move. Live. I chant those words in my thoughts, but the first two have become impossible. I cannot move, can no longer breathe. Panic fills me to the very core of my being. I cannot die, but the pain is overwhelming. To die now would be a blessing, an escape from the agony.

I TRY TO SCREAM AS I BURST AWAKE, but no sound escapes. I am just as trapped as I was in the nightmare, only this is real. Demeter stands over me with an expression so dark and fearful, I wasn't even aware she was capable of producing such malice. The same vines she had used against the Titans are clutching me like a starving python, trying to crush my bones into dust. My gaze flies around frantically and I see Evaristus in a very similar state. I struggle all the more, pulling at her power, calling up my own to summon shards of gems from the earth. They rain upon me, lacerating my skin, but their sharp edges, guided by my own magic, are enough to free me.

I leap up with a roar, initially ignoring Demeter and go immediately to Evaristus. I tear at the vines, panic and fury fueling me. His head lolls to the side, unresponsive and I realize that if he does not wake on his own there is nothing I can do to help him. I have no powers of life, no magic to heal him. My throat burns, stifling the urge to call out to Persephone in the frantic hope that wherever she is she may hear me and break the contract to save the dæmon.

Demeter flies at me, knocking us all to the ground. "Cerberus!" The name roars from my lips and an answering howl rumbles the ground beneath us.

"You monster! You stole my daughter from me, turned her against me and now you seek to have your disgusting mutt attack me?" She shrieks, flinging pockets of power at me. They sting, burning my flesh, but she's so riled up that they do little more damage than that.

The ground shakes from the force of Cerberus' footsteps. My faith-ful hellhound bursts into my chambers, immediately tossing her aside with his heads before clamoring over to pin her carefully beneath his feet. He growls down at the Goddess of Grain, spittle hanging from his many lips. She shrieks and squirms and I do not approach her until I have given myself a moment to think.

I collect Evaristus from the ground. He fits easily into my arms, tucked there like a child. His head fits in my hand and I just hold his silent form for a few moments. Evaristus has never been silent in all the millennia I have known him and it chills me to the bone to see him in such a state now.

I cross the room to Demeter. "You have invaded my realm and attacked both myself and someone I hold very dear. Whatever you believe transpired between your daughter and I, you are gravely mistaken in thinking that your actions are justified here."

She looks at me with eyes sharper than blades. "You and your brothers are scum and somehow you have poisoned my daughter against me."

"*You* poisoned your daughter against you. You trapped her and coddled her and denied her the birthright of a Goddess. You may refuse to see it, you may deny it with every breath in your body, but there is no way to escape the truth. If you had taught her your craft, taken her out into the world, you could have built a foundation that lasted through eternity, but you left her with a crumbling sense of self and no purpose to speak of."

She doesn't speak, only continues to glare at me. I cannot tell whether or not she believes me, or is even capable of considering such a thing. She shoots vines at Cerberus, but he is quick and decisive, his heads moving to bite at the vines and tear them to pieces.

"Demeter, I know you believe that I am evil and that I will likely never change your mind about that, but I swear to you that I would never intentionally hurt Persephone. Now, I am going to remove you from my realm and if you return to it ever again and harm anyone that I love, I will feed you to Kamp."

Cerberus snatches her up while she screams and I escort them both to the Gates of the Underworld where she is unceremoniously tossed out. The barrier around my realm solidifies, no one else will be able to break through it without my knowing.

I return my attention to the dæmon in my arms. "Gaia," I whisper, feeling my voice catch in my throat. "Please, I have no magic to help him, please undo the damage Demeter has done."

I sink to my knees at the shores of Styx, Thanatos hovering nearby. I pray fervently, my thoughts pouring into the ground, the realm of the Earth Mother. It seems like an eternity passes as I kneel there, clutching Evaristus. I feel her energy creep up, caressing my skin like a soft breeze. It wraps around Evaristus, so potent that he glows. Seconds pass in agony before finally he begins to stir. His eyes flutter and I feel his muscles tense as he tries to sit up. Dæmons are only technically immortal; they will live forever, but only if nothing manages to kill them. Evaristus could have succumbed to the force of Demeter's attack and he would have been lost to me. My realm holds the souls of human mortals, but Evaristus' soul would have dissolved into the æther, rejoining the primordial spirits.

"My Lord," his voice croaks, "I am so sorry, I never should have led her to you."

"Hush, we will speak of it when you are recovered."

Thanatos rests his palm on my shoulder. "Lady Demeter is far too accomplished an actress, she fooled us all. She came in tears, appeared repentant of her actions and told us she only wanted to apologize, if only she could speak to you. You must have been deep in dream, for you did not answer when we called. Evaristus escorted her, but it would appear when she was gone from our sight she sought to cause trouble."

"None of you are to blame. How were you to know her nature when you have never encountered her? I certainly never divulged what I knew of her to you. I never thought she would come here, nor that she would commit such acts as she did." I sigh and drag a hand through my hair. It's only then that I even notice the red welts across my arms. They are likely all over my body, but I dismiss the deep ache in my bones and carry Evaristus back to the Palace.

I install him in his private quarters and place two dæmons in charge of his well-being until he recovers. Gaia saved his life, but he is far from healed. When he is safely settled I return to my quarters, the thrill and terror of the fight long gone, forcing my awareness to recognize how much pain my body is in. My movements grow slow and when I strip off my clothes to slide into the baths, I hiss when the heat strikes the flesh wounds. Persephone could heal us both instantly, but it is still months before she returns to us, so we will both have to simply heal in our own natural time. I have imposed upon Gaia's good will enough for now. She avoided disaster for Evaristus and I cannot ask her for more. I'm lucky she answered me at all as her interventions since the creation of this world have been minimal. She coaches Persephone, a gentle guidance and perhaps it was only my connection to Gaia's protégé that prompted her assistance, but whatever her motivation, I am grateful for it.

37

PERSEPHONE

The fields lay barren or filled with shriveled crops, dry as dust. I have never seen such destruction of flora like this before. Everywhere I turn the landscape seems lifeless. The mortal world has been devastated. With the lack of my mother's blessing it is almost as if the rain refused to fall and the Sun conspired with her desires to desiccate all hope in the fields. My mother said it was the Sun, Helios, that told her where I had gone and the rains are controlled by my father. Nothing like this should have occurred without cooperation between all three of them. I have never met Helios before, nor know of any association he might have with my mother. If my father was involved, keeping the rains in the heavens, what might his motivation be in doing so? He came for me to save the mortals, but that makes no sense if he had a hand in the famine. He could have lifted it himself if that were the case, why has he not done so already? Why is Helios involved at all? Questions plague me, but there are no answers to be found in my own thoughts and I can hardly ask any of them right now. I will get to the bottom of this, but for now there are larger problems at hand.

The sheer magnitude of the task ahead of me is slightly terrifying and away from my mother my bravado fails me. I truly have no concept of how to apply my magic on such a colossal scale. I breathe, using the soothing internal motions of pulling in air and pushing it out again to build my energy.

"Great Mother Gaia, please guide me. I seek to replenish your soil, to allow the seeds planted by mortal hands to grow strong and bear fruit. Those who live upon you are starving, help me to save them."

I wait in silence until I can feel her energy stir beneath my feet, her power pulsing up and through me. I follow her lead and allow my energy to reach out. I kneel down and place my hands upon the ground, pushing down as she pushes up and together the energy of life flares out around me. It winds through every blade of grass, every seed and leaf, infusing them with renewed life and vigor. The sad golden brown color slowly turns vibrantly green. Hope floods my chest and contributes to the outpouring of power. Mortals flee their homes as the green floods through the fields.

An old man falls to his knees at the edge of the fields and cries out. "Lady Demeter has taken mercy upon us!" Others join him, many collapsing into tears, some even growing hysterical as the prospect of the famine ending fills them to bursting with hope.

"*Persephone.*" We all still as my name is whispered out of the Earth. "*Demeter has not returned her favor, it is her daughter that saves you now.*" The Great Mother falls silent once more and even her power retreats. She has intervened as much as she deems appropriate and now has returned her spirit to the depths of her body.

I am nearly as agog as the mortals at hearing Gaia speak. We all fall to our knees, the mortals praying and I pouring out my thanks to the Earth Mother. Women begin to wail, keening out with bright voices, overcome with emotion. It's traditionally a sound reserved for grieving, but somehow it seems to match the situation perfectly.

With Great Mother Gaia's blessing and initial guidance I travel onwards, pouring my very life into the soil. With every blade of green that breaks through the soil the mortals weep with gratitude. It is a tired gratitude, much like someone who has been kept from sleep for a long time and is finally allowed to rest. They are so thankful to just close their eyes, unable to muster the strength to voice their praise they simply emanate it from the core of their being. The use of so much energy is difficult, even for an immortal. I want to allow myself to rest, but I press on. Word spreads quickly about the resurrection of the food supply and by the time I reach the end of my journey I am almost disoriented by the scent of smoke and fragrant herbs burnt in my name. The sound of prayers has become a constant buzzing in my ears and it overrides my ability to hear anything else. I follow the smell of herbs to an exquisite stone temple. I realize belatedly that the temple is dedicated to my mother. Three women are clustered around an altar, casting dried herbs onto a bright flame.

"Persephone." They whisper my name in reverence, swaying gently to a silent tune they share between them. Unsure as to why they speak of me within my mother's halls, I wait and listen to what they have to say. "Goddess of Spring, of life beyond the darkest winter. Lady of Flowers, bursting forth under your gentle hands, we speak your name in praise."

I drift closer and examine the women. They are all painfully thin from the famine, their dark curls and warm brown skin look in poor shape from malnutrition, but they are outfitted in their best clothing. Their simple white gowns are of fine fabric, well made and decorated with green sashes and dried flowers adorning their hair.

"Beautiful Lady, Goddess Eternal. She Who Is The Intercessor, She Who Banishes The Cold, She Who Cares For Our Souls. Bright Maiden, we speak your name in praise."

The tallest of the women bows low, pressing her hands together and her forehead to the floor "Forgive us for the use of your mother's temple, Lady of Light. Construction will begin on your own, but our praise for the bounty you have brought to the world could not be delayed."

My mother has turned her back on these people, allowed them to succumb to starvation. When Great Mother Gaia spoke my name there had been a very audible shift in prayer. They continue to speak, praising me, still using my old epithet, Daughter of Demeter, but now a new one follows it: Wife of Hades, Queen of the Underworld.

They take jugs of oil and wine, carefully hoarded by the temples during the many lean years and carry them in a short procession out of the temple and pour the contents of both into the Earth. There is precious little left, perhaps a handful of each, but it is all they have left and they are giving it away with a prayer. "Praise to thee also, Earth Mother, from whose body the bounty of Persephone grows. We are eternally grateful for the nourishment drawn from your breast." Clouds gather in the sky and release a gentle rain to quench the parched soil. "Praise to Zeus, God of the Heavens who brought Spring from the Underworld and blesses our fields with rain."

I look up at the sky. My father brings the rains. He had starved the fields of water just as much as my mother had starved them of her blessings. I push my parents from my mind and take on a corporeal form and approach the women from the temple. The tallest of them notices me first. She gasps and collapses into the dirt, moving to prostrate herself at my feet. Her companions follow her actions immediately. My body shimmers, glittering from so much power flowing through me.

"Please," I implore them, "please stand."

"We are in the presence of the divine, it would be improper for us to stand." They visibly tremble.

When they refuse to rise I settle onto my knees before them. "I have something to tell you that must be spread, tell everyone you can. What has befallen this world will happen again. I cannot say for how many years it will occur, only that I know it will and you must all prepare for it. The crops will likely wither and die, cold may sweep the land and chances are good that many will starve again. When I return to the Underworld I will care for the souls there, but I cannot guarantee that my mother will care for the crops in my absence. I promise when I return I will personally make sure that the world is reborn so food will become plentiful once more. People must preserve their food, save it for the long months when nothing will grow. Please remind them to have faith, I will always return to save them."

"Is there no way to prevent the hardships from occurring again?" Their noses are all pressed to the ground, so I cannot tell which one asks.

"I wish there were, but I cannot control the happenings of this world when I am in the Underworld. If I remained here to ensure bounty then the souls I pledged to care for would become neglected in my absence. I promise I will do everything possible to prevent widespread famine, but you all must play your part. I cannot harvest the grain, I cannot preserve the food; mortals must take a hand in their own success. Have faith, I am here for you all."

I fade out of a visible form and call up the last dregs of my power. The fields have been cleared, but I sift through the memory of the soil. The Earth always remembers, always knows what it has previously nurtured. I need only lock onto the memory of what began to grow here before the famine overcame it and then I can craft it into existence once more.

Delicate leaves and buds poke out of the dirt and the edges of the fields flood with people. Their faces are coated with filth and tears. "Praise be to the Gods!"

My priestesses clamor up from their prostrate position and yell out to the people. "It is the Lady Persephone, she is the one who has heard our prayers and answered them!"

I need to craft a symbol of hope, something that will see them through the coming cyclical famine. I press the last of my energy into the Earth and coax up a pomegranate tree, its emerald leaves and ruby fruits fanning out before the golden sun. I am emptied of energy, but filled up with pride and happiness. These people are weeping and their gratitude fills me to bursting. It is more than I can hold inside of me, so I do not. I fall to my knees and join them, pouring out a river of praise to Gaia who has enabled these miracles and taught me my gifts so I could bring this joy.

38

PERSEPHONE

The sun is gone and the people retreated to their homes by the time I raise myself from the fields. I rub my hands over my arms, a bone-deep exhaustion slowing my movements. I need to rest and so I return to Olympus, intent on my bed and a large cup of nectar.

Instead I find my mother perched on my bed, waiting for me. Oh, Gaia, I do not have the energy for a fight. I ignore her at first and shuffle to where a silver pitcher of nectar stands next to a series of matching cups. I fill one carefully and swallow the lot of it before refilling the cup again. I sip this one, giving myself a few moments to collect myself. The nectar forms a hot swirling in my belly, spreading slowly through my limbs. It brushes away some of the mental cobwebs, but such a large undertaking will need more than a couple of drinks to restore the energy lost.

"The mortals are pleased with you." I focus on her and note that she sits very straight and her eyes are wary.

"I'm glad I was able to assist. I had to repair the damage caused by my leaving. My words were not intended to spark any reaction. My thoughts are so focused on sleep that it is hard to even form coherent sentences.

"I was too distraught to care for them, I was too busy trying to find you." She defends, her muscles growing rigid and unyielding. "I gave no thoughts to their needs."

"You are a Goddess," I remind her. "You taught them how to grow food to begin with, your duty should always be to them before any other. You should not have abandoned them."

"So I should have abandoned you instead?" She rises up at me like a snake. She's looking for a challenge, for a fight, but I am too tired to give her what she wants. I sigh, unable to stop myself.

I rub my face, willing my energy to perk. "That is not what I meant. I wish things could have been different, honestly I do. I'm sorry my choices hurt you, but I saw no other way. I felt so choked off, so trapped and pressed down by your need to control me. In your mind it was for safety, but in mine I was caged eternally. If I had told you I was visiting the Underworld you would have found a way to stop me."

"Of course I would have." Irritation sparks off her like embers as her voice picks up volume. "I am older and have infinitely more experience than you. I could have easily told you that such a notion is incredibly foolish. Parental concern is not controlling, Persephone."

"Yes it is!" I cry out, suddenly swept away by emotions bubbling deep inside of me. "Mother, please at least acknowledge what you did to me. There is an enormous difference between concern and controlling every moment of my life. You never gave me any freedom, never gave me any reason for how or why something occurred, I was just expected to follow you blindly. You never even let me talk to anyone except for companions that you personally selected for me."

"Are your companions not suitable to your taste?" She asks, disregarding the rest of my statement.

I feel a vague urge to pull out my hair. I press my hands to my face before shoving them through my hair. "That is not the point I am trying to make."

"Our kin are selfish and capricious and other immortals are no better, you would not want to talk to them even if I gave you the opportunity."

Her energy is exhausting, flying at me with such force it's a struggle to remain standing. The surge of emotion fades, unable to maintain itself. I swallow more nectar, the sweetness fortifying me. "But I do want to. I have always wanted to know them. All I ever wanted was to be able to help you in the mortal world, to learn your craft and make myself useful while enjoying a little freedom to speak to whomever I might wish to speak to, but you have never once allowed me to do so."

She reaches out to me with smooth golden hued hands. I stay still, stopping myself from shrinking back. "You are mine, Persephone. I don't want to share you with others. I love you and I want to protect you from this world."

"I do not need your protection, Mother. Please have enough faith in your abilities as a mother to have raised me into a capable person. Allow me to believe that you at least entertain the concept that I might be capable of making intelligent decisions."

She drops her hands and her eyes narrow. "I can hardly entertain such a thing when you were deluded and tricked into a marriage."

"I was neither tricked nor deluded." I pull some of her furious energy into myself and allow it to push me over the edge. "Marrying Hades was not a snap decision. I took the time to consider what I wanted before I agreed. While I feel guilty for having to hide it from you I wanted my freedom and his love more than I wanted your approval. I thought at one time that there would never be anyone that was worth causing you pain, but he is. I love him and he loves me."

"You think Hades will give you freedom? That is he even capable of love?" Her spine stiffens to the point I fear she might break at the slightest movement.

"Yes." I cross my arms over my chest, stubbornly defiant. "Hades trusts me. He allows me to go wherever I please in his realm and he has entrusted souls into my care."

"So he gives no consideration to your safety when his realm is filled with monsters and darkness and he has offloaded his work onto you."

"There are no monsters in his realm, save those safely tucked away in Tartarus. His companions are kind to me. There is also a difference between offloading work and taking the time to teach and cultivate confidence in the student. I felt useful for the first time in my life."

"His companions are horrid. I have seen that miserable three-headed beast, was nearly mauled by it."

I stop suddenly, my mind churning despite the cobwebs. "When did you see Cerberus?" She averts her eyes and does not answer. "Mother, tell me."

She shrugs and turns her back on me. "Whatever your delusions about them might be, I do not want to hear them. What is done is done and there is unfortunately nothing I can do. You are with me now and I will hear no mention of them. When you are taken from me again I will cope the best I can knowing what you are truly in store for. Until that time you will be silent on the matter."

39

HADES

Thanatos has placed Evaristus in an enchanted sleep so he might heal faster, but Demeter nearly crushed his bones when she attacked. Before falling into the sleep he told me that he had only hoped that Demeter had truly come to apologize, that she truly wanted to make things right between us all. He had forgotten his protocol in his joy that Persephone might be allowed to freely move between all the realms. Demeter had slowed behind him and when he had pointed out my room all had gone black.

I wanted to scold him for allowing anyone into the Palace, for not waking me to meet her at the Gates, but his mottled skin and slow breaths still the words in my throat. He has paid enough for his mistake, I will not add to it. None of us here have healing magic, but his sleep at least removes his pain and when Persephone returns she can complete his cure.

She has done well, Hermes reported not long ago that the fruit trees swell to breaking point, the grain grows tall as a man and animals grow fat with babes in womb. The world rejoices in having Persephone while we languish in purgatory.

The group of souls electing to wait for Persephone to judge them is growing daily, though not so quickly as when the famine was in place. I miss her terribly, but I'm so proud of what she has done. Her freedom is so precious to her and for her to give it up, not knowing whether it might ever be regained is an act of true devotion. The mortals are lucky to have her.

I have tried to work through the remaining months until Persephone's return, but the dæmons are rather vigorous in their insistence that I rest. They pull longer shifts and report to me with anything they cannot solve themselves, but for the most part I have been turned away from my usual duties. I wanted to just work through the pain at first, but damage such as this takes as long to heal as if I were in a mortal body and discomfort slows time so I have no choice but to acknowledge my wounds. I had initially debated going into an enchanted sleep as well, but couldn't justify leaving the realm unattended for so long. The days move slowly, but each moment that passes is a moment closer to the return of my Queen.

"Hades," I glance up through the steam of my bath to see Hermes hovering at my door. "Demeter has issued the terms of the exchange. You are to fetch Persephone from her meadow and she will be accompanied by several nymphs. She is using them as spies, that much is obvious, but they do not seem to be malicious."

Hermes pads over and slips off his winged sandals, popping his feet into the water. Persephone will return in two days time and I will be ready to receive her the moment Eos brings the dawn. I nod my acknowledgement. "She may have whatever attendants she desires, but they will be guests here, not spies. I will be there with a full reception party."

Hermes shakes his head. "Demeter wants you there alone. She is fighting a losing battle, grabbing control where she can. Have the reception party wait for you before the light is visible, they will be close if you require any assistance, but far enough away that Demeter need not know they are there."

"Very well." My sister has earned what is likely a permanent position on my bad side, but she is Persephone's mother and I will be civil for the sake of my wife. "Do you think Demeter will always view us as the villains in this?"

The question was more rhetorical than anything else, spoken to myself, but Hermes shrugs his shoulders in response. "You are one of three of the brothers of Olympus. She doesn't see beyond that. We are all filth by association in her mind. The Gods have long memories when it comes to wrongs against them, I doubt she will ever move past what they did to her. It's a shame that you and Persephone must suffer for the actions of others, but I can see little way around it. For her to go to Zeus at all shows how much she feared for Persephone, but I cannot believe that your Queen would stay silent on how she was treated here. Demeter has no reason to continue her mistrust of us."

"Were life so easy that a few words could correct a misunderstanding so great. We must all live with the choices made."

"I looked in on your bride," Hermes says. I face him directly, trying not to appear like a dog waiting for a treat. "She is resting, nearly in a God Sleep to recover. Gaia only knows where Demeter has gone, but she has rarely been on Olympus since Persephone returned." God Sleep is an extreme measure taken by worn out immortals. They essentially descend into a comatose state, their ancient link with Gaia providing them with healing energy. They expend no power and simply wait and heal. Some deities fall silent for so long that the people who once worshipped them forget they ever existed. There are a few who enjoyed the solitude and peace of the experience so much that when they woke to find they were no longer remembered, they simply enter the state again and rest eternally. "She is young still, her strength will grow and in time she will not need to sleep to recover."

40

PERSEPHONE

I'm roused from sleep by Chloe jostling my shoulder. I stretch slowly, allowing my body to adapt to the movement and let the sunlight coax me into a wakeful state. I consume the cup of nectar she offers and breathe in the delicious scent of ripe pomegranates and rose petals.

"You return to the Underworld with the coming Dawn, are you ready?" Her words spark a fire inside of me, joy rushing through my blood. Chloe hoists me with her arm hooked around mine. "Are you well, my Lady?"

"Yes, only tired. I didn't realize the restoration would be so difficult, or that I would sleep for so long." My legs feel like jelly.

"It's not so long, only a few mortal months." She assures me as she props me onto a stool and fetches a comb and another cup of nectar. I sip slowly while she gently wrestles through the tangles and combs until my hair falls in a sleek rolling waterfall of hazelwood locks. "The others will be waiting in the meadow, but I thought you might like some company. We all worried for you, working so hard like you did."

"I had to work quickly," I remind her, "the growing season is cut in half. If my mother doesn't care for the crops while I'm away they will die again."

"Slowly yes, but they did not all die at once when you left before, maybe some things will have time to finish growing into the cold season. The biggest risk would be if she lets Boreas fly unchecked, bringing his ice winds with him. He froze the crops in their fields and Helios' Sun hid behind clouds that never gave any rain." I feel a well of anxiety in my belly. I cannot stop Boreas from coming again or coax the Sun and rain to shine or fall. "I can feel you tense, you must relax. The mortals are resilient, they will survive with your aid."

"You're right, there is nothing I can do now." I turn my focus instead towards my return to the Underworld. It's so close now I can all but taste it. "We have only one night to wait, one more blanket of stars pulled down by Nyx and one more slow rising dawn as Eos awakes."

She braids my hair, lazily twisting the strands as she moves without urgency. "I cannot decide if I'm excited or terrified. You love that realm, but I confess some of the stories are still trapped in my mind."

"I doubt we'll ever truly escape the legends, but so long as a few know the truth I will be content." The stories of Kamp, of Cerberus, even of Hades or Thanatos will follow the Underworld into eternity. Mortal fear will always outweigh fact.

Chloe and I talk all through the night and just before the Goddess of the Dawn wakes my mother appears. She is decked in finery, a formidable beauty with a sharpness in her eyes that seems so at odds with the softness of her cheeks. They are wet with tears. She has slipped back into the role of grieving mother.

She walks over to me in silence and wraps her arms around me, pressing a sodden cheek to mine. Tears drip down onto my shoulder and I wrap my arms around her as well in comfort. "I will return so quickly you won't even have time to miss me."

"I already miss you and you have not even left me. If you have need of anything you must promise to send a nymph to me at once. I will beg the Thunderer to intercede on your behalf."

"I promise." There will be no need, but I assure her anyway. The first signs of Eos, gentle Goddess of Dawn who heralds the coming of the Sun, breach the horizon and my mother grows ever more solemn.

She clasps my hand and draws me out of my quarters and into the night air. "Come now, I must deliver you to your jailer." She doesn't look at me when she speaks and I don't correct her. Instead I follow her in silence to the meadow where I had first gone to the Underworld. The other nymphs are there waiting, their hair piled high with flowers. Chloe follows a moment later, right as the first reaches of Apollo's Sun chariot peek past Eos' painting.

The ground trembles beneath our feet, the soil rending and roiling before it splits apart with a thunderous roar. Preceding Hades are his four horses, rearing with squeals and hoof beats as they ascend into the dawn. Their nostrils flare and their eyes flash with dark fire. As a unit they charge towards me, causing my mother and the nymphs to scatter. I fling my arms open and revel in the rush of air and force of fur as they all shove themselves at me.

Hades lets out a sharp whistle that stills even the air around us. Everyone stares at him, the nymphs totally agog while a visible anger boils in my mother. I move slowly, skirting the horses until I can properly see my husband. He looks nervous under his fierce expression, but when I smile at him the wariness melts away. He nods his head and holds out his hand for me. He lifts me easily, like the wind catching a flower petal, and settles me delicately onto the chariot next to him.

I'm overwhelmed with anticipation, but I force myself to exhibit restraint in front of my mother. His display with the horses is ostentatious and I can see that it's infuriated her, but I'm secretly thrilled by it. He nods curtly at my mother, but she doesn't acknowledge him at all beyond a fiery glare.

He turns the horses sharply and we descend into the ground in a whirlwind of metal and fur. We pass a collection of dæmons as the horses careen down the pathway and I turn back to see them breaking through to the surface to gather up my nymphs. The horses stop so quickly in front of the stables that the chariot is nearly overturned. Hades holds me tightly while the tilting vehicle rights itself and settles with a plume of dust. Safely on the ground once more he wraps his arms around me and presses his forehead to mine.

"I've missed you." We have only a short time before we will be required to attend the nymphs and greet all those I have not seen for two seasons. I stand with my husband, enjoying a few heartbeats of silence in his presence.

Eustathios appears to unharness the horses and it's then that I notice a familiar, exuberant face has not yet appeared. "Where is Evaristus?"

Hades' expression falls. "There was an incident, he is resting. I had hoped you might be able to help him." I agree immediately and follow him to the quarters where Evaristus resides. I clap my hands over my mouth to silence the shriek of dismay when I see the state of the dæmon.

I rush to his bedside and kneel upon the marble floor. His usual golden glow is gone, only an ashen face and too thin features remain. I reach deep, to the small well of power that has managed to restore itself since I brought about Spring. Calling it forth I sweep my hand over the dæmon's brow, pushing his curls off his face. I feel my energy drain, but Evaristus needs me. His bones have already begun to heal, some of them mere dust and shards beneath his skin. I concentrate until I break out in a sweat, willing the minuscule bits to reassemble, to withdraw from the surrounding tissue and become whole once more. I pull back my hands when I feel my legs start to tremble. I try to stand, but find myself staggering. Hades catches me easily and sets me on the bed before fetching me a cup of nectar. "I'm sorry, I want to be able to help him."

"You have, see how his glow is returning, his skin shimmers." I turn hazy eyes onto the dæmon to verify Hades' words and find that he does indeed look a little less like he may perish at any moment. "I shouldn't have called on you so soon after the restoration, I should have allowed you time to rest."

"He needed me, I had to try. I will keep trying as my strength recovers." I smile at my husband and lean into him. He winces and I withdraw. My hands fly of their own volition and draw a reading from his body. He is healing, but appears to have similar injuries to those that Evaristus bears. "What happened?" When he does not immediately answer, I question him further. "Was it my mother? She was gone for days and avoided me when I questioned her as well."

He nods slowly and I curse. "She came without warning, attacked us both." Hot tears flood my eyes and I dissolve into sobs. Hades pats my back awkwardly.

"I'm such a failure. I can do nothing to help you and I couldn't stop her from doing this." He gathers me into his arms, tucking me like a child as he strokes my hair.

"You have performed a great duty and it is not your job to monitor your mother's behaviors. You have done your best and no one can ask anything more from you." He holds me tighter. "My love, do not be distressed, I will heal and so will Evaristus, you must not let our condition upset you."

"But I love you both, I want to help."

He presses a finger to my lips, shushing me. "And you will, when you have rested and are able to do so. You must restore yourself first before giving everything to another."

I struggle out of his grasp. "The nymphs will be here by now, I must go to them. They will be frightened until they are settled." He helps me walk and I focus on taking long, slow deep breaths, pulling in the essence of the Earth. I pause on the walk from the Palace to the Gates and mutter to myself. "I should never have come here."

Hades stops short. His dark eyes fasten on me, feeding the guilt that chokes me. Every death in the famine is on my head, every choice I have made has caused heartache and chaos. "Have I done something to offend you?"

"Never," I reach for him, but he is tense and does not embrace me in return. "I only wish that I had been less selfish, had not caused so much hurt." Tears well up and my exhaustion leaves me with little defense against them. "If I had never left Olympus in the first place none of this would have happened."

"Would you truly prefer that?" I realize then that my words have been disregarding his feelings, that my desire to correct the wrongs would also have erased everything I have with him. I reach out to him, but he moves just beyond my grasp. "Please just answer, I have suffered in my long existence, I should like to know whether it will be something that continues."

41

HADES

Persephone shakes her head slowly. She looks fragile, like a child who has long been sick. I don't think I could bear to exist with a Queen who regrets her decision to be with me. That head shake is everything. I know her words are spoken in grief and exhaustion, but they still cut deep. When she reaches for me again I don't avoid the contact, instead I gather her into my arms as she sobs. My bride has lost her freedom and her relationship with her mother and she has given everything she was able to give to the mortals to save them from the consequences of her choices. She has repaid her debts, but they still weigh too heavily upon her. I cannot begin to say whether or not those burdens will ever be relieved for her, but succumbing to them is beneficial for no one.

She clearly needs rest, but I'm at a loss as to how to restore her. The dæmons have already prepared a welcome feast, but she's in no condition to enjoy it. They will all be waiting for us, and there are souls that have postponed Judgement just for her. "Many are waiting for you, but I will dismiss them all if you would prefer a respite to recover."

"No, I have to go, I'm expected and there's so much to get done."

"It can all wait, I promise you. Don't overextend yourself."

"I'm fine, really," she gives me a fragile smile, "I won't stay long."

I keep an arm secured around her as we walk, wishing that I had the energy she needed, that either of us knew how she might draw it from another source instead of always providing for others.

When we arrive at the Gates her nymphs are huddled in a group. The dæmons do their best to entertain them, but they are just as bewildered by the nymphs as the ladies are by their new surroundings. The nymphs visibly perk when Persephone comes into their line of sight. Cerberus catches her scent and bounds over, causing the nymphs to shriek and scatter. The hellhound bowls us both over and rubs his heads upon Persephone's outstretched hands. Thanatos floats across Styx and ushers Cerberus' frantic form off of us. The nymphs fall silent as the grave and stare at Thanatos in awe.

"We have missed you," he offers his hand to my Queen and helps her to stand, his brow creasing over how much she depends on the action to rise.

"Ladies, if it pleases you, the dæmons have prepared a welcome feast for you all in the Great Hall, please allow them to escort you." My voice shocks them out of their stunned silence and they awkwardly loop arms with the dæmons who are considerably shorter than they are. As a group we venture through the outer recesses of the realm until we pass through the Palace gates.

The tables are decked out with silks and little pots of the roses and other blossoms Persephone had previously grown in the courtyard. With a snap of my fingers I summon the throne I had installed for her and set it at the end of the table for her. The shimmering black stone seat is draped with indigo silk and adorned with a matching plush cushion for comfort. She slides onto it, giving me a relieved expression when she is finally off her feet.

A gnawing worry ravages my belly, she needs God Sleep to recover, but who knows how long she could be out for. Once she enters it she won't awaken until recovered and that is a difficult matter when she must be shuttled between her mother and I twice per mortal year. She needs to rest within Gaia, but I can only imagine what might happen if I allowed her to do so and her time here elapsed before she awoke.

She grins sleepily when the dæmons pick up instruments and fill the Great Hall with lively music, while those not playing fall into a patterned line dance. The nymphs take mere seconds to join in, their awkwardness and unease forgotten in the face of music and dance. I fetch my bride cups of nectar and as many bowls of ambrosia as she willingly consumes and it seems to help, but not as much as I hoped.

The celebratory atmosphere is fueling in itself. Happiness feeds her power and this room is filled to bursting with it. The array of colors on the dancing nymphs is dizzying and they tug dæmons out of their dances to join their own and soon the whole room, even the musicians, are swirling in an intricate dance around us. Persephone's eyes shine and I know that she wants to join them. I scoop her up and spin us both, she laughs, the sound of bells filling my senses. I take nearly all her weight so only the tips of her toes need touch the ground and move us with all the grace I can manage despite having no idea what the steps might me. Her weight, though slight, makes my barely healed bones burn with the effort, but I want her to be happy, so I continue. I dance on instinct and Persephone seems so pleased that I don't even worry about fumbling the steps.

Intoxicated by joy, the nymphs seem to have a boundless energy and dance so long into the night it's a wonder that their feet don't simply fall off. Persephone's moss green eyes glimmer, soaking in the festivities and allowing me to assist her in dance whenever she becomes too restless to remain seated. She is magnificent, even in her depleted state, a splendorous beauty of warmth and life.

Long before the festivities are over we both retreat. The energy of the nymphs and the newfound celebratory bliss of the dæmons far outpaces us both. I have almost forgotten the sounds of such things, realizing that they have long been denied to the dæmons. I'll have to ensure that this feast occurs regularly and let them enjoy themselves more often with no thought of duty upon them.

As we near my quarters, walking arm in arm, a sense of awkwardness slows my steps. We still have separate quarters. I didn't want to presume to combine them without her and she was gone too quickly. As we move closer, I begin to wonder whether or not she will join me or if she will continue to stay in her own rooms. The question lodges in my throat like dry bread and I have neither courage nor wine to wash it free.

I walk with her to her door, the quarters across from mine and I wait in silence. "Let me stay with you," she whispers, but does not look at me. "I do need rest, but I would take it by your side."

I turn us, still in silence and part the double doors to my chambers. The austere black seems too harsh for her. I had not the foresight to add some color, a flower or two to brighten things, but she doesn't seem put off by it. She settles herself on the black silks, a spot of light among the dark.

I settle next to her and tentatively reach for the multitude of blossoms in her hair. She turns her head to accommodate and I spend a few moments in silence plucking them from her hair and unbinding the intricate system of braids. Her hair falls in waves as soft as a cloud and the strands shimmer in the low light so she's surrounded by a halo. A smile tugs at my lips and I allow myself to enfold her in my arms, resting my chin upon her shoulder and inhaling the sweet scent of Spring.

42

PERSEPHONE

Hades' closeness sparks gooseflesh up and down my arms, despite the warmth of his rooms. There is a light humidity from the expansive baths and it fills me with a deep sense of comfort as I lie tucked against him. "You were the only one who believed I could do something so grand." My voice is a whisper, but I know he hears it when he tenses.

He sighs and pulls away so he's sitting upright next to me. "Were I the only one who had ever believed in your abilities, Persephone, then you would never have accomplished all that you did. You believed in yourself and Gaia obviously did as well or she would never have trained you to begin with. You are greater than you believe, I just wish that you could accept it. You were unafraid to reach for new heights and you achieved everything I knew you could. In time it will become less difficult, you will learn to build your power and to tap into Gaia without her directly providing for you." He trails his fingers through the tips of my hair, re-establishing the gentle intimacy between us. "You have become a powerful Goddess and I could not be more proud of you."

A quiet sense of deep love, all pervasive and surrounding, fills me so completely that I do not know how it can possibly be contained within my body. My soul reaches out, overflowing with this love. This God has believed in me from the very beginning, has given over his time and energy in order to help me grow into the Goddess I am meant to be. He offered these things to a stranger and gently encouraged me until I had enough confidence in myself to take charge of my own life.

Love, compassion and trust pulses between us. Shimmering crystals dance along the ceiling and walls, refracting the light like the sun through water. Their subtle light grows dimmer and I lean forward to place a light kiss upon his lips. My soul surges as tendrils of our magic, power and essence reach for one another, blending our souls as our corporeal forms embrace. Every ounce of my being pours out of me and into him, as I am filled up again by his own energy. His soul threads through mine in an experience I can only describe as shattering. I am complete and destroyed at the same moment in time.

Overwhelmed and drowning in the intensity of emotion I can do little but try to breathe. We are as one being, strung together by an all-encompassing love that arches in spirals through every level of existence. Touching his soul leaves me blinded, flayed open and vulnerable, but I am not afraid. I could never be afraid of him, for he too is before me, blinded and exposed to the depths of his being. It is this vulnerability, this pulling apart of ourselves that allows us to reform and embrace what the other is offering.

I am shaken to my foundations, poured over by a sensation so hot and vibrant that I could be at one with molten rock. Breathless and clinging, the sensation slowly drips away, replaced by something so light and beautiful I could swear I was floating, though I can feel the silk beneath me.

The concept of time is lost entirely as we disappear into the night. We float together on a tranquil sea, beauty surrounding us as our bodies rest, our souls gently brushing one another in a sweet symphony of adoration.

I spare a glance over at Hades and find him dazed and enraptured, his dark eyes shining like stars. My churning mind slowly settles and it occurs to me that much of the confusing imagery flitting through my mind is memories. I stare at Hades, slowly comprehending that his entire life is now part of my own memories. I am privy to the entire history of his being. I feel the acceptance he craved and had been so ruthlessly denied, the self-sacrifice he continuously made to please others and ensure that the souls are receiving the best care possible. I knew some of it, as he had told me, but it is entirely different to know something from being told and knowing it from having the experiences to call upon. I know his thoughts, his emotions and desires. I have always known there was a light in him, a brightness just below the surface that needed to be given the opportunity to shine, given the joy to spark it into the open. I feel the flickers of hope that had come to life when he met me and the slow building of an internal fire as our relationship progressed.

I am humbled by this knowledge. It's incredible to me to think that I, the once unknown, unskilled Daughter of Demeter, had been the one to give him that light. He has the acceptance he has so desperately craved since his birth into this world. A fresh surge of love fills me and my lips curve into a smile.

It occurs to me all at once that if I have been given his memories then surely he has been given mine as well. Uncertainty blossoms in my chest. He has seen every moment of insecurity, powerlessness and lack of direction.

"Persephone," I jump a little, lost in my own thoughts. His voice is a rough whisper, as though he has been silent for years and only now speaks again. He tangles his hands in my hair and gently massages my scalp. "I could never have hoped for a more perfect partner in my life. Thank you for what you have given me."

"Given each other," I whisper, cupping his cheek in my hand. "I can never repay all that you have given to me, but it is heartening to know that I have been able to offer some of it back to you."

I snuggle in close, resting my chin on his chest. "Do you think the others have ever experienced such a thing?"

"I have my doubts that they are even capable of such a thing. They do not often join together out of love," Hades tells me. "More often than not it is a physical desire or want of power that brings them together."

"Surely if they knew of this they would want to experience it with someone they loved." It seems impossible to me that no one else knows about what we felt. How can they forge relationships without love and settle for less than this wonder?

"Do not trouble yourself with the motivations of our kin, they are senseless at the best of times." His hand glides down my hair and hooks over the curve of my hips. "I am emotionally drained and filled all at once. We should both rest."

I grin at him and he smiles in return. The bone-deep exhaustion that has been plaguing me is hardly noticeable now, tempered by our extensive exchange of energy. I pull the silks over us and settle in and together we drift through the realms of Morpheus. Soon enough the outside world will draw us back, but not yet.

43

HADES

A knock wakes me. I struggle for a moment to place the sound and fight my way through the haze of bliss that has settled over me. I walk to the door with eyes closed, groping for the handle and open it a few inches.

Ariston, one of my dæmons, stands at the door. "My Lord, I hesitate to disturb you, but the Gods are fussing and have sent us a soul they demand go straight to Tartarus. Also, I have heard news that Evaristus has awoken from his sleep."

The news, more of Evaristus than Olympian drama, jolts me fully awake. Persephone stirs and sits up slowly in bed. I take a deep breath and mentally shake myself down, forcing myself to return to my usual role. "Bring him straight to Judgement, I will be there shortly."

Before I return to the bed Persephone is already up and pulling on her gown from last night and tugging her fingers through her hair. "I want to see Evaristus before we go to the Towers."

I tug my own clothing on and we rush from the room and I lead her through the halls to where Evaristus is quartered. He is tucked securely in bed, propped by pillows and watched over by two dæmons.

Theophanes and Zoticus, who take care of his comfort and ply him with cups of nectar. They bow and excuse themselves when we enter the room.

Persephone rushes around me and takes up a post on her knees at Evaristus' bedside. "My Lady, such a pleasure to see you." He smiles brightly, albeit with a slight tremble to his lip, and Persephone slips his hand into hers. He gasps and his back arches as light pulses between their joined hands. He twists, writhing, but her grip is firm and her brow creases with concentration. When she finally releases her grip he falls back against the pillows, breathing like he has run from one end of the realm to the other.

I approach the end of his bed and am pleased to note that the ashen tones of his skin are gone, replaced by the pink flush of health. As the daze clears from his eyes he grins at me, his old sparkle present in the gaze. He continues to stare, almost unnervingly. "What?"

"Happiness suits you, my Lord." Evaristus grins, his ivory teeth gleam brightly before disappearing behind his lips.

"How do you feel?" Persephone runs a hand over his brow, her fingers fluttering over his limbs to check their condition.

"Much improved, my Lady, thank you for the healing." He sits up slowly, and untangles himself him the layers of fabric keeping him warm. He wiggles his bare toes before hefting his legs over the edge of the bed and slides off to stand. He wobbles a moment, but grins at us both when he gains his footing and stretches.

"Now that you are well," I say to him, "we must attend to our duties, but we will speak when I return." Evaristus nods, suddenly looking abashed. I give his shoulder a light squeeze before Persephone and I head for the Towers. Ordinarily I'm comfortable with allowing the Judges to oversee things, but when a soul is condemned by the Gods to Tartarus I must be present for it.

From the top of the Towers we stare down at the soul bound in shining gold chains. He is ancient, wrinkled like fruit left in the sun, with wispy hair, spindly arms and a significant belly paunch. A cruel glimmer sparks in his eyes. We look to Minos as he speaks. "My Lord and Lady, we have been commissioned by the Gods to pass Judgement on Tantalus. Zeus invited him to dine at the Table of the Gods and Tantalus insulted the Olympians by bringing the butchered body of his son, disguised as garnished plates of roast meat." I glance over at Persephone as she makes a sound of revulsion. Her hand is clasped over her mouth and her eyes are impossibly wide. "This atrocity is to be reversed, with orders from Zeus for the Moiræ to rebind the thread of life for Pelops, son of Tantalus. The Gods will gift him with his former body, with the addition of an ivory shoulder, which had been mistakenly consumed by the Lady Demeter." Persephone grips my arm fiercely at these words. "My Lord and Lady, have we approval to send Tantalus to Tartarus and restore his son to life?"

I nod my head. There is no point in denying the sentence, even had I thought it a good idea to do so. The murder of his child would have been enough to ensure punishment, but to have tried to feed the boy to the Gods is beyond reprehensible. Tapestries do not show thoughts, only actions and events in mortal lives, there is nothing to indicate that Pelops was anything but a kind, obedient son. Why Tantalus thought to mur-der the boy is beyond my understanding. I drape on the metaphorical cloak that turns me from myself into the iron-willed Lord of the Realm. "Tantalus will spend his eternity in Tartarus." The slithering black smoke that makes up Kamp, Jailer of Tartarus, slinks over the ground until it finds what it seeks. Tantalus lets out a ferocious scream as the tendrils snake around him, ripping away his unfortunate soul to torment.

Minos seats himself at the table before addressing us. "It would appear that Lady Demeter was not herself at the feast and did not notice what she was eating until the others grew upset and pointed it out." Persephone shudders at my side and grips my hand like a lifeline.

A cool breeze ripples over the back of my neck and I know at once that the Moiræ have appeared. Clotho, Atropos and Lachesis move like mist, one after the other, until they all stand before us. Clotho speaks for the group. "Lord Zeus knows not what he is asking. It is against the natural laws to restore the life of the dead and against the laws of our realm. Restoring his thread of life will put him on a new path, he will not be the same person, his line and house will be tainted by this resurrection. What say you Lord Hades?"

"Let them see what their demands create. Go to Olympus, Moiræ, make things as the Gods believe it should be and we will receive the aftermath of their decision." They are visibly displeased, but they nod and carry out my orders.

"What happens when someone is resurrected?" Persephone looks at me with plaintive eyes.

"As the Moiræ said, they will not be the same. Whatever sweetness that boy possesses will fade and he will grow an evil heart. The core of the soul does not want to return to the body after it has been freed and it will never be comfortable there again. Zeus will strike the body with lightning and seal the soul within the flesh once again. Resurrections are infrequent, this is the first in many millennia, and although I disagree with it, having the Moiræ restore the boy is the method of least upheaval for my realm."

She crosses her arms, a hard look in her eye. "Olympus should keep a closer eye on the mortals and things like this would not occur, and would therefore not need to be rectified. Tantalus was a human king, was he not?" I nod, having seen it on his tapestry. "The ruling mortals are paid more attention by the Gods, why was my father not aware of this?"

"I'm afraid he is easily preoccupied."

Persephone huffs peevishly. "It is their duty as immortals to care for the creatures created in their likeness." Her skin is glowing as though she has a blanket of stars beneath it. "Zeus himself commissioned them from Prometheus, he needs to take proper responsibility for them."

"Zeus will never take responsibility for their failures, only their feats of glory," I remind her.

"That time needs to be over. I am a liaison between Olympus and the Underworld. I am Queen here and daughter to the King there, there must be something I can do. We must be able to regulate our own realm. Bowing to pressure from Olympus is only disruptive to our purpose and harmful to the souls and mortals. I will speak to the Gods, make them understand that their time to intervene is in life, not after death."

I tug her close, and although she does not sink into my embrace, she does not protest. "I admire your motives, Persephone, but I cannot tell you it is wise to challenge the Olympians. Zeus does not take kindly to threats against his power."

She deflates in my arms at these words. "One day they will understand. I swear it."

44

PERSEPHONE

Brooding in my baths amid the steam and pomegranate oil, I mull over how to make Olympus respect the boundaries of the Underworld. Logically I know that Zeus is a formidable opponent and not someone to be trifled with, but I find I remain adamant that the Underworld should be beyond his sway. I settle back against the warm stone, letting the weight of my head rest on the edge while the rest of my body floats freely.

The Underworld is entirely separate from Olympus and the visible world which it rules, Hades should be able to be an autonomous ruler. It is a disservice to all that we are under the thumb of Olympus. They disregard mortals in life and then try to meddle with their souls when they are delivered into our care. The irresponsibility of it leaves me fuming.

Too restless to enjoy my soak, I haul myself up and out of the bath and dry myself off before selecting an ivory comb from the vanity. I pull the comb through my hair in a gentle, rhythmic fashion and become so entrenched in the task that a series of cheerful knocks at the door startles me into dropping it. I wrap a length of fabric around me In a make-shift gown and pry open the doors to find Evaristus backed by the nymphs. They each carry a woven basket of shining fabric; the tapestries of life.

"I hope you will not take this as an impertinence, Lady Persephone, but I thought since I am recovered I might take over the role of guest relations. I have provided your companions with the tapestries you will be needing to perform your Judgements on the waiting souls. I thought perhaps they might enjoy seeing your work." Slightly astonished at their eager faces, I nod in approval. Evaristus snatches a dæmon passing in the halls, one I have yet to learn the name of, and instructs him to escort the nymphs to the Great Hall before he slides through the doors into my suite.

I do not protest as he rifles through my clothing while I retrieve the comb and finish freeing any lingering tangles. He whips me through preparations, styling my hair into elaborate coils adorned with a gold and emerald diadem before handing me an emerald green gown, the same deep color as my eyes. "A vision of Spring, my Lady," he pauses, suddenly uncomfortable. "I have not yet apologized to you, for my behavior endangering Lord Hades."

I pull him into a hug on impulse. "There is no need to apologize, Evaristus, you thought of our happiness and only wanted to correct the barriers between us all. I am proud to have someone as loving and loyal in my life as you are. Promise me you will not feel guilty. You're both healed now and there is nothing more my mother can ever do. No one will fall for her tricks again."

Evaristus gives me a wobbly smile before he manages to collect himself. He brushes at his eyes where thin lines of tears gather on his lashes and gingerly extracts himself from my embrace, standing tall once more.

I allow him to escort me to the Great Hall where the nymphs are milling about, their baskets stacked along one of the side tables. Evaristus gives a nod to the two dæmons at the doors and they disappear to collect the souls. He bows at the door with a smile. "Please summon me if you require anything."

With Evaristus gone, the nymphs crowd around me. "You look so happy, Lady Persephone," Charis grins at me, "there is so much love in your eyes. I confess it is not something I even believed the Olympians to be capable of."

Chloe gives her a light smack on the arm. "You insult our lady by insulting the Olympians."

Charis only laughs. "I have never considered her to be the same as them, our Lady is special."

"We have explored much of the realm with a dæmon escort," I catch Zoe's voice in the sea of nymphs, "they speak very fondly of you, my Lady."

"How do they keep from fighting?" Eumelia wanders over to toy with the tapestries. "There are thousands in the employ of Lord Hades and never have I seen such a number of immortals cooperate without any animosity. Usually you can feel the tension when so many gather."

I usher us all around the table to answer their questions while we wait for the souls to arrive. "Each dæmon works where they are best suited, in the place they most enjoy. In positions that are less desirable they are rotated accordingly so no one need work where they dislike for long. Hades also takes the time to speak to them. If there is ever an issue he receives their concerns and deals with it accordingly."

We're interrupted by the dæmons bringing in the first souls. I instruct the nymphs in the unrolling of the tapestry and together we read over the lives. I listen to their opinions and after I make my Judgement more dæmons arrive to escort the souls to their respective eternities. There are quite a lot of unborn children and very young babies admitted to Elysium and we carry as many of them in our arms as we are able.

As we breach the borders we find that the realm of paradise opens proudly, tendrils of mist and light reaching out to lift the babes from our arms. The nymphs stand transfixed and Chloe openly weeps at Elysium's reception of the children. The little souls float, bright as tiny stars, cradled in the arms of paradise.

The air ripples around us and erupts into sun-dappled forests decorated with bubbling streams and more flowers than I have ever seen. The souls gasp in pleasure and run into the forest, laughing as they roll through the blossoms and scamper between the saplings.

Elpis tugs on my arm, eyes shimmering. "My Lady, it's so beautiful. We were afraid of the old stories, but this is so much more than I could have ever imagined."

We stand huddled together amid the radiating joy as the souls begin their afterlife free of all pain and worry. Hades created this world, crafted Elysium so painstakingly that it responds to the smallest thought. He had come to a barren world, containing only the deepest part of Tartarus and the rivers that divided this world. In the Titanomache, the Great War between the Olympians and the Titans, those who had fought against my family were relegated to an eternal prison. Hades had begun his post as their guardian, aided by Kamp, and it was many millennia before the rest was built. He had been so alone and the Titans were rather poor company in their prison. None from Olympus saw any reason to alleviate him of his duty. It was only when humans were first created that he had begun to hope there could be more to his existence. When the first of them died, Thanatos carried the soul to Hades, searching for a place to let it live out its new life. The gradual increase of souls had brought out the dæmons who offered their service and when Hermes was born he became the Psychopomp. Hades, Thanatos and Hermes became the Lords of Death, the caretakers and guides of all the mortal souls for the rest of eternity.

Hades gave everything to this world. It is an affliction we both share, this desire to give all of ourselves to help others and it draws us deeply into a life of servitude. We look upon things and see ways to make it better, ways to bring kindness and fairness into a world so often bereft of both. I feel a tingle of energy at my feet, a gentle reminder of Great Mother Gaia. Perhaps she had been waiting just as much as Hades for the birth of humanity. They had crafted this magnificence together, an infinite realm to house the souls for eternity deep in Gaia's body.

"My Lady," I snap out of my wandering thoughts when I hear Zoe's voice, "should we get more tapestries?"

Eumelia props herself on the table and groans. "Does the work here never cease? When are we going to have fun?"

Tryphosa nods her head. "While I hesitate to agree with Eumelia, I do want to know if you plan to spend the whole of your eternity like this. You spent all your time in the mortal world working and then sleeping to recover and now you gave yourself but a few moments of celebration before falling into a new routine of work."

"I feel guilty," I say, the confession making me feel oddly light. "When I work I feel useful, like I am repairing the damage done."

Chloe rubs my arm softly. "My Lady, you have the rest of forever. You need to give yourself time to establish a method that works for you."

"It's the way it has been done here for millennia." I argue, but their faces are impassive.

"It's the way it has been done until you arrived," Elpis counters. "If Lord Hades wanted things to be as they always had then he would not have married you. We know the inhabitants of this world work hard, they are dedicated to their craft and we understand that. We are happy to assist you with your tasks, but you did not bring us here for that." I can only nod. "Let us help you bring more joy to the Underworld."

45

HADES

Persephone curls against me, tucked beneath the silks of my bed. We have retreated in the last moments before she has to leave. Any moment now Evaristus will knock on our door and inform us that the nymphs are ready and we must greet the dawn.

The knock comes and I move, oddly numb, towards the door. Evaristus hands me a bundle of gold fabric topped by a wreath of Asphodel blossoms. "The nymphs are ready, everyone is waiting to see Lady Persephone off."

I stare at my Queen for a few moments after accepting the fabric. Each breath feels like diamond shards are churning in my chest. She crawls out of bed and wraps me in her arms. "Do not look so sad or I will not be able to leave."

I suck in the lip that traitorously slipped into a pout. Half a year is a short time, but it feels substantially longer when one is waiting for every moment of it to pass. It is sobering to realize that this will be the rest of my forever. We will both be trapped in this endless cycle. I will always wait for her to return, celebrate the time we have together while at the same time dreading its end.

She kisses me quickly before changing into the gown Evaristus provided. The fabric shimmers like real gold in sunlight and her hair gleams as she combs it through before settling the wreath over her brow. She combs my own hair and fastens the brooches at my shoulders that keep my cloak in place. Both as ready as we are able to be, we clasp hands and move slowly through the halls to the courtyard where the nymphs and a surprising number of dæmons await us.

The nymphs did much better than I was expecting, integrating themselves into the realm by making sure that everyone was kept engaged. At first the dæmons were startled by the attention, but they adapted quickly and soon I could see them looking forward to speaking with the nymphs upon the occasions they encounter them.

I cast my hand up to the sky and a staircase falls, settling itself as the ceiling above us splits open. We walk up, hand in hand, the nymphs following us and a horde of dæmons following them. They are peculiarly silent. I kiss my wife just before we reach the surface, cursing her mother and my brother in the back of my mind.

I can feel Demeter before I see her. At first she ignores us, instead focusing her glare on the nymphs so that they instantly retreat behind her. She is resplendent in pale gold, crowned with ripe wheat stalks. Her eyes are diamond hard and all around her the meadow grass is shriveled and dead, flowers drooping sadly.

Persephone squeezes my hand and kisses my cheek before moving towards her mother. Demeter embraces her daughter with fervor, no doubt she believing I've kept her squirreled away in the bowels of Tartarus. The meadow bursts into life under Persephone's feet. The nymphs wave shyly to the dæmons, their hands retracting swiftly as Demeter turns her gaze upon them. Scarce moments pass before Persephone is whisked away, leaving us all behind.

Chloe maneuvers through the crowd to stand before me. "Do not worry for Lady Persephone. She has grown strong and will continue to become the Goddess she was meant to be. We will watch out for her as well. I would be pleased to pass any messages to her that you might have."

I stare at the nymph for a few moments, absorbing her petite form and overly large brown eyes that give her a distinctly child-like appearance. "I will not ask you to risk Demeter's wrath."

"You are not asking, my Lord, I am offering. Lady Persephone is not the only one who is changing."

"I appreciate your loyalty to Persephone, Chloe." She smiles at me and I leave the nymphs and dæmons to their own devices as I retreat back into my realm.

46

PERSEPHONE

I catch the barest glimpses of the abysmal conditions of the mortal world before my mother deposits me on Olympus. Laid out in the courtyard between our quarters she has a long table laden with fresh bread, ripe fruit, bowls of ambrosia and jugs of nectar. She snaps her fingers and one by one the nymphs appear, summoned like dogs.

My mother smiles cheerfully at them, but there is a tightness in her expression. She pushes us through this feast as though we are automatons, able to manufacture joy at a moment's notice. She enchants a harp and it plays while the nymphs dance at her urgings. They cast awkward glances at me. I settle next to my mother and stare at her until she acknowledges my gaze. "Mother, I know you're upset, but please know that I *am* happy. Everyone in the Underworld is very kind to me and the work is fulfilling."

She doesn't believe me, refuses to believe me, and soon tears are rolling down her cheeks. She is making an odd snuffling noise as she tries to control her imminent sobs. "You do not have to lie to me to make me feel better, Persephone. Whatever delusion they feed you, whatever words you feel you must say to hide your suffering, I do not want to hear them. I only want the truth so I may have some hope of intervening on your behalf."

She clutches at my hands suddenly, causing my goblet to clatter against the marble, its contents sloshing over the floor. The nymphs fall silent and still, acutely uncomfortable and unsure as to whether they should stay or go.

"Mother, please, it's the truth. You can ask the nymphs yourself. Nothing bad happened to any of us and they had a pleasant time. Why are you not capable of understanding this?" I struggle to keep my voice sympathetic, but this is all so completely ridiculous.

She flings herself away from me, the twirling motion turning her gown around her like a vortex. I can no longer tell if she is sorrowful or enraged. Her energy spikes and her hair whips around her. "Why couldn't you have just stayed on Olympus?" She shouts, lashing out power and words. "None of this would have happened if you had simply listened and stayed where I told you to."

I bristle and clutch my fingers together to control the urge to start tugging out my hair. Fighting directly is new ground for me, but I cannot cave. If I fall I fear I shall never regain my footing with her.

"Mother!" I don't scream the word, but I pour as much power into my voice as I can manage. She freezes for a moment, wide eyes staring at me as though I am a monster from the primordial depths and not her own daughter. "I am going to speak and you are going to listen. I swear on the River Styx that what I have told you is true. I swear on Styx that I truly love the Underworld and its inhabitants and I love Hades. He has never been anything but kind to me and if you would remove yourself from your prejudices for one moment you would have known that without the need for an oath."

Her anger disappears immediately and she begins to bawl, great sobs heaving her shoulders. She wails, clutching at her gown in an overt display of emotions usually reserved for funerals. "You are leaving me, you have let yourself run away to that horrible place and you have abandoned me here. Why do you hate me, Persephone?"

I struggle with my own reactions, the conflicting compulsion to soothe her and to lash out against her. I force myself to remain impassive, unwilling to placate her or scream or break down. Mothers have a curious power over their children. The babes they carried in their womb are ever connected to them. The bond that many mothers and children forge is a wonderful thing, but in others it becomes a tool of manipulation, guilt and control. In those corrupted bonds the child ceases to be a separate entity, instead becoming an extension of the mother. The child must bend to the mothers will as surely as her own body responds to her thoughts. My mother has lost sight of the loving connection that should be there and now, under the guise of loving protectiveness, seeks only to control.

"Mother, I love you. I have not abandoned you." I allow myself the luxury of a sigh. "Please take a moment and remember who you are. You are a Goddess and you have abandoned the mortals. Do you want them to abandon you and turn to me? You cannot keep this up or they will lose faith in you." I knew it had been fortuitous to warn the mortals last spring. Without my intervention the mortal world would again fall into famine and war. My mother has become a fair-weather Goddess, only helping the mortals so long as things are going her way. As soon as things become difficult she abandons her duties and leaves them to starve. She doesn't respond and I don't have the time to wait for her to figure out what she wants. "I need to begin the restoration."

I extract myself quickly and am gone before she ever answers. Free of Olympus I feel I can finally breathe. When I set foot on the first field and the first touch of green appears a shout is raised. "The Goddess has returned!" The mortals pour out of their homes, dressed hastily in colorful fabrics and they sing, throwing their hands into the air. They chant and sway to the music as people pick up instruments, their voices praising the Earth and Sun and my return with Spring.

The work is easier this time as the mortals prepared everything. Seeds sit ready in the fields, fruit trees have been pruned, gardens planted and livestock penned to allow the tender shoots to gain a foothold in the soil. Great Mother Gaia guides my hand delicately, pushing lightly only when I become distracted by everything around me. My thoughts become laden with prayers, whispers and shouts, vying for my attention. Every prayer directed to me enters my thoughts, a momentary intimate connection with the mortals who send them.

By the time I arrive at the temple that had been converted for my use there is a great bonfire blazing where the mortals are tossing in offerings. My initial group of three priestesses has swelled to a dozen and they lead the people in celebration, several of them dancing around the pomegranate tree I gifted them, which has already produced fruit.

A tall man with a crown of gold upon his brow speaks loudly to the people. Celeus is the king where my mother's cult at Eleusis began. He accepts a pomegranate handed to him by one of my priestesses and breaks apart the rough skin to bite into the ruby pockets. A trail of juice slides down his chin, but he's so engrossed in the fruit that he doesn't wipe it away. The pomegranates are cracked into small portions and passed around to all those present. They might only get a few seeds each, but the sweet tartness, after many months of preserved and dry food is a welcome treat.

As they eat, Celeus addresses them all once more. "Persephone, Goddess of Spring and Queen of the Underworld, we give thanks for this bounty. We give thanks for this show of your favor and offer up our gratitude to you."

"Hail to Spring and the warmth that She brings." The mortals chant when Celeus falls silent. "Hail to the Guardian of our Souls who feeds us in life and cares for us when life is within us no more."

My priestesses share a pomegranate between them, each tossing a single seed into the writhing flames. "Hail to our Lady, our patron Goddess, She who blesses our fields with life."

I watch the festivities, inhaling the sweet scent of their offerings. The exhaustion that overtook me at the first restoration is still there, but I am stronger than I was then. The smoke from the fire curls into the air, twisted by a gentle breeze. The air is warm, enlivened by Zephyrus, the God of the West Wind. He is the opposite of Boreas, banishing the cold northern winds with the warmth of the West.

I have never met the West Wind before nor seen him, but if I focus I can see transparent flashes on the breeze. Sparkling green eyes appear mere inches from my face and before I can cry out a hand materializes and clasps over my lips. A rainbow shimmer floats in the air before it forms a solid person. He has quite a winsome smile, set on a face of warm, dark gold skin and a breeze keeps his hair in constant motion, a perfect tousle of russet locks.

"Persephone, I am most pleased to meet you. The mortals have spoken of little else." He steps back and holds out his hand until I belatedly place mine into it. He bobs his head and places a quick kiss at my wrist. "I am Zephyrus of the West Wind, and you are fast becoming a legend. Tell me, how have you fared as the Bride of Hades? The things one hears on the wind are so often embellishments, and I have never taken the time to go and meet him for myself."

"I have fared very well. He is a fine husband and an exceptional ruler of his people. I am proud to be called his Queen." I am wary, not knowing this God, and not keen to reveal too much to him.

"Curious," Zephyrus whispers more to himself than to me, or at least I assume since he stops looking at me altogether and faces the sky, "The stories spin him into almost as much a monster as the creature that guards Tartarus. I should know by now not to believe such fantastical tales when reality is never so thrilling."

"Thrilling or not, he is not to be trifled with." I slip the barest edge of warning into my voice, making it quite clear I will tolerate no slights against my husband, however flippant they might be.

A quick flash in his eyes reveal that I startled him. "The insult was not one of intent. I am the wind and subject to the flowing whims of my power." He swirls in the air, caught in his own breeze. "The world needs a little more warming up, I must ensure your plants do not suffer any ill effects from the Boreal frosts." He looks at me contemplatively for a moment. "You are quite unlike your mother, Lady Persephone. At one time I aided her, but she has given Boreas free reign to run rampant and his power has gone unchecked. I do hope that you and I will be able to renew balance to the winds. Farewell, Goddess of Spring, I look forward to the world you will create."

47

PERSEPHONE

Time passes, cycles renew, life and death, winter and spring, turning the year over and over again. We all grow accustomed to the transitions, each easier than the last. My chambers are overflowing with reminders of the Underworld. Vases of Asphodel blossoms adorn each end of my bed and the evergreen I planted ages ago has grown tall enough to brush the ceiling. The wait to return is not so long, but these reminders help temper the loneliness.

With time my mother has given up on trying to make me say that I loathe the Underworld and all those therein. She now spends much of her time stubbornly ignoring my presence. Perhaps I only exist in her world when I am obedient and agreeable to her misguided opinions. After a few decades it all seems so normal, as though I have simply always lived this way, passing between one world and the other.

My skin prickles and I turn from my garden to see my father standing at my chamber doors. "My dear, how are you?"

Zeus has never shown any interest in me before and he has most certainly never taken the time to seek out my presence. He seems to be an absentee parent to majority of his children so I have never felt singled out by his lack of attention. In fact, his volatile energy frightens me and I have been rather grateful for the blind eye he turns to me. "I am well, Father, thank you. Might I be of assistance?"

The air crackles with energy. "You have never told me of your time in the Underworld. Is Hades a suitable husband for you?" The hair on the back of my neck stands on end and my fingers fly up to clutch the pomegranate pendant hanging between my breasts.

"He is most suitable, my Lord." I speak stiffly, trying to put some verbal distance between us. He makes me uneasy, but he is my father and king and I cannot offend him by leaving when he has sought me out for the first time since my birth. I force myself to remain still, though his gleaming eyes and crackling energy make my skin itch, goosebumps racing down my arms.

"I wanted to ask you about the famine," I tell him. "You stopped the rains from falling. Why? You could have lifted the famine without taking me away."

He shrugs. "You get so few opportunities to be viewed as a true hero in the eyes of the mortals. I was the one who rescued you from the Underworld, brought Spring to the world and became their savior for a new age. Besides, Hades is dull, I'm certain you would rather a little spark in your life." He steps closer and my muscles tense. He holds out his hand, beckoning me to take it. "Come here." His storm-gray eyes are dark as thunder clouds, roiling with the same level of intensity as he stares me down, almost willing me to disobey his order. I quell my discomfort and place my hand into his, reminding myself that he is the ultimate authority while I am on Olympus. Power shoots up my arm and I bite my lip to stifle the cry of pain as my arm goes numb. His hand closes like a vice around my wrist, trapping me in the manacles of his fingers. He tugs me forward so suddenly that I stumble and fall against his chest. His other hand reaches around and braces me about the waist. His lips fall against mine, but I turn away sharply. His lips continue downwards and he murmurs something, but panic blurs the words. "When I agreed to support your union I had not yet thought of the payment I desired. Now I think I might like to claim it."

"Let me go." I try to pry myself free, clawing at the hand that binds my wrist, but his power courses through him and he feels infinitely larger and stronger than me. I try to vanish, willing my form to lose substance and disappear to somewhere safe, but I only flicker in place. Terror strikes me deep, panic rising up and choking out all rational thought. Some part of my mind is whispering that I have to be calm to control my power, but that part is quickly drowned out, overwhelmed.

"Now, do not be coy, you share the bed of one brother, but not the others?" My blood turns to ice at his words. "That will never do. Perhaps I shall share you with Poseidon when I'm done with you." He grabs the pendant around my neck and yanks the chain so it snaps and cuts into my neck. He smashes it against the marble floor, the rubies scattering in flashes of red.

"Let me go!" Hysteria works its way in, turning my voice shrill and terrified. He twists me sharply and he brings his arm around to clamp a hand over my mouth. His eyes sharpen and I shriek into his flesh as lightning flares, shooting electric bolts of pure pain skittering over my skin. I tug ever more frantically, lost in the panic, but his grip does not yield.

"I am King here and you will obey." He jerks my arm so fiercely I almost feel my shoulder leave the socket. My knees fall hard to the marble floors and my eyes water from the impact. Tears roll over my cheeks, the fear making my heart gallop like a frantic stallion.

I try over and over to free myself, gathering power, surging it up, but I only flicker at best. The lightning strikes me again, a hideous sizzling sensation creeps over my skin. I have never had to defend myself before, I know nothing about combat. He slaps me hard across the face with enough force that I sprawl on the floor. My vision swims, the world swirling around me until I feel nauseated. Lightning flashes against me so many times that my eyes become unseeing and my limbs no longer respond. They feel so heavy, as though they are filled with hot lead. I try to curl into myself, but there is so much pain that I can only lay, whimpering.

A haze of shadow intermittently fills my vision. Tears flow like a river, scorching my cheeks, but I cannot staunch them. In a brief moment of coherency I realize that this must have been what my mother experienced, what she had wanted to protect me from, what my father had once done to her. Hades was never the risk, I have always been more in danger at home than anywhere else, but she never saw that. Two of her three brothers have done this to her. I cannot imagine what would possess anyone to put another being through this. I cannot imagine the depths of darkness in a soul that fills it so completely and spills out in this form of torture.

His touch is worse than the lightning, deliberately cruel and unyielding. I properly register very little, only that my nerves are on fire and each caress is like acid upon my flesh. It is the opposite of everything I have ever known. There is no love, no trust, no sharing of souls. There is not even an inkling of concern for my well-being. This is the plundering of a physical form, the utter destruction of peace and the blistering corruption of familial bonds.

The sensations fade so slowly that it takes me some time to realize that he is gone. Still unable to move or see, I lay there in agonizing darkness and wait for my immortality to begin healing my battered form. It feels as though a millennia passes before I can feel my fingertips again. I sit up slowly, moving gingerly as every movement nearly cripples me over again.

I bring my hands to my face, just in time to catch the cascade of sobs that crawl out from such a depth that my entire form shakes as violently as leaves in a storm. I cry for a long time, hoping the tears will pour out the memory of what just occurred. The lightning has scarred me badly, a fractal pattern of blistered red covers near every inch of me. I rub at the marks as though the action might erase his touch as well. A new wave of tears flood as his eyes come unbidden into my thoughts, storm-gray and full of hate. I nearly collapse anew under the rise of panic, but I turn my attention instead to gathering the shattered bits of pendant. The bits shimmer in my hands and I pray it is not a symbol of my relationship with Hades. Exhausted beyond all measure I sink into sleep. Perhaps when I wake I will find this has all been a dream.

48

PERSEPHONE

"My dear, you look a little worse for wear." I peel open my eyes, the movement far more difficult than it should have been. Someone I have never seen before stands over me. She glimmers, shifting through a thousand colors, her hair floating in a brilliant cloud around her.

"Who?" My voice croaks and I fall silent, closing my eyes against the light.

"Iris. My husband mentioned he spoke to you and I was overcome with curiosity and decided I must see you for myself." Vaguely I recall that Iris, Goddess of Rainbows and Messenger for Hera is married to Zephyrus. "Are you well? It has been months since the crops were restored, but none have seen you since. Have you been here asleep since then?"

I sit up slowly, taking stock of my body. My stomach roils as though I am being punched from within. My eyes fly open with panic as I realize there is a spark there, a touch of life causing the sensation and not just part of the healing process. I sit bolt upright, startling Iris before collapsing again from the pain. Desperate fear consumes me as I understand that there's a little God growing inside of me, the child of my father. Immortal gestation varies wildly depending on the nature of the deities involved. I could bear this child tomorrow or in a century.

I stare at Iris until she begins to look uncomfortable. My mind is whirring so fast I feel dizzy. Iris is in the employ of Hera and the Olympian Queen is a Goddess of Childbirth. She would know how I might be rid of this child. "Iris I need you to tell your mistress that I would like an invitation to the Hesperides." Hera's secret garden is the only place I can think of where my situation might not be overheard. Her eyebrow quirks upwards, but after a moment of hesitation she nods and vanishes on the breeze, returning after several agonizingly long moments bearing a gold coin. I snatch it out of her offering hands. One side has an apple impressed upon it and the other bears a side profile of the Olympian Queen. The coin pulses with energy, holding within it the path to the Hesperides.

Iris clasps my wrist gently and tugs at me to stand. I hold the coin tightly and allow Iris to pull me along through the æther on the path provided by the coin. We emerge into a lush oasis under a vibrantly blue sky and grass so fresh it springs beneath my feet. Iris leaves me there to await my Queen. Alone, my attention drifts to the massively tall tree that is growing hordes of golden apples. The tree had supposedly been a wedding gift from Gaia upon Hera's marriage to Zeus. A coiled dragon wraps around the base of the tree and a few feet away is a man that bears a hundred eyes over his skin. Hera emerges from behind the tree and speaks quickly to the man.

I run, forgetting all composure and the searing sting of the movements. I throw myself into her arms. She freezes awkwardly, but by this point I'm sobbing beyond control. The man clears his throat. "I will excuse myself, my Lady, please call upon me if you have any need."

"Thank you, Argus." She pats my back, but after a few moments becomes tired of my display and pries me out of the embrace. "Persephone, take a breath and calm yourself. What is the matter?" Her voice is level and cool, a calm and reassuring sound.

"Hera, I know you have no reason to love me because of how I was born, but I am in need of your help."

She nods slowly, the level of her tone never fluctuating. "I can hardly assist if you have not told me what the problem is."

I hold her forearms and take several deep breaths, grasping for words. "First, I must ask you to not reveal what I tell you to anyone, not even my mother. You must also agree to not tell anyone that we have met or spoken." She nods and my throat swells shut at the words and more tears warm my cheeks. "I am to have a child."

"There is nothing so terrible in that. Is your husband not pleased by the news?" She seems confused by my declaration and tears so I elaborate.

"I am sure that he would be very pleased, but for the fact that he is not the father."

Her eyes widen in shock. "Who is?" I burst into sobs again, unable to voice the name, but I see her expression turn dark and furious. I know that she knows now and she is angry.

"What can I do?" I bury my face in my hands, just trying to get control of myself.

She remains unnervingly silent and when I can bear it no longer she finally speaks. "Does he know? What about Hades?" I shake my head to answer both questions. "Do you plan on telling either?"

I swallow another sob and suck in as much air as my lungs will allow. "Only if I must."

"Did you consent?" Her eyes are sharp as obsidian glass, shoulders stiff as marble.

"Never!" My voice is tight and squeaky as I rein in the urge to cry again. "This child is not wanted. I love Hades, I don't want to hurt him with knowledge of its existence and how it came to be. I tried to stop it from happening, tried to get away, but I wasn't strong enough."

She gazes at the sky and heaves a great sigh, dragging her fingers through her hair. She cups my sodden cheeks and pulls me close so she can kiss my forehead. A wave of relief spreads through my being. "Do not worry, we will rid you of this child. We cannot erase what has happened to you, but we can at least remove the product of it." My shoulders sag and my knees give out as I slide to the ground. Relief, hot and potent, crashes over me. Hera's little dragon marches over and flicks his tongue at me. He bops my ankle with his head before deciding his mistress is much more interesting. He climbs up her body to settle across her shoulders like a shawl. "We must go quickly, every moment we wait is a moment we allow this God-child to grasp more firmly to life. Argus, take Ladon."

Her many-eyed guardian appears as though from the æther and collects the little dragon. It hisses in protest until Hera gives it a few strokes on its head. She kneels down and grasps my hand. Her magic pulls us both down into the Earth, down and down into Gaia's body, beyond where even the Underworld reaches. We emerge into a spacious cavern that is bisected by a flowing river. Glowing crystals light the interior and there are several women there who turn speculative eyes upon us.

"Daughter, granddaughter." A woman gowned in violet with ebony curls approaches us and hugs us each one after the other. I blink several times before grasping that the woman before me must be Rhea, mother of the Olympians. Rhea's sweet face twists into worry as Hera explains why we've come. Telling Hera has passed over the burden and all the stress of my situation begins to fade, vacating my mind and body to be replaced by a delightful numbness. In my daze it takes several moments to identify the gentle energy that floats off another woman whose quiet presence envelops me. She is translucent with swelling breasts and hips, dark hair that falls to her feet and green eyes that glow in the dim light.

"Gaia," I whisper, transfixed by her. Her spirit comes forward and presses a hand upon each of my shoulders as she forces me to lay back in the soft dirt. A flick of her finger diverts the river to flow around me with a barely discernible current. Tendrils of power coil around me in the liquid warmth so I fall into a dazed sleep. They circle around me, the hands of a dozen women pouring power into me. At first the tendrils are gentle, but they grow more forceful, insistent and invasive. I bite my lip to keep from crying out. The Great Mother's energy plunges into my womb and with a frighteningly intense tearing she removes the child that had burrowed into my flesh. I shriek, unable to contain the sound. All around me there is a flood of chaos and movement, voices shouting and people rushing about.

Nudging me out of the chaos is Rhea, pulling me out of the water. "Go home now and rest, do not speak of this to anyone. Do you understand?" I nod dumbly and move on wobbly legs. It's only an extra push of energy from her that gives me the strength to leave. Pressed into the æther I deliberately avoid my home on Olympus and tumble into existence in my meadow. I stumble through the grass, following the sound of water, seeking out that reassuring warmth of Great Mother Gaia's embrace. I fall headlong into the stream and lay there trying to focus my thoughts. I reach out for Gaia with a desperation until I feel her energy cocoon me. I let myself drift into sleep, letting my battered body rest before I have to return to the world and pretend everything is fine.

49

HADES

The Moiræ find me on my rounds in the realm of Asphodel. They seem peculiarly nervous, a most unusual state for them to be in. Atropos wrings her hands and her sisters look frantically between themselves. They hiss at each other so quickly I cannot catch the words. They cast a final, almost terrified glance at me before disappearing as quickly as they had come.

I stare blankly after them. My curiosity is piqued, but unease quickly overrides it. The Fates rarely leave their alcove where they weave the tapestries and for them to come to me without known cause usually means they have something rather life-altering to report. It's possible they miscalculated their timing, coming to me before I'm supposed to know the details, but now I crave the knowledge.

I let it slide for a few days, but when they approach me and disappear twice more my patience reaches its limit. Before they can retreat again I slam my foot into the ground and spires of gold erupt, trapping them in a gilded cage.

"Tell me what you've come to say, Moiræ." The dark sisters stare at me, liquid black eyes deep as the sea daring me to challenge them.

Lachesis demands I swear on Styx that I will harm none of them for the news they bear. Dread fills me at these words, but I do as they ask. They sag with relief.

"Very well," Atropos chews her lip, selectively choosing her words. "Lord Zeus has taken Lady Persephone."

Without blinking I find myself against the gold bars, fury welling in my throat. They all leap away despite my oath. "What?!" The word echoes and I struggle to breathe through the vitriol that is quickly overtaking my every thought.

"Lady Persephone loves you, my Lord. We never thought he was capable of this. His crimes are well known, but he believes her to be his daughter and he has never before forced himself upon his own child."

I cannot speak. A black fury swells inside my body and clouds out my vision. The spires shatter and the Moiræ shout in alarm. The power of the oath keeps me from reaching out to strangle them for not having told me sooner, or warning me before such an atrocity was able to happen. They could have at least given me the chance to save her.

The sound that escapes me is barely human and shakes the walls. It sends my power rippling through the realm, the souls screaming in response. I fight to breathe, to control myself so I can spare them from absorbing my anger, but my chest heaves and shakes with the effort. I sink to the ground and drive my fingers into the Earth, through the stone, just to feel as though I have some sort of anchor in the chaos.

Thanatos appears instantly and he reaches out to me. His power calms me, the potent mix of death and sleep that settles me enough to begin to think once more. I am sick and furious, outraged at Zeus and desperate to see Persephone. "I will care for the realm, do what you must and return to us safely."

I vanish into the æther, locking onto my brother's location. He's at the city of Olympia when I appear, watching some ritual sacrifices to himself and admiring the massive gold statue the mortals had built for him. It's a perfect likeness seeing as he filled the minds of its creators with images of himself.

The air shivers around me as I adopt a semi-corporeal form. It catches his attention and he turns to look at me. "Hades? What brings you to my temp-" I drive my fist into his face before he can finish his question. The feeling is magnificent, propelling me to strike again and again before he can recover enough to defend.

The temple shakes violently and the mortals below us look around in terror. They hesitantly continue the ritual, trying to appease the Thunderer. When my brother is able he gathers handfuls of lightning and hurls them at me. The impact sends me crashing into a pillar that immediately collapses. The mortals scream and scramble out of the temple to safety. They cannot see us, but the results of our interaction mimics the violent upheaval of an earthquake.

We grapple, shoving power at one another, the waves of energy making the columns shudder and crumble around us. Lightning flares and I throw chunks of broken columns at him. Explosions fill the air, dust and rubble raining over everything. Every issue I have ever had with Zeus comes pouring out, riding on the wave of rage that swells out of control when I think of what he has done to Persephone.

"What is the matter with you?" Zeus demands, striking my cheek with lightning. The skin crackles, but I press onwards.

"You took my wife!" The dust is so thick I can barely see him. Only the flaring lightning around him serves as a beacon for his presence.

"I had to, Demeter was letting the mortals die, you know that." He claws at me, electrified fingers digging deep into my flesh. The scent and sensation brings to mind the Titanomache, but this time there is fury driving me and not fear.

"She is your daughter, how could you be such a monster?" I bellow at him, the roof of the temple collapsing around us. The gold statue is bashed to pieces by the falling rock. If only he were so easy to tear apart.

Finally understanding what I am angry about, he shoves himself away and smirks at me. "So you found out? I am honestly surprised the little bitch had the gall to tell you about it." He shrugs. "She is beautiful and she was yours. How could I be expected to resist?"

His words are a poison that curdles my blood. I grab him by the shoulders and fling him over and down into the Earth. The stone in the earth burrows him into a tomb, leaving only his eyes visible. "Hear me now, Zeus of Olympus. I swear on the River Styx that if you ever touch her again I will tear down Olympus with every ounce of power in my body. I will not rest until you have paid for what you have done."

50

PERSEPHONE

Storm clouds gather around me, so thick there might be nothing in the world beyond them. Thunder claps reverberate so loudly my bones rattle. The clouds creep closer and swallow my limbs inch by inch until I have lost myself in the storm. A scratching on my arm starts small, but becomes increasingly more desperate despite my attempts to swat away the invisible annoyance. A bird call echoes through the clouds, muffled and distant.

A frantic flapping and cawing in front of my face snaps my eyes open. The storm clouds are gone and I am in my meadow, half in the stream and chilled to the bone. A black bird hops around me, cawing and tugging at my gown. It keeps up this behavior no matter how many times I swat it away. It just keeps cawing at me and dancing around as though it weighs nothing.

"Leave me alone," I hiss at it. It hisses right back and I'm caught so off guard that I laugh. It hops over and shoves itself under my hand, self-petting its glossy feathers. It hops out of reach when I try to pet it myself, so I heave a sigh and get up to follow the insistent creature. It hops along, flying every so often before dropping back to the ground. I follow it until the forest begins to change, spindly pine trees blending in with the chestnut, apple and almond trees. The stifling heat brings out the sap from the pine trees, turning the air rich and sweet.

It stops under a towering pine and settles itself, looking like a puffy ball of black rather than the sleek bird that it is. I sit next to it before sprawling back on the bed of dry needles. They prickle my skin and stick to my hair and gown, but the scent is comforting. I dig my fingers into the dirt, the sting of the needles on my hands is a welcome anchor to keep my thoughts from flying too wildly. A sense of fragility overwhelms me. I feel like even the lightest breeze might shatter me if I let my thoughts fall too often on what I dare not think about.

The little bird hops up again and scratches at the ground, digging with feet and beak until it lets out a delighted squawk and pulls up a chunk of silver from the dirt. It walks over awkwardly and proudly deposits it in my lap. A good scrub from the fabric of my gown reveals the silver setting holds a thousand minuscule diamonds forming the shape of the Asphodel blossom. It squawks at me and hops onto my knees to rub the top of his head against the underside of my chin. It gives an undignified protest when I scoop it into my arms and rub my cheek on the silken plumage. The small comfort triggers a fresh rush of tears. It wriggles free as my tears soak into its feathers. It meticulously plucks pine needles from my hair as I clutch the pendant, wishing with a fierce desperation that the earth would open up and reveal my husband.

I rest my forehead against the cool silver. "Please, please come to me, I need you."

The bird ruffles, fluffing up into a perturbed ball. It quivers and energy erupts as the little black bird slowly morphs into a human form. I recognize him immediately and before he solidifies I'm in his arms. He crushes me to him so tightly I fear I might burst. Coaxing tendrils of his soul reach for mine, the light and peace tugging at the knots of pain and sadness in my belly, struggling to unravel them.

I cling to him, my anchor as the dam of emotions collapses and sobs wrack my body. Tears pour out over my cheeks, a manifestation of my trauma. His hands smooth over my hair and cheeks, brushing away my tears before his lips brush against mine. Light pulsates between us and I reach towards it. I need that light, the blinding power that courses through me, burning away Zeus' touch and the memory of his stormy eyes.

The radiance bursts as our souls frantically tether each tendril in rapid succession. It grates against me, but instead of being irritating it is as though it relieves a deep itch, scouring me gloriously clean.

His memories slip through mine, visions of his brawl and the destruction of the Temple of Zeus at Olympia. A bitter part of me is blissfully pleased to see Hades pummel my father. It's suddenly a sobering thought as I realize that he is being fed my own memories too.

His lower lashes are lined with tears. "What became of the child? It is not so easy to kill a God."

"My memories are yours, I don't know what occurred after I left." He gathers me close and just holds me for a few moments. He's tense and I know he is dwelling on the memories I unwittingly shared with him. "Please, don't think on it, I just want it to go away. I want to come home."

"Soon, only a few days remain," he sighs. "When we're together the time seems to pass in moments, but when you are gone it seems as though it drags into eternity." He bends his head down and kisses me softly. He is my home and soon I will be back with him.

A cold wind lashes us, the harsh touch of Boreas clawing at our skin. "You know the rules." My whole body tenses as my mother's voice fills my ears. We part reluctantly and turn to look at her. Boreas must have alerted her that Hades was here. I fear I shall never be free if she has the very air itself keeping watch over me. "You stay in your Underworld when she is with me. Begone."

Hades nods stiffly and gives my hand a squeeze. He does not address my mother, only looks longingly at me as the earth opens up for him to make the journey down to his realm. I feel the light leave with him and I fortify myself against the ache in my chest with energy borrowed from Gaia. The Earth Mother is a stabilizing force that I desperately require.

51

HADES

"I fail to see how being angry now will resolve anything." Thanatos watches me pace back and forth in Erebus, his features placid. Seeing Persephone's memories made me want to maul Zeus all over again and feed the remaining bits to Kamp. I fume, letting my emotions run wild despite the effect on the souls. It's too potent to contain so Thanatos floats over, his gossamer wings twitching with vague annoyance. He clasps my arm, forcing me to pause my tirade, and pours an overwhelming amount of power into me. The effect is immediate, like water being thrown in my face. It leaves me chilled, but calm as I sink to my knees. "You have taken your retribution and have comforted Persephone."

The rage is still there, but is now weighed down by an ocean of Thanatos' power. "If you saw it you would not believe my retribution was near enough."

He crosses his arms and eyes me speculatively. "I agree with you that I would not, but the fact remains that you have already taken action for the crimes committed. Your anger serves no further purpose. All you are doing is hurting yourself and frightening the souls." Damn his cool logic to Tartarus. "You have carried the punishment as far as you are able to at this time. If you continue to pursue it you will bring all of Olympus into this matter."

"Perhaps they should be brought into it." I snap, but I allow myself to give in to his potent mix of death and sleep, letting it drown out my anger.

"This is likely the first time in his entire existence that Zeus has been punished for anything. I know it is not enough, but it is more than any have been able to do before. Persephone had you to fight for her, but all the others Zeus harmed were swept under the proverbial carpet. He may yet be judged," Thanatos whispers, "even an immortal could one day face me."

"Special delivery!" Hermes shatters the mood, zipping past us with a soul bound and dangling from a gold chain. He always did have all the tact of a rampaging bull. "I have one fresh from Olympus and bound for Tartarus."

I suppress a sigh. "What now?"

"This is Ixion." He drops the soul at my feet. "Poor bastard was fried to a crisp after Zeus invited him to dinner and he developed some inappropriate intentions towards Hera. Not entirely his fault, mostly stupidity, Zeus orchestrated the whole thing for fun. He got the bright idea to force Nephele, that cloud nymph he had a fling with, to take the guise of Hera and behave as though she was in favor of a sexual encounter. He knew all along that Ixion was interested in Hera, but rather than stopping him at the beginning he thought it better to catch him in the act. Now Ixion will burn for eternity for sleeping with the wrong woman."

"No, I will review his tapestry and get to the bottom of this." Hermes sighs at my response, but hauls Ixion into the inner recesses of the realm. Normally the cases for Tartarus are clear cut with obvious crimes, but in this case I do not feel that Ixion warrants eternal punishment.

His tapestry unfurls and while my Judges explore his earlier life I move straight to his last moments. Had Ixion actually copulated with Hera he would have been violating the laws of guest-host relations, but since Zeus replaced her with Nephele there is no crime under that law. Nephele is effectively a neighbor and there is no law against pursuit of the neighbor of the host. Nephele did sleep with him under coercion, but Ixion was not the one coercing, nor was he aware of it. Ixion's only crime seems to be stupidity and desiring the most unreachable female in existence. Zeus' actions negate the existence of any legitimate crime. I counsel briefly with my Judges and we agree quickly. "Ixion, you are for Asphodel. We have studied your life and deem you to be innocent of the crimes of which you are accused." Incorporeal tears blossom from his eyes. He is still bound by the gold chains or he would have openly wept. "Kamp, free him from his bonds, but leave him be."

The smoke tendrils slither through the fires of Phlegethon and tear apart the Olympian chains. They are powerful enough to contain a soul and designed to only be removed when they are siphoned into Tartarus. A shiver passes through me as a sudden realization forms. This is the first time I have overturned an Olympian sentence. The first time I have achieved dominance in my realm when Olympus is bearing down upon me. It doesn't matter that Zeus will likely never find out where Ixion truly ended up. A quiet sense of satisfaction settles into my blood.

Hermes plunks himself down on the table the moment my Judges have rolled up the tapestry. "Now that the unpleasantness has been dealt with, I have some good news to bear. The mortals have started a little cult to you, your bride and her mother."

"What? Why?" I ask and Hermes shrugs in his usual, non-committal way.

"They fear the annual famine. They know Persephone will return, but Demeter still destroys their crops when she's gone. The mortals have been trying to cultivate Demeter's good will so she might spare them and they build shrines to you to honor your guardianship of Persephone. They have even begun calling our Queen the Mistress of Life and Death."

A grin creeps over my features, pride swelling brightly in my chest. "She has done so well, I'm pleased the mortals love her."

Hermes nods his head in silence, staring at me oddly. "I heard you destroyed Zeus' temple at Olympia." My mood instantly plunges. "I should have looked out for her more carefully, I never thought she was at risk."

"The fault lies with no one but Zeus, do *not* take any guilt upon yourself." I stamp down on the simmering fury that swirls in my belly. An idle thought flits into my head. "Did you know if he were a mortal he would have earned Tartarus multiple times?"

"I have no doubt of that." Hermes looks somber and out of character. "There are men far kinder than he suffering for eternity on his whims."

"His actions are inexcusable and were it up to me he would be condemned. I would lock him even deeper in Tartarus than the Titans who tried to slaughter us." A new, forbidden thought springs up. "One would think he would tread more carefully with me given that I am the Guardian of the Titans. It would be an easy matter for me to free them. A simple oath bound by Styx could direct their fury to him."

"War in the heavens is a very serious matter, Hades." Hermes admonishes, but there is a tremble of fear in his voice, a spark of terror in his eyes. Freeing the Titans would bring about another Titanomache and the memories of the first are more than enough to stay my hand.

"I know, but sometimes he tempts me." Hermes puffs out a breath, shoulders relaxing. "That is only an action I would take if Zeus repeated his most grievous offense. I swear if he touches her again I will see Olympus destroyed. It is a fact and a threat. I am no longer content to sit by quietly and watch his path of destruction when it has led to my own door." It would be the end of me as well as I swore on Styx long ago to accept Zeus as my King. Following through on such threats would eliminate me from existence. An oath sworn on Styx binds into the soul and breaking it consequently causes the soul to be destroyed.

"That's fair," Hermes nods, but there is still an edge in his eyes. "I suppose if any were to oppose him you would be the most likely to succeed in such a venture. I hope it does not come to such a confrontation, but if it does, I will support you."

The Messenger God could not have surprised me more than with those words. "You would pledge your allegiance to me?"

He gives a non-committal shrug. "Why not? You have treated me with more kindness than my father ever has. I believe that you respect me and I consider you to be a very good friend. If Olympus were to get a new King you would be a very capable candidate."

I embrace Hermes forcefully and for a moment he squeezes his eyes shut and clutches me just as desperately. "Thank you. I will never rule Olympus though, I would leave Hera as Queen."

"You are a most unusual God, Hades." Hermes cocks his head to the side and smiles at me.

52

PERSEPHONE

"You will take two more nymphs with you. Minthe and Leuce will be a good influence on your horde." Mother combs my hair forcefully, snaring through tangles with vigor. I wince, though she cannot see me, when she yanks on my scalp. "Wear the violet, it is a Queen's color. You might be Queen of Hell, but you are still a Queen." She turns sharply from me, the ivory comb clattering to the floor. She snatches a pile of deep violet fabric and tosses it to me. The linen is finely woven, soft to the touch and a brilliant color. "I spun it myself."

The gesture surprises me. Her behavior has been alternatively smothering and distant, but there is a hesitant sweetness in the fact that she made this dress for me to wear. When I'm dressed I am carried off to the meadow for the exchange. Gentle hands embrace me and crown my brow with irises and myrtle blossoms. The nymphs are gowned similarly in lavender, a matching entourage with white blossoms tucked into their hair. The two new nymphs stand towards the edge of the group, segregated, but I cannot tell whether it is by choice or not.

Moments later the earth trembles and Hades emerges riding Archihippos. Xanthippe erupts after him and trots immediately to me and nuzzles my face. She lips my hair and dances in place. My mother appears at my side and slaps Xanthippe's nose. "Back, beast."

Xanthippe snorts and turns flaring eyes upon her. Mother moves to hit her again, but my hand shoots out and snatches her wrist before she makes contact. "Leave her be, she is no harm."

"Filthy creature," Mother spits on the ground before my beautiful horse. "Spawn of hellfire."

"Goodbye, Mother. I will see you in the autumn." I stroke Xanthippe's smooth flank and she lifts one foot for me to use as a step to swing onto her back. I do not look at my mother when I speak the words and there is no kindness in the tone. Xanthippe is a sweet creature and does not deserve to be spoken to in such a manner. She tosses her head and charges towards the chasm. Quick as the wind she carries me down. I can hear Hades and Archihippos following us in a storm of thunderous hoof beats.

Xanthippe slows to a stop at the stables, but Archihippos roars past us. My equine beauty snorts and charges after them. I clutch her mane in a panic as I nearly fly backwards over her rump. As we breach the borders of the Isles of the Blessed an emerald grass sea forms into being, dotted sporadically with trees so laden with blossoms you cannot even see the branches. There is nothing around us for miles but rolling hills of green. Archihippos trots contentedly ahead of us, snatching up mouthfuls of fragrant grass. Xanthippe tailors her gait until we are finally riding abreast.

"I wanted a few moments with you before our duties descend," Hades says with a smile. He flicks his wrist and the valley before us fills with water. I leap off Xanthippe and run towards the water, tearing off my gown right before I plunge into it. It's warm as a bath. Steam rises up in pale, snaking tendrils and my hair floats in a spiral around me. A cool wind ghosts over me, dispelling the soothing warmth for the barest of moments. Hades descends off Archihippos with a little more grace than I managed and he joins me in the water, shedding his shoes and clothing on the shore.

We touch, first lips, then hands, then souls reaching as we pour into one another. Our memories blur together until they swirl in one pool of thought. In the water we ride a wave of ice and fire, searing bliss and heart-rending peace. The water helps to wash away the memories of the burden we now share, pouring it out as our souls fill one another. It's exquisite, the complete shattering as our souls join together and rebuild as one entity.

The horses neigh and paw at the shore, drawing our attention away from one another. Hades sighs and presses his forehead to mine. "I love you more than my own existence and it burns me deeply knowing what you have suffered."

I pull his mouth to mine and spend a moment just memorizing the sensation of our lips touching. "You are my heart and my home. I would dearly love to tell you that all is well, and someday it may no longer haunt me, but that day is not yet here."

The desire to hide here, deep within the Isles of the Blessed, is overwhelming. The foreseeable future would be nothing but paradise. Still, is paradise devoid of purpose truly paradise? Reality and duty hold me too strongly to give hiding in Elysium true credence, but it is a fantasy that I cultivate far more often than I should.

The horses lose patience with us and march into the water. Hades lifts me onto Xanthippe and pulls himself onto Archihippos when he reaches the shore so he can collect our clothes and shoes. They take a slow walk back and we talk to pass the time. We pull on our wet clothes, but I tuck my shoes into my sash. "My mother's cult at Eleusis now includes us both. You can be sure that she loves sharing her worshippers with us."

Hades laughs, but then his face sobers. "I worry you are taking on too much. There are souls waiting for you here and you overtax yourself with the restoration."

"I must respect the decision of each soul that waits for me." There's not really a way around either duty, that I can see at least.

He reaches out and squeezes my hand lightly, a nervous energy sparking off him. "If we had a daughter she could be your partner, take on some of the responsibility. She would be free to move between Olympus and the Underworld as she pleased and the souls would love her as they love you."

I suck in my breath and feel my heart thrum in my chest. I have honestly given children very little thought. All notions of motherhood had been stamped down when the unwanted child my father begat upon me was torn out of my body. I can only begin to wonder what it might be like to allow my body to harbor a child I actually desire.

Hades fumbles and mutters about withdrawing his comment. "I should not have spoken."

"We are married," I remind him, "you have the right to desire children. Perhaps it is poor timing to voice those desires right now, but I will not fault you for them." I squeeze his hand in return and smile. "One day you will be a father."

53

HADES

I brood much of the remaining ride. It was thoughtless of me to speak of a child between us when she has only recently purged one from her being. Persephone has already given me the gift of her love and company, and it is more than I could have ever dared hope to have, but I cannot help but want more. The thought of a walking, talking physical representation of our love fills my thoughts. I will put aside that desire for her sake. She is not ready to be a mother and I can respect that. We have the whole of forever laid out before us and there is no need to rush anything.

By the time we return to the Palace the welcome feast is in full swing. The dæmons and majority of the nymphs know the standard practice by now and have already filled the Great Hall with music and laughter. An overly excited Evaristus greets us at the stables and ushers Persephone off to her room to freshen up.

When she joins us in the Great Hall she is drawn into the fray immediately, plucked from my arms by exuberant nymphs. Most of my employ is dancing, arms flung in the air and swaying to the fanciful tune. I should be pleased. I am pleased. Persephone is so happy with them, the nymphs shuffle her into the heart of the revelry and they all laugh excitably. I should not be jealous of them or her ease in integrating with them, but I still wish I were so comfortable with them or that I could keep her to myself instead of sharing her with everyone else. One of the new nymphs approaches me. She hooks her arm through mine and pulls me forward. It's typical nymph behavior, but her usual group is reasonably well mannered and not a single one has ever touched me. I don't enjoy strangers touching me and this type of emboldened action is why I have avoided nymphs for centuries.

"You must dance with us, my Lord." She coos and slides a hand up my arm.

I stare at her, agog, for a moment. She is lovely, with milky skin, golden brown hair and pale green eyes with a crown of leaves twined across her brow. I am fully on board with the dæmons letting off steam and engaging in social activities, but I have my limits. I slip my arm from her grasp. "Your name?"

"Minthe, my Lord." She wraps herself around me and pulls me into the steps of the dance. I repeatedly extract myself from her grasp and push her away to create space between us. She simply pushes harder, pressing against my will. She leans herself against me again and I feel her lips against my ear. "You must dance with me, my Lord. I can promise you I am a better lover than your Lady."

Her words catch me even more off guard than her actions. I shove her away so forcefully that she stumbles. She catches herself quickly, before anyone else notices her display. She turns smoldering eyes on me, burning her pale eyes into sharp emeralds. I stand ready to defend, but she slips away and draws one of the dæmons into the dance.

"Come, my Love, dance with us," Persephone grins and tugs at me. The steps are easy, a simple repeating pattern that lets me lose my worries in the monotony of movement. Step, step, back, down, step, we move in a rotating circle and circumnavigate the Great Hall multiple times. The nymphs add in additional flourishes and turns, so quick they flow in and out of the line without interrupting anyone else.

Minthe doesn't approach me again, a fact for which I am grateful. Persephone and I take our leave as the party dwindles. Several of the nymphs slip out with dæmons in tow. They are happy and Persephone's return is cause for celebration so I will look the other way in the face of this dereliction of duty. Minthe's words and behavior replay themselves in my mind as we walk back to our quarters. I wonder if I should mention it to Persephone, but she kisses me, pulling me through the doors and I opt to let the matter rest for now. If Minthe pursues her behaviors I'll ask for her to refrain from joining Persephone's party, but only if it persists past tonight. It's beyond rude for her to attempt an intrigue with the husband of her mistress and I won't have her disrespecting Persephone.

My bride pours us each a cup of nectar before slipping into her baths. I sit on the edge and sip at my drink while she floats on her back. "One day," she smiles back at me, her hair swirling around her, "I will break free from this contract. One day I will go where I please whenever I please."

I swirl the contents of my cup and drain it before joining her in the water. "You have handled the restrictions remarkably well so far, though I must agree that I prefer you in freedom."

She laughs. "I have never been completely free before. For all you know I am an entirely different person in such circumstances and you may not even like me."

She is a spectacular sight with skin glowing pink from the heat of the bath and the rose quartz crystals that light this part of the chambers. "I doubt there is any incarnation you might become that I would not like." I slip into the water, the rush of liquid warmth enveloping me up to my chin. She moves through the water with the ease of a seal and swirls around me before moving to snuggle into my arms. "We must find a way to free up more of your time. It has been decades and the process has not improved."

"What am I to do?" She asks.

"Perhaps we could gather you some assistance."

She is suddenly giddy, a blissfully excited grin lighting up her features. "Judges!" She exclaims. "I could have my own council of Judges, just like yours."

"The souls want you, if they wanted Judges they would just be served by mine."

She shakes her head. "Your Judges are male. Perhaps it is not me specifically they want, but a female touch. They want someone who will listen and connect and hear out their side of things as the tapestry is studied. They want more than a simple Judgement."

I should feel offended by this, that the souls do not believe my own Judges or myself do an adequate job, but she may be right. The slip in quality has been slow, so minimal over time that perhaps it had crossed a barrier and I had not been aware of it. If a fresh set of Judges is what Persephone and the souls need to increase the quality of their experience then that is what I am willing to provide.

54

PERSEPHONE

I wake still in the water, wrapped as cozily in the steaming water as I am in the arms of my love. A day where I do not have to move from this position until I desire to seems too distant to visualize. Before long it might become a reality. I mull over the concept of my own Judges, excited, but a touch lost as to how I might proceed with selecting appropriate souls. I push aside the guilt that picks at me for not delving straight into my work and those waiting for me. I owe myself to the souls, to the mortals, but I also owe myself to Hades and to myself. I cannot sacrifice the relationship we have cultivated together. The realm will be at peace if its rulers are at peace.

I know when I leave this bath and throw myself into my work that I will blink and my time here will have elapsed. I feel as though I only get started and suddenly I am forced to stop and move onto a new task. I don't feel as though I have the time to accomplish anything meaningful. I have seen a similar occurrence with mortals. When they begin a task about which they are passionate they fall into a trance-like state and when they emerge a great deal of time has passed unnoticed. I am not so different than they, the only difference is that my impassioned task is never ending. Half a year passes so quickly, even now.

My shifting wakes Hades and he smiles at me with sleepy eyes and reaches out to stroke my cheek. An idea dawns on me. "I thought of a way that could give the souls of unjust heroes in Elysium a proper afterlife." He nods for me to continue. "They were often cruel in life, abusive and condescending, some even brutal killers. What if there was a way for them to experience their lives from an alternative perspective?"

"How so?" He quirks his head in question and crawls out of the baths to wrap himself in black silk.

"I don't even know if it is possible, but I thought since Cocytus collects the memories of the souls, perhaps there is a way they could be transferred to those who are unworthy of Elysium. The victims, of the heroes, I mean, their memories would show them the wrongs they committed in life."

Hades' eyes flare briefly, excitement flooding his face. "You want their own actions to create an internal Tartarus for them? If we could do it, there would never be any issue from Olympus ever again, they would never find out anything was amiss with their favorites." He sweeps me out of the bath. Water soaks his robe and covers the floors, rolling down my body in rivulets. "My brilliant Queen, I cannot believe I never thought of such a thing."

Though I'm anxious to get started, my desires of hastily dressing and running to test out the idea are thwarted when Evaristus announces himself with a knock on the door. He shuffles in quickly and shoves a sunrise pink gown over my head. While I dry the unruly and sodden locks he makes quick work of Hades. He zips about like a fruit fly, so nimble and seemingly directionless that you cannot tell where he might land, but he always gets exactly where he intends to go. Within moments my husband is adorned in fresh silks and soft lambskin sandals and I have my hair coiffed and pinned with slivers of gold.

"Your nymphs await you in the Great Hall, my Lady."

I look at Hades expectantly, but he nods to the dæmon. "Go for now, I will experiment with drawing the memories from Cocytus and when I have done that we will see what we can do with the heroes."

Slightly disappointed, I follow Evaristus to the Great Hall. My nymphs are gathered around the long table, chattering away in between bites of fruit they pluck from the silver platters between them all. I have many souls to work through, but I also want to find my Judges. "Evaristus, please instruct whoever controls the archives to bring me the tapestries of all the women of influence who have earned Elysium. I need women accustomed to authority, ones who have experience with power and justice. Tell them to look for any that fit that criteria." He bows and scampers off to complete the task.

They bring tapestries as they find them, brilliant works of art trimmed in gold. Ultimately they bring us very few. There are a decent number of women in Elysium, but few queens or other leaders among them. We unfurl them, their shimmering length drawing my eye to key events. We sort through them all, compassionate and vibrant queens, wise and fierce princesses and founders of great cities. In the end I am left with fifteen potentials. Some are new to Elysium, while others have rested there thousands of years.

They are remarkable women in unusual situations with the men in their lives fully supporting their abilities and dreams for improving the world. Many of the princesses served their fathers wisely, with some taking to battle to defend their homes. The queens' rule in the stead of their kings when needed and otherwise devoted themselves to creating social institutions that served the needs of the people.

"How am I to choose between so many capable candidates?" I slam my cup down on the table. "I am spoiled for choice."

Leuce, one of my mother's latest additions, raises a hand to catch my attention. "Must you choose, my Lady? What about a rotating panel of Judges?"

"That's true," Chloe agrees. "You are asking these women to remove themselves from Elysium to serve you. Some may not agree to the terms of service, but those that do, if there are still many, could be rotated so they may still enjoy paradise when they are not needed."

The two are seated next to one another and I hug them both fiercely. "You are both brilliant. I hadn't considered that they might refuse. We may as well ask them all."

My flock of nymphs follows me into Elysium and I call each potential by name. They assemble slowly, moving like mist. Some retain only vague resemblance to the person they once were, their memories long separated from their souls. They bob slow bows and stand silent waiting for me to speak.

I explain carefully; the need for them, their absolute ability to refuse with no repercussions and what their accepted duties would entail. Ultimately only three refuse and retreat back into the Elysian light. I end the day with twelve women agreeable to the terms laid down. I will keep them in Elysium for the time being and present them to Hades when we are next in the realm of paradise. Equality is coming to the Underworld and my freedom is coming with it.

55

HADES

Thanatos appears on the Towers while I'm engaged in Judgement. His wings flutter gently, a silken aura around his body. "Forgive the intrusion, but there is a mortal at the edge of Styx requesting entrance."

The only mortals who ever want to enter my realm are demigods. I hate demigods. As a general rule they are the most arrogant, cruel and obnoxious of all mortals. The sons of Zeus are usually the worst of the worst, with a few exceptions, such as my own Judges. New ones are introduced to the population so frequently I have long since stopped trying to keep track of the ones that end up at my door. Every so often one comes charging up the Gates and tries to beat them down. Thanatos is a barrier that few dare to challenge, but I would bet my kingdom that it is a son of Zeus banging on my doors now.

I suppress a sigh and follow the God of Death to the Gates. On the opposite side of Styx waits an old man. His clothing is coated in dust and sweat from travel, but he has a regal bearing despite the stoop of his shoulders. A thin gold circlet binds back wisps of gray hair. At his side is a statuesque woman with deep olive skin and black hair bound up in a laurel wreath and gold pins. She is gowned much more splendidly in a meticulously cared for gown the color of wine. A large yellow stone in a sun-shaped gold setting hangs between her breasts.

The old man genuflects with considerable difficulty, but keeps his eyes firmly upon me. "My Lord Hades, Ruler of the Underworld, I have come to beg your permission to visit my father."

Taken aback, I study him. A polite request does not often come from a child of Zeus and my curiosity is piqued as to the identity of this mortal. Most demigods who seek me out are in their prime and they spread rumors of fierce trials so they can grab at glory. I had always hoped that the fear of those imagined trials would prevent others from trying their hand at entering my realm, but somehow they just keep trying. This mortal also requests to see his father, which means he is either searching for the mortal who raised him or he is not a son of Zeus.

"You are near death now, why not wait until Thanatos comes for you to see your father?"

"Would you truly allow my soul to visit my father?" He asks sincerely. He has me there. I wouldn't be likely to grant his request were he already dead. Not that I'm likely to grant it now.

"Tell me your name, mortal." I ignore his question and pose my own.

"My Lord, I am Aeneas, the son of Aphrodite and Anchises." I stare at him in vague shock for a few moments. Demigods born of Goddesses are significantly rarer than those born of mortals. The woman at his side stares at me with an unwavering, almost defiant gaze. Signs of age creep onto her flesh, but her souls glows through like an internal flame. "My companion is the Cumæan Sibyl, the Prophetess of Apollo."

The doomed Sibyl nods her head almost imperceptibly. I remember Hermes mentioning her years ago. Apollo had granted her eternal life, but not eternal youth. She will age into eternity and one day her body will crumble into dust. She had requested the extended life for herself, but neglected her youth in the equation.

"I have no reason to grant you entrance to my realm when you are still in possession of your body." I wonder if his mother will intervene if I refuse him admission?

He struggles to his feet with assistance from the Sibyl. She barely touches him, retracting her hands as soon as he stabilizes. "My Lord, I beg of you, I long to know that my father is properly cared for. My wife has also passed, I would visit her as well if you would give me leave." He clasps his hands in a desperate prayer.

"Aeneas, I am sorry for your mortal losses, but you do not belong here. Be on your way."

His eyes flood with tears and he clutches at his clothing over his heart. "Please, please, my Lord." He prostrates himself on the ground, grasping handfuls of dirt and rubbing them upon his face. "I wish only to know that they are happy, that I will not find them in Tartarus." His tears spill into the dirt, muddy trails smearing down his cheeks.

"My Lord, Hades," the Sibyl interjects, "Aeneas fully realizes that it is not your custom to allow mortals into your realm, but I beg you to reconsider in this one case. He has done great things in his life and I have foreseen that he will live many years yet. I implore you to grant him this wish so he may live the remainder of his life knowing that his wife and father are cared for as they should be."

Annoyance and anger flare sharply in my belly and the Sibyl steps backwards as they flare outwards. "Are you suggesting that I am providing incompetent care and have improperly judged the souls in my realm?"

She lowers herself to the ground beside Aeneas, knees bending to accept the dirt. Her expression twitches and she tries to brush her gown clean of the dust plume that floated up when she landed. "I mean only that when the Gods are angry with mortals they may sometimes force the hand of one such as yourself. It is possible that they persuaded you to place him in Tartarus when he did not deserve it."

The Sibyl is fast getting on my nerves and I am not afraid to let it be known. "I assure you, whatever force may be employed, I have never sent someone to Tartarus when they did not deserve it." Irritated and ready to send them away, I am distracted by a tap on my shoulder. Clotho and her sisters hover behind me.

"Allow him entrance, just for a few moments. The dæmons can bring forth Anchises and Creusa. Aeneas will go on his way once he has seen them both. He is going to lead his people to war against Carthage, he needs this or he will fail and the Gods of our pantheon will be forgotten in his new land."

My annoyance shifts between Aeneas and his Sibyl and the Moiræ. They all press me to break my rules, just like the Olympians. The Moiræ know our laws as well as they know their own being, and it is only because of their respect for the realm that I will allow such a breach. "Very well. Ariston," the dæmon appears immediately, "please bring Anchises and Creusa from Asphodel."

"Asphodel!" Aeneas cries out and clasps his hands together. "Please, my Lord, my father and wife were good people, they should be in Elysium."

I choke back the sigh and hoist them both Aeneas and the Sibyl over Styx and into Erebus. "If they deserved Elysium they would be in Elysium." I snap as a flare of anger overtakes me. "Their eternity is based on their choices and actions, not on your personal opinion of them. Every word you both have spoken to me has been an insult to my judgement and I do not appreciate it. We do not throw souls at random into eternities. Each life is carefully reviewed and the choices they made in their mortal lives dictate where they spend their afterlife. If your father and wife wanted to end up in Elysium they should have made better choices when they were alive. It may be you do not know either of them so well as you believe, but there are no secrets in my realm. The Moiræ tell me you are a great man and I can only hope they are correct, but right now you are not proving their opinion of you."

The Sibyl reaches out for me, but I step away from her grasp. "My Lord, we do not mean any offense." I have no desire to hear her out as her very presence offends me.

"Do you not? I could be made the fool for believing otherwise. I have heard of you, Sibyl. You made a deal with Apollo for your immortality and then reneged on that deal. You offered your body for eternal life and then decided you would rather keep your virtue and the gifts you intended to sell it for knowing it could not be undone. Who are you to be trusted in anything when you cannot even keep your promises to the God who blessed you with your gifts? You have made a poor choice in your companion, Aeneas, she does you no credit when you come before me requesting a dispensation I grant to so few." The Sibyl had ended up with immortality and visions of the future, both gifts from Apollo. I'm mildly surprised the Sun God didn't take what he wanted, but then he has always had more care for his lovers than most Olympians do.

Aeneas falls to his knees in Erebus. "My Lord, you have granted me so much, might I put forward one more small request?"

"Speak your words, mortal." He cannot ask for anything more insolent than he has already.

"Cassandra of Troy, my Lord, the oracle priestess and princess, where does she rest?"

The question catches me off guard. "What interest have you in the Trojan princess?"

He looks at the ground shyly. "I love her, my Lord."

"Then why do you seek to speak with your wife and not Cassandra?" He appears more a young man now than the ancient and gray man before me.

"I love my wife as well. Cassandra was never for me. I loved her in my youth and married her sister. In our many years together I grew to love my wife very much. I have always wondered what became of Cassandra. I might have married her instead, but she devoted herself to the life of a priestess. I know now that my family at least has peace, if not paradise, it would do my soul well to know the truth of Cassandra as well. Did she die in the war?"

Perhaps it is the longing in his voice or the confession of a young man from aged lips that sways me. "She did not, she was captured and raped by Ajax, but he was sent to Tartarus for his many crimes. Your princess was taken as a concubine by Agamemnon. They were both murdered by his wife, along with the child she bore the Mycenæan King. She is in Elysium." Aeneas' eyes fill and then overflow with tears. "Your sorrow is unwarranted, Aeneas. She shed hers long ago and has rested in paradise for many years now. She does not remember her pain." I remember the judgement of the Trojan princess. Unlike the Cumæan Sibyl, Cassandra received her gifts by honest means although it was the same God that cursed them. Apollo merely altered the perceptions of Cassandra's prophecies, but he could not take away her gift since he had not granted it to her in the first place. "Would you request her presence?"

He shakes his head. "I could not pull her from paradise, not when I failed her in life. She is a magnificent woman who deserves every moment of Elysium."

Ariston appears with Creusa and Anchises and Aeneas rushes to them. They released their memories, but passing across Acheron allows them to temporarily access their mortal memories so they may recognize Aeneas. I stand by, forgotten by him, but now the Sibyl moves to stand close. "Forgive me, Lord Hades. I know I was a poor companion to accompany Aeneas, but I offered to come with him. I only wanted to experience your world once, since I shall never come here."

"If you are expecting sympathy for your plight you will not find it here. You cannot proposition a God for eternal life and then refuse him the agreed payment. Any mortal must know how short-sighted such an action would be. You know there had to be some kind of retribution after you spurned the advances you elicited from him."

"I was young then," she whispers. Her eyes connect with mine and she stares audaciously. "I assumed that he loved me and though I rejected his advances I believed he would not want to hurt me."

It is an incredible struggle to not roll my eyes. "I had hope that the plethora of legends would have taught you mortals something by now. You should be aware of the nature of the Gods before you attempt to trifle with them. You cannot take without giving, there must be balance in any deal with them. Besides, he has not hurt you. Not yet, at any rate. Thus far you are immortal, as you requested. There is nothing to say you will encounter any issues with your health in the future, so in all likelihood you will be able-bodied for many years to come."

"And when I have reached my ninth or tenth decade and beyond? What then, Lord Hades?"

Exasperated, I shrug my shoulders. "What do you want of me, Sibyl? I cannot undo your curse. It might seem extreme when you reach later years, but that is the choice you made and you must live with it. You have no hardship now and whatever punishment you believe Apollo has bestowed upon you, do remember that you are the one who forgot to request eternal youth. It is no fault of his if he granted your wish exactly as you asked it."

Her eyes well with tears and she clutches at the stone around her neck. "For the love you bear your Queen, take pity on another who fell in love with an inopportune choice. Intervene for me, let me die."

"Do not try to use Persephone to sway me to your desires, Sibyl." My voice drops into a deadly tone and a shiver slips through the realm.

I do not take kindly to her attempt to manipulate me via Persephone. "When Aeneas returns you will leave and you will not return here once more. Your quarrel is with Apollo. If you must press the issue, turn your manipulations upon him. Until you are relieved of your mortal body you are no concern of mine."

Her shoulders quake, but the sobs do not make their way into existence. She stands in abject silence, tears flowing in slow streams down her cheeks. The son of Aphrodite bounds up to us with all the vigor of a child, despite the years clinging to his body. He genuflects, a grin plastering his features as he clasps his hands before him. "My thanks and praise to you, Lord Hades. I have been blessed beyond measure by your graciousness. Thank you so much for granting me these moments with my loved ones in your realm. I know I am one of very few allowed such magnificent privilege. I swear to you, before my life is over, I will build you and your Queen a temple. I will personally see to it that it is brilliant enough to reflect your majesty."

"I appreciate the sentiment, but I would be most pleased if you would both take your leave of my kingdom now."

Aeneas bows and cups his hand beneath the Sibyl's elbow, guiding her towards the edge of Styx where they are both swept over by Thanatos. The God of Death turns back to me after Aeneas and the Sibyl fade from view. "That could have gone a lot worse. A son of Zeus would probably have tried to wade through Styx and ignore us completely."

I laugh, shaking away my annoyance from the encounter. "Let us be thankful for small blessings."

56

PERSEPHONE

Olympus is quiet today, most of the Gods are away and there is little beyond the soft breeze and sunlight to keep me company. A flicker of gold catches my attention from the corner of my eye and I turn to see Hera, resplendent in gold and copper, approaching me. Her hair is loose and there is a rare smile and a calm aura about her today. I see her so infrequently that I never made the connection between this look of quiet pleasure and the absence of her husband before. The sternness of her expression, the constant edge of worry that painted her features had always given her an appearance of someone much older, but she looks rather youthful today.

"Hello, Persephone, are you well?" She settles next to me on a bank of cloud.

"I am," I smile at her

Her brow suddenly creases. "I have something to tell you about the child." Fear claws at my belly and I clutch it with both hands. "The reason you were sent away so quickly was because of Athena. Zeus must have felt the disturbance, the energy that is created when a God is being destroyed. He must have sent her and she stole the heart. The child lives, Persephone."

My child is alive. I am filled with both wonder and revulsion. "How? Why?"

"I didn't know what had happened to it until a mortal became pregnant with the child."

"How can a mortal birth a God?" My mind is reeling and my stomach churns uncomfortably.

"Zeus impregnated one of his priestess's, put the heart into her womb to incubate it. By the time I found her she was almost dead, the child had grown so fast and she was being torn apart from within. I tried to help her through it, used my magic to numb her pain, but I could not remove it all. She died in agony, the birth of the child burning away her mortal body in a burst of power. The child is growing, a bit more slowly than is usual for an immortal, but he is nearing adulthood. The other priestess's care for him."

"What," my voice catches, tongue suddenly thick, "what is his name?"

"Dionysus."

"What should I do?"

She shrugs and pats my arm sympathetically. "Whatever you want to do. He doesn't know that you are his immortal mother and I will not be the one to tell him. You must know though, that he is a full immortal, a full Olympian. He will come to live here when Zeus remembers him. He does not keep close tabs on his children, so who knows when that will happen."

Tears breach my eyes and fall hot on my cheeks. "How am I to look upon him and not remember how he came to be?"

She embraces me fiercely. "You will survive it, just as I have with every immortal child my husband has brought into my home. Every one of them I see is a reminder that he went outside his marriage bed, that there was another woman I could not save from his brutality. I will be here for you, Persephone, whenever you have need of me."

I find myself wishing that Hera was my mother, but such thoughts make me feel disloyal. The concept of looking upon the child I carried as a result of my father's actions makes me feel sick. Maybe if I were a stronger person, had more of a mothering instinct I would be able to love my son, but all I can remember is my own pain.

"You have been so good to me, how can I ever repay your kindness?"

"Try to heal. You will see your father and son many more times in your life. Do not to let your fear change who you are." Tears coast down her own cheeks and she strokes my hair. "You are sweet and loving, you did not deserve what happened to you. I would change it if I could. You are very loved, Persephone and love is greater than fear. Find your strength and stand in front of our King and take back your power. I truly hope you do and I will support you however I can."

57

HADES

Cocytus is so large that it seems it might be an entire ocean rather than a lake. Its waters are black and placid, save for the edges where the souls pour out their sorrows and their memories. When I was a young God and had only the Titans for company I would swim in these waters, lose myself in the cocoon of peace they brought. I have not been able to swim here for millennia, not since humanity first came to me. If I tried now I would be assaulted by all that they shed into the depths.

Some of the souls are openly sobbing, but most sprawl languidly and trail their fingers over the surface. A shriek draws my attention and I race towards it. The dæmons struggle with one of the souls. "Agamemnon!" I roar and they all fall still and silent for a moment. "Cease this nonsense at once." I grip my hand and shackles form about his limbs and bind him together. The dæmons release him. I have long since tired of his presence. He is belligerent, but something inside of me gave me pause and I did not send him directly to Tartarus when he died. Now a spark in the depths of my mind gives me the reason. "You created misery in those around you and now you will know that misery yourself."

A quick flick of my fingers has him twisting in the air and landing flat on his back. I request a chalice from the dæmons and one dashes away to collect one for me. I stare at the darkness of Cocytus and hold the fetched chalice out in front of me. "Sacred water, pull for me the memories of those Agamemnon has harmed. Bring forth only the memories in which he is directly involved with those people." Droplets float to the surface and float one by one towards me and deposit themselves in the cup. I still the water before it overflows the chalice and pour the contents into his mouth.

He chokes and protests, but the chalice fills three more times before Cocytus brings nothing else forward and I pour it all down his throat. As soon as the last drop fills up his shade form he freezes. He shouts and struggles against the bonds after a moment, but he is no longer with us, lost in the memories of others. I touch his forehead and am drawn into the memories. His thoughts flit around, caught in rapes, beatings, murders, everything that Agamemnon ever used to fuel his blood lust is turned back upon him. It is a sweeter torture than Tartarus could have ever given him.

Agamemnon writhes in his bonds, tormented by his own actions. I snatch him up on a bubble of power and he floats along behind me, shrieking. I snap my fingers and muffle the sound so he does not disturb the others. Cocytus soothes them and memory of the disturbance fades instantly. I cross the raging fires of Phlegethon with my kingly bounty, closing my eyes as we pass through the flames. The heat is uncomfortable, but it does not burn me. My skin tingles all the same, remembering the burns that it once endured.

Kamp greets me as I enter her realm. As much as a half-formed primordial creature with no language can greet someone, at least. Her smoke tendrils relieve me of Agamemnon and I follow her through this ashen world. There is little light, the water is bitter and unholy screams echo in my ears.

What most people don't know is that the punishments in Tartarus do eventually end. It may take millennia for that to occur, for it only happens when the souls are completely broken down. All sense of ego must leave them and they must repent for their crimes to the very depths of their being. Until that time the punishment continues.

Tartarus is full of labyrinthine caves, but it is mostly empty. All of the souls housed here are kept in the deepest part, nearest to the Titans so that Kamp can easily keep an eye on them all. We walk for a long time before the caves start to fill, each one we pass containing a single soul experiencing their comeuppance for horrendous crimes.

Kamp tosses Agamemnon down and a plume of dust floats up around his prostrate form. I unbind his voice and his whimpering turns into a series of sharp yells and then into hysterical sobbing. There are so many things in his life that could be cause of such a reaction, but out of curiosity I check in to see. Black hair and blood fill my vision as I watch him plunge his knife downwards and tear it through the tender flesh of his daughter, Iphigenia. I retreat away from his thoughts, disconcerted by the look of twisted satisfaction I had seen on his face.

I turn my back on the Mycenæan King, pleased to leave him here until the end of my days. Tartarus unnerves me. It never used to bother me before it was filled with souls. Back when it was only the Titans it was relatively peaceful. Now it houses misery as well as chaos. Kamp gives a sigh and the rest of her half-formed visage dissolves entirely into smoke. Her smouldering body ghosts out, spreading like mist over a lake in the earliest hours of morning. It is how she surveys the realm and makes sure everything is as it should be. If she encounters any issues the smoke instantly reforms where it is needed. If she encounters any souls that have reached their full repentance she summons me and we return them to Judgement. I doubt I will ever see Agamemnon returned to me for Judgement. There are few souls in here that are crueler or more arrogant and that combination will keep him occupied in misery for the better part of forever.

58

HADES

Eager to shed the energy of Tartarus, I head towards Erebus and a waiting Cerberus. I stroke his fur absently while watching Thanatos. He stands at the shore of Styx, wings outstretched as his form flickers, transitioning from light to shadow and back again. Much of his essence is out gathering souls. He effectively creates doppelgangers of equal power so he may retain his position guarding Styx. The air around him ripples with power and the scent of ice and pine wafts towards me, a cool balm against the stress of experiencing Tartarus. I can feel his essence probing my thoughts, popping the bubbles of distress and replacing them with calm. At times I forget just how much power Thanatos wields. He never abuses it, but if he ever decided to do so the results would be devastating. He is strong enough to extract the soul of a God, effectively leaving them alive, but powerless, a shell of what they once were. He is a primordial spirit, one whose influence extends far beyond controlling mortal death. He contents himself here, serving the purpose carved out for him, rescuing mortals from the suffering their bodies inflict upon them. His invasion of my thoughts, even in this healing manner, is a stark reminder that his power far outreaches mine and he follows me only by his own choice.

Ever so slowly his wings close, giving him a halo of midnight black feathers. His eyes open as he turns to face me and a handful of souls appear behind him escorted by barely visible phantoms of himself. Each doppelganger returns to the source in a brief shimmer of light. His wings usher the souls forward, sweeping them across the River Styx to await Charon.

He nods to acknowledge my presence. "Is anything wrong, Hades?"

"No, only the remnants of Tartarus." A sweep of his magic is like a cleansing bath, washing away the misery that clings to my flesh.

He smiles shyly. "Lady Persephone will be returning soon, do you think she will be returning with the same companions?"

The question catches me off guard and I instantly think of Minthe. "I should think so. Have any been giving you trouble?"

"No," he shakes his head, "I was merely curious if Leuce would be returning. She is a lovely creature." I scour my memory for the nymphs he speaks of. Vague impressions of dark green eyes and silver-blonde hair come to mind. She is quieter even than Persephone's favorite companion and I cannot even remember her speaking a word while she was here last. Not that I pay much attention to them anyway. They are often a giggling herd, but they do well enough to bring up the spirits of the dæmons.

An amusing thought crosses my mind. "Are you sweet on the little nymph?"

He shrugs, non-committal. "Her face and nature are pleasing, but I cannot say I am sweet on her." The barest hint of color on his cheeks betrays his words.

"Use Elysium to get to know her. I can always guard Styx while you engage in some socialization." He looks positively stricken by the very concept. I bite my lip to tame down the smile that attempts to form. This is new ground for him and I must tread softly. "You say she pleases you, so would it not be logical that spending more time with her in a quiet setting would also please you?"

"I would much prefer to simply observe from a distance." He averts his eyes. I don't press the matter further, but I make a mental note to speak with Persephone about it. If Leuce's gentle spirit is appealing to Thanatos there is no reason why they should not spend more time together to see if something develops. I will not force anything, but the least we can do is put her in his line of sight a little more often.

59

PERSEPHONE

I lose myself and my worries in the music. Hooked arm in arm by a nymph then a dæmon and tossed between someone new each moment as we fling ourselves through the steps of the dance. I can forget that I am a mother while my own will barely speak to me. I can forget the stormy eyes that strike me full of terror and I can forget that far too soon I will be forced to remember all that again. I dance until I no longer know what direction I am moving in, until my body begs for rest and my throat begs for drink.

Hades steals me from the fray and plies me with nectar and spring water. He leans close to me while I drink and whispers in my ear. "Send Leuce to dance with Thanatos." The God of Death hovers reluctantly in the corner, looking uncomfortably out of place.

Riddled with curiosity, I put down my drink and press Hades for details as to what prompted his request. I swallow a gasp so I do not draw attention to myself, but a grin spreads over my features and a swirl of giddy joy leaps in my belly. I discretely watch them both and notice that Thanatos is watching Leuce. He's not obvious about it, but his eyes keep drifting back towards her. He likes her, but he's shy and she has an equally hesitant disposition.

I throw myself back into the dance and strategically work my way towards the silver-haired beauty. As we swing towards each other I tell her I have a request to make of her. We swing away and mix through partners and when we are tossed at each other once again I instruct her to bring Thanatos into the dance. Her eyes grow wide, but she bobs a little bow and slips out of the pattern as a new dance begins.

I catch Hades as the circle passes him around and he joins in with a practiced flourish. At one time I had to drag him into this, but now I think he loves it just as much as the nymphs. He is graceful, as Gods are wont to be and it is beautiful to watch. I overflow with glee when I notice the flutter of black wings out of the corner of my eye and see Leuce followed by a very nervous God.

"Do try and be a little less conspicuous about it." Hades whispers, slipping his arm about my waist. Thanatos and Leuce look so beautiful together, contrasting loveliness. One as fair as moonlight, the other dark as deepest night, a delicate play of light and darkness. Leuce's cheeks flush pink and her easy laughter brings a ghost of a smile to Thanatos' lips. He lasts only a single dance before the push and pull of the other nymphs becomes too much for him. He retreats entirely, leaving the Great Hall for his sanctuary on the shores of Styx. "Do not press them, even with your thoughts. They might be immortal, but they may still be susceptible to the desires you're wafting at them. Aphrodite would not thank you for putting her powers to shame in such a matter."

"I can really do that?" I find the idea absolutely fascinating. Thanatos is a relatively solitary being and the thought that he might find love is wonderful.

"There is little in this world that can stand up to the singularly focused desire of an immortal, especially when the motivation is genuine. They may be on the threshold of something, but it would be unfair to let your own excitement over it be the tipping point into whatever relationship might form. Let them develop at their own pace."

If I stay here I know I will not be able to stop myself from thinking about it and I tell Hades as much. We excuse ourselves from the festivities, leaving them all to revel, and we set off for the depths of Elysium.

"Elysium, show me something new, something I have never seen before." It ripples at my command as white sand forms beneath my feet and azure water spreads out before me and disappears into the horizon. "Is it broken? I have seen the ocean before."

Hades laughs. "You're not looking at the big picture. You have seen the shore and the surface, what about beneath the waves?" Water crashes in gentle waves against my ankles as I contemplate his words. "I asked Elysium the same question once and it brought me here too. We are nearly as far from Olympus as one might be able to get, on the other side of the world."

I march into the surf and plunge beneath the surface. The Elysian water is warm and my vision instantly fills with a swarm of multi-colored fish. A sea turtle glides by me as though it might be flying. A whole world exists under the water. I should have assumed there would be something, Poseidon never would have taken on an empty realm, but I have never given thought to it before. I had no idea there were such wonders here. It occurs to me that the Olympians probably have the same misconception of the Underworld.

Little white and yellow striped fish glide around us in a living cloud, prodding at us with their tiny trumpet noses. They scatter like seed puffs in the wind when a sleek gray creature glides towards us from the depths. Sharp fins jut out of its huge body and a pointed tail propels it forward until its rounded nose smacks me in the belly. It sweeps a wide circle and smacks me again, this time in the backside.

We surface and Hades holds a hand so the beautiful creature can slide under his palm. "Sharks are found in our waters, but they are wilder here and have more space to grow. They are master hunters in this realm and are the fear of sailors the world over."

He hitches a ride on the shark's dorsal fin, hooking his arm around my waist and the great creature carries us along. A rainbow of coral flows up the side of the land for miles, every color imaginable and fish of every shape and size I could ever conceive of. The abundance of life flows all around us, a reminder that there is more to this world than politics and duty and that I need to take more time to enjoy it.

60

PERSEPHONE

$\mathbf{S}$ till dripping from the ocean and determined to take back control of my own time, I gather the souls I had selected as potential Judges so that Hades can meet them. I call the women one by one and they appear in a slow blaze of light.

These women are founders of cities, queens, princesses and political leaders. They have strived for equality, served their people faithfully and many had sacrificed their very lives for the well-being of those under their care. They are examples of honor, intelligence, kindness and integrity; beloved leaders, wives and mothers. Hades approves of each in turn, not saying a word about the number I chose.

"Ladies, you are all exceptional women. You have been through hardship, but you have done your utmost to keep to your personal values and have cultivated strength and virtue. You have the nobility of spirit far beyond your stations in life. Being a royal or a leader is not a necessity in this arrangement, but possessing experience dealing with people, with diplomacy, is a skill that you will require. You all have experience navigating politics, yet you retain your virtues. You will each be gifted with the ability to take corporeal form as you see fit and you will be given chambers in the Palace to use whenever you please." I grasp each woman's hands, light flaring between us as I bestow both blessing and form to them.

We move as a unit from Elysium and Evaristus summons a fleet of dæmons to prepare quarters for each of them mere moments before we enter the Palace. Each is gifted with an opulent chamber and they fill the remaining rooms in the south wing.

"Why did you choose so many?" Hades and I walk hand in hand to the Great Hall which has been emptied and cleaned. Several neat stacks of tapestries await me lining the one wall.

"If I have twelve, but only require three at a time, that means they are only giving up Elysium for one quarter of their remaining eternity. I thought it might be a more reasonable request. I know your Judges agreed to be out of Elysium forever, but none of them have been there. My Judges are plucked fresh from paradise and it must be a hard thing to lose having experienced it. Were I in their position, I would have likely declined. Since they agreed I wanted to make it as easy as possible on them."

He looks contemplative. "I had not considered that. You are correct in that mine cannot miss something they have never experienced, but perhaps it's something I should look into. My Judges earned Elysium, but they have never been there. Have I been cruel in my choice to have them serve as my Judges?'"

"I do not believe so. They made the choice and they were free to decline. Even now if they wanted to leave your service I don't think you would stop them. You worked for millennia without them, and they are grateful for the trust you place in them. They were good men with great souls who know how to speak to anyone, even a God. If they wanted change they would ask you for it. You can be certain that Aeacus would never stay silent for long about something that upset him." I am secretly pleased he even contemplates that one of my own ideas might be superior to his. We work from different directions, he from experience and I from instinct, and while they might yield similar results, the means to our end can diverge quite drastically. "I would not worry on it tonight, for now I will let my Judges adjust to their new home and tomorrow they will begin their study of Judgement with yours."

"As you will."

61

HADES

I should not still be surprised when Persephone takes charge of her own life, or even parts of my realm, but it's still a delight to watch. She handled her selection perfectly and now she fills the Great Hall with many of her nymphs, her Judges and mine for a study session. I take only a few moments to see them all settled, eager to engage myself at the Towers while they are occupied. As my Judges will be helping Persephone with training I will be handling Judgement exclusively for all those not waiting for Persephone.

The entire company is quite beautiful, but I notice that it is only my Judges that adorn themselves with lumbering crowns atop their heads. Persephone's chosen are simply dressed in fine fabric with only thin gold bands or flowers adorning their hair and no baubles on their necks and arms. It is still easy to tell that they are noble ladies, though it shows in their demeanor and not their finery.

They listen raptly to Persephone and my Judges explain the process. Everything seems under control so I take my leave of them. I pass through the courtyard and a sweet, peppery scent overpowers the usual aroma of flora. Hands like silk ghost up my arms and a warm body presses against my back. I recoil and spin around sharply, snatching at the hands. Minthe stares at me with wild eyes, rimmed with red and tears. Her gown is shucked and pooling at her waist, leaving her breasts bare. Her hair spills riotously over her shoulders as she shakes her head and strains towards me. She is slippery as an eel as she frees her hands and clings to me.

I scrabble for purchase on her and force her back. "Minthe, stop."

"Please!" She cries out and wriggles harder, tears running over her cheeks. "Please, please, do not turn me away, I cannot return again having failed."

She crumples to the ground and despite myself I kneel next to her. Hot tears fall onto the marble and she hugs her arms. "What do you mean? How have you failed?" Her words confound me and I want to understand.

She catches me off guard when she literally throws herself at me, springing off the ground to cling with all four limbs like a parasite around me. We crash to the ground as I topple backwards. She is surprisingly strong, lithe limbs wrapped in muscle. No matter how I try to wedge my arms between us I am unsuccessful in removing her. Her lips fasten to my throat and she mutters something I cannot quite understand. She rotates her hips in a way that makes me hope to all the Gods Persephone does not encounter us and misunderstand. Her face whips before mine and she kisses me with a kind of desperation I have never experienced before. It's so deep I can taste it, a sad and bitter flavor. I struggle against her, but it is like trying to win a battle with a very enthusiastic octopus and I don't want to hurt her. She is terrified over something and attacking her will not improve matters. I just want to get free and contain her enough that she can speak and tell me what is going on, but each time I free myself from one limb another takes its place.

I place both palms against her face and quite unceremoniously push until she lets out a screech and limb by limb, releases my body. She is not even off for a second before she reaches for me again, but she freezes halfway through the movement. Her eyes become sightless, mouth partially open as her back arches and she hovers motionless.

I glance behind her and see Persephone. Her eyes are snapping with a fury I never considered her to be capable of. Her hand is outstretched before her, glowing with power as she crushes her fingers into a fist. Minthe shrieks as her body twists and contorts. Her skin melts away and her bones shatter to dust. She shrinks down until she is nothing more than a vibrantly green clutch of leaves.

Persephone's eyes glow white and she moves as though in a trance. I cannot help but be rendered speechless as I watch her glide towards me. Her face is set in a frown and her shoulders are rigid. "Explain yourself, Minthe."

A minuscule voice quakes from the leaves. "I am so sorry, my Lady. I was only following orders. I was so afraid."

Persephone's body heaves, a sigh forcing its way free as she crouches to the ground. The wild light fades from her eyes and she looks like my bride once more. "What were you afraid of?" She spares a glance at me. "Do not look at me so, I only forced her transformation back to her true form. It is a little startling and much more vivid when they do not choose to do it themselves, but there is no permanent damage."

Minthe's leaves tremble. "Lady Demeter told me that I must find a way to come between you and Lord Hades. She hoped you would become displeased and desire to return home. She threatened to destroy my life source if I did not comply. Had Lord Hades the countenance of any other God I would have succeeded easily. I felt terrible when I realized that he loved you, but my life was at stake, you must understand."

"You could have told me. I would have found a way to protect you." She looks sadly down at the little plant. "I will protect you, all of you. Your life sources will be transplanted to the Underworld, you need never fear her retribution again." She turns to me again. "I can gather the nymphs and harvest their life sources, we could keep them here, keep them safe." I nod and she scoops up Minthe. "Please prepare a place for them before I return."

62

PERSEPHONE

O nly a nymph knows what plant serves as her anchor to this world so I need them to be with me in order to find and save them. A few well-placed bribes of apples have the horses cooperative and laden with nymphs. Between all four horses we are cramped, but they manage the weight with relative ease. The sun is blinding when we surface from the path Hades opened for us into the meadow. The nymphs are nervous and rightly so.

"How many of you were tasked with the same assignment?" All of them raise their hands and Minthe trembles from her place in my lap. Only Minthe had followed her orders. I cannot think too poorly of her. She made a very unwise and destructive decision, but Minthe does not know me or the others. Leuce does not either, but her nature is not as bold and it is possible that she noticed Thanatos as much as he noticed her and knew such actions would destroy all possibilities of a future with him. Minthe was entirely alone in our new world and afraid for her life. I should have made an effort to help her feel included, but that is hindsight and I can only deal with the repercussions now.

Each life source we arrive at involves careful magic. The applicable nymph cradles their plant and each root must be extracted from the earth, each leaf infused with my power to keep it alive until it is replanted. If I make any mistake it could cost a life. I rub the Asphodel pendant and in response a shaft opens in the ground, leading to the Underworld. In a bubble of magic the nymph and life source are lowered and accepted by Hades and the dæmons who are ready to receive them.

More than half of them have life sources near the meadow, but the rest are stretched further afield. Most of the day elapses by the time I am down to Chloe and Leuce. The horses returned as they were unburdened and now it is only us three on Xanthippe. An icy wind needles through my gown and cold fear swells. Chloe's life source is closest and I urge Xanthippe to hurry. Boreas has seen us, his winds know what we are doing and it's only a matter of time before my mother knows too.

"There, my Lady." Chloe points to a velvet Centaurea plant tucked amid a sea of ferns. I fly from my horse and with trembling hands I begin the intricate process. Nerves assail me. I should have been faster, should have thought that Boreas would be watching. Chloe hugs the fuzzy silver leaves and shivers as I tug the roots from the soil. I want to rush, but she is already struggling with her discomfort. I breathe slowly and wrap my magic around every fiber and secure her in a safety bubble. A quick swipe over the pendant has another shaft opening and I lower Chloe down. She stares at up at me with frightened eyes and I know I have her entire existence in my hands.

Leuce screams and I almost drop Chloe, but catch her after a moment of free fall. I force her descent a little less gently than I should and shout out for Hades to catch her before I release my hold on her. Leuce writhes on the ground.

"What is it? Leuce, tell me what is happening!" I snare her around the waist and toss her up onto Xanthippe's back before climbing up myself. Boreas' icy wind comes for us again, this time carrying the scent of wood-smoke. "Xanthippe, run, find it!"

The horse takes off in a burst of speed and I cling to her mane as she and the wind nearly unseat me. Leuce sobs and clutches at the fabric of my gown. "She knows," she croaks out, "my Lady, your mother knows where my tree is. She made me show her before I went to the Underworld." The smoke grows thicker as we get closer and Xanthippe bursts into a clearing where a white willow is lost in flames. "She promised me she would keep it safe while I was away."

My mother is nowhere to be seen, but Boreas sends his winds to coil around the tree, fanning the flames. Fire and water are not my domain and I cannot drown it with soil for fear of shattering the brittle branches. I shove my hands at the Earth in a blind panic and call up vines of honeysuckle and ivy to race up the tree and smother the flames. Leuce hangs lifelessly from Xanthippe's back, but there is still a delicate rise and fall to her chest. Agonizing moments pass until at last the worst of the flames quell and the tree stands smoldering. The vines fall away and the branches disintegrate into ashes.

My knees hit the ground before I realize I am falling. "Gaia, save her." I haul Leuce off Xanthippe and carry her to the tree. The fire was too far gone by the time we had reached it. I scour the tree, searching for some sign of life.

The air stirs behind me. Black wings stretch into my field of vision and I turn to see Thanatos. "She is gone, Persephone."

I clutch the body of the nymph I barely knew. Nymphs do not have souls in the same manner that humans do. Like dæmons, if they die they are dispersed into the æther. Thanatos reaches out and strokes her brow.

"No." I set her gently to the side and scrape through the charcoal. Desperation and blackened fingers digging deeper. It's ridiculous to argue with the God of Death in such a matter, but I keep digging anyway. Leuce's pale form flickers and he scoops her from the ground and cradles her. "Thanatos, no, don't send her away. There has to be something we can do."

"Persephone," he speaks gently and places a hand on my shoulder, "the mortals cannot return their dead, nor can you return yours."

"You never even had a chance to be happy with her." Tears blur my vision and I crawl into his embrace so that Leuce is tucked between us.

"It was not to be." His calm irritates me. How can he not be upset about this?

"Let me take her to Elysium, there might be enough of her soul left." He gives me a look to suggest that my endeavor will be fruitless and painful, but he indulges me.

By the time we reach the Isles of the Blessed Leuce is transparent. I had been unresponsive and determined passing through the throng of nymphs and Hades, so they had all followed me. The nymphs are a cacophony of wailing. The heart of Elysium opens itself and I take Leuce from Thanatos and lay her upon the ground. I move the soil by hand and the nymphs ground around me, each pouring handfuls until Leuce is entirely covered except for her face. I lean over to kiss her forehead, bestowing power and blessings upon her. She flickers and Elysium pulls her in deeper.

"This is unacceptable." I grind the words out, furious with my mother. I should not be surprised, given her hostile reaction to Hades and Evaristus, but I never thought she would go this far. "I will not tolerate this abuse of my own people. This has to stop, here and now."

63

HADES

"What precisely are you trying to stop?" Furious anger is building in her and I know I need to quell it before she does something she will regret.

"This interference, this complex my parents have that makes them believe they have the right to play with the lives of others. Mother attacked you, Evaristus and now Leuce and my father has attacked me. How much more are we expected to endure before we strike back?"

"I understand, truly I do, but what do you even intend to do?" If I can question her enough, bring her logical mind into this, perhaps she will see reason. "You cannot fight both your parents. Don't act rashly, Persephone. I was a poor example.,I was impulsive when I took on Zeus, we cannot afford to start a war with Olympus. "

Hysteria works its way into her voice and her eyes implore me to simply support this madness. "Hades, please, we have to be able to protect our people or what is the use in us ruling them? You took your vengeance, why do you try to deny me mine?"

"I only want you to be safe," I plead with her, but her eyes do not soften. I struggle with myself, combating the same desire to keep her tucked away that her mother must have felt. She is too precious to risk, but she is mine by her choice alone and I have no right to command her.

"We are not safe, here or anywhere. My mother attacked you in your chambers and my father attacked me in mine. If you think they will not consider doing so again then I must believe you are mistaken." I could try to command her to stay here, but that could irreparably damage our relationship and I would never forgive myself. I have to swallow my own fears and reservations if I am to support her in this. She will never find peace if she does not confront them. "My father knows you are not to be trifled with, but he thinks me weak. I don't want to be afraid of him, please let me do this."

I cannot turn down such a request, despite the risk to us. I stroke her hair, soothing myself as much as her. I love her, but this is a difficult task she asks of me. I have no desire to send her to battle against Olympus. Hermes' words echo in my thoughts. If handled improperly this could tear Olympus apart.

"I cannot say if it will be liberation or tragedy that awaits me, but I do know that I have lived too many days in fear. There is too much anger inside of me, I shouldn't feel this way Hades."

The hesitation from only moments ago flees from me. My bride needs this and I need her so there is only one course of action available to me. Once I thought so carefully, tested theories and pondered intently on the outcomes, but since Persephone has come to my life, impulse has been a more constant companion. I once pledged to support the person she wanted to become, to offer her opportunities and I would be a poor husband if I retracted that pledge now simply because it's more complicated than it once was. "Then you will not. If this is what you need to do to feel empowered, then I will stand behind you. I hope to Gaia that it does not lead to war, but you *are* right. They have come for us once and I have already pledged to destroy them if they do so again. My Queen, your kingdom stands behind you."

Persephone is Spring, the earthly symbol of change and rebirth. I may have praised her position in the mortal world and enjoyed the light she brought to this realm, but mayhap there is more to it than that. Perhaps she was born to be the catalyst for change. Olympus has been unchanged for millennia; the same Gods; the same conflicts and issues ruling their world. Spring is coming to Olympus.

64

PERSEPHONE

My energy swells, churning like a tempest, crashing up, around and over me. The nymphs will remain here as they are recovering from the transplant and in no fit state to fight. I would not have them or the dæmons fight my battles regardless of their condition. The largest threat we have backing us is Thanatos. His primordial power over death is a force to be reckoned with and is something not even Olympus will take lightly. I do not want it to come to battle. I pray to Great Mother Gaia for reason to lead us, for Olympus to think clearly on what I'm coming to say.

Hades and I are gowned alike in black, amethyst and gold, an appearance based show of solidarity. My husband is my support and I will lead. If necessary, he will back me, but this is my battle to wage. I am ready to go toe to toe with the King of Olympus. Part of me wonders if I even possess the strength to face him. Should I approach this all with more subtlety, work to undermine his control over time? The greater part of myself demands action and there is no internal force that will quiet it. I thought that perhaps I should go alone and without adornments, only as myself and not with my titles and husband behind me, but I think I must approach my parents as their equal.

"Gaia, be with me." I pray to the Earth Mother, invoking her guidance and pleading for her strength to face this. Panic still seizes me when I see my father and I cannot even begin to imagine the anger that might appear when I see my mother again. All that is left of Leuce is ashes. I can barely tell what I feel when I think of everything that has happened, but I know that the emotions are not positive. Dwelling on them makes my vision blur and a coaxing brush from Gaia brings me back into focus.

I have no concept of how this will go, how I will even begin. I have no intentions of direct battle, but there are things I can no longer keep silent on. I have only the fire burning inside of me to move me towards action and the knowledge that if I do not stand my ground the Olympians will forever continue their abhorrent ways towards us.

I slip my hand into Hades' and a burst of power turns us into particles on the wind, whipping up through the earth and into the sky. Olympus blossoms before us like a vibrant flower in the heavens. It is a pity it is a poisonous flower that is watered on intrigue and fed on corruption. I search out my parents, finding them both near.

We appear in a massive courtyard lined with white marble and gold pillars. The air is warm today despite the altitude and a coaxing breeze reminds me that we have friends here. Zephyrus appears atop one of the columns, perched like a bird and smiling at me. He acknowledges us with a nod of his head before fading from view again. I feel Great Mother Gaia's energy ripple up through my feet. *"Be strong, I am with you."* She whispers to me and the fire in my belly rises to fill my whole body.

Her energy surges and makes Olympus shiver and crackle. Shouts of alarm echo through the Olympian forum and faces begin to emerge. Hermes arrives on Olympus and moves to stand behind us, his eyes wild. "I am with you, whatever the cost."

Gaia's power springs each step forward, urging me in my choice. Others appear and an auburn haired God with sparkling green eyes catches my attention. His visage hooks inside me and pulls. My son. Gaia pushes at me. Now is not the time, there is no sense in reaching out to him when I have come to challenge everything he knows. I turn away from him, pushing down the nausea and uncertainty that settles over me.

I direct my energy down and it blends effortlessly with the Earth Mother, a ripple racing out, searching for my father and mother. The doors of the throne room of Olympus rise before us, ostentatious monstrosities of pure gold. Another surge of power slams them open, the resounding crack as loud as thunder. My father lounges on the throne and jumps as we enter. He doesn't bother to sit up. He's so used to flaunting his authority that he doesn't even pretend to respect others.

My mother bursts from her own chambers and rushes towards us through the throng of creatures and Gods now clamoring to see what the commotion is. "Persephone!" She charges up to us, skidding to a stop when she realizes Hades is with me. She tries to disguise it, but her displeasure can be keenly felt. Prior to her attack on Leuce she might have believed I was here because Minthe's orders had been completed. My vision goes dark for a moment before it fills with the flames of Leuce's burning tree. I squeeze Hades' hand as the fury grips my heart in a pulsing staccato. "Daughter, what are you doing here?"

"I wanted to ask you why you thought it appropriate to act so blatantly against my marriage and to murder one of my own companions." My voice slips into a deadly tone. Zeus snorts, a low chuckle erupting from his throat. "I am here for you too, Father." He sits up a little and raises his eyebrow. I'm surprised my voice does not crack or quiver. "Answer me, Mother, why did you do it?"

"Persephone, my darling, I only ever loved you." Her hair flies around her as she reaches for me.

"No, you loved who you wanted me to be, not who I am. Perhaps I could have one day forgiven how you confined me and manipulated me, but I cannot forgive you attacking my home, my husband and my companions." Tears pour down her cheeks and whispers erupt from everyone around us watching the exchange.

Zeus laughs, a hateful chortle that makes the bile rise in my throat. Gaia's energy floods me and I breathe deeply of it. I turn to my father, hardening my features. "The contract you set up is ended."

He rises from his throne with all the foreboding of a coming storm. He slithers towards me with the feral grace of a cobra. "What makes me you think you have the right to negate the terms I set out?" His voice is sharp, the words dancing on the tips of knives. The hair on the back of my neck prickles, but Hades' grip on my hand is an anchor against the torrent of Zeus' rising energy. I gather my courage and step away from my husband and meet my father in the center of the room. His hand shoots forward and grips my chin and mouth like a vice. Hatred sparks in his eyes. The grip is crushing, threatening to slice the inside of my lips against my teeth. I hear Hades call my name, but I hold up a hand to assure him I can handle this myself.

I summon up the power of the Earth Mother and the shock of energy burns his hand. He leaps back, shaking the offending limb. "I have the right because I am the one it involves. I am the one being controlled and I am tired of it. I call upon the Gods of Olympus!" The strength of my voice, the sheer volume and power projected forth is startling. It is Great Mother Gaia's doing, ensuring that others will listen to what I have to say. Hera enters the throne room from the opposite side, her lustrous auburn hair flowing free around her. She moves to stand behind me and as I turn to follow her with my gaze I realize that I am flanked by a veritable army. Hermes, Hestia and Hera stand just behind Hades and behind them is a gathering of sky nymphs, the Moiræ and other beings that call Olympus home. At the back of the crowd is Thanatos with midnight wings outstretched, a very real expression of power poised and waiting. They look to me for guidance, but for now I need them to do nothing more than show Zeus that we do not stand alone. Zephyrus winks at me from a new perch and cocks his head to the crowd to tell me he is the one who brought them.

"I command you all to bear witness on what I say. I declare the contract controlling my access to Olympus and the Underworld to be invalid. I declare that I am free to make my own choices, that I will no longer bend to the will of others without a greater purpose. I am the Goddess of Spring and new life cannot thrive when it is pressed down."

By the time I finish Zeus is marching towards me in a fury. Lightning sparks around him and it is only the comfort of the crowd and the steadily flowing power of Gaia that keeps my mind from descending into memories better left untouched. The edges of panic claw at me and a sweat breaks out on my skin. My whole body trembles with remembrance, freezing in terror for a moment before Gaia releases it once more. I square my shoulders and face him, standing tall and letting my own power course through me. We are both light, one creative and one destructive. His hand shoots out and I can see the lightning flashing between his fingers, but this time I am ready. It stings, but there is no paralysis and my own power flares back in a bright wave.

He stares at me incredulously, the hair of his beard faintly smoking from the contact. His eyes turn to stone and he gathers his strength again. "Stand down." The order weighs on me, his force of will like a boulder trying to drag me to the depths of the sea. The magic in his words shoves at me and fills me with foreboding as the sound of thunder rolls through the cavernous hall.

"No." His storm-gray eyes are full of hate. He is so used to his authority being unchallenged that I'm not sure he really knows what to do with me besides attempting to intimidate me into submission. He thinks I'm an easy target because he broke me once before. He thought he had crushed me, destroyed what Hades and I had together, but he was wrong. I am not broken and I refuse to be afraid anymore. There is too much counting on me, I cannot stand down.

"Stand down!" He shouts in my face, spittle flying as he rages. His voice pitches in volume and he punctuates his words with lashes of lightning. I do not allow myself to flinch away. The lightning slips across my skin like fire, but I push back and I can feel my eyes begin to glow. My whole body shimmers with power, shining out through my eyes and a brief look of panic fills my father's eyes.

"No! I am not a cowering child anymore." The words escape me with brutal force and he stumbles back from the accompanying rush of energy. His lightning flares again and my hand swings forward almost of its own accord. A blinding flash erupts as our powers collide.

"Worthless wretch." He gets right up in my face and shouts, his temper quickly overcoming him. "I am your King and you will bow down to me." A cruel smile twists his mouth. "You have done so before and you will do so again. Do not make me prove it in front of all these people."

I haul back and slap him across his smug, hateful face. My hand connects to his cheek in a burst of light, all my power focused into the movement. Absolute astonishment overruns his expression and he careens to the side, stumbling against the wall to catch himself. "I am not who I used to be, Father. I refuse to be a pawn of Olympus. I may be your daughter, but that does not give you the right to treat me as you have done or to threaten to do so again. You have disgraced yourself by your treatment of others and despite all the power you possess, you are without question the weakest in character of any man I have ever encountered. You deserve neither loyalty nor respect from anyone here." My fury drains away. He is still using the wall to support himself and his features are painted with fear and pain. No one has truly fought back against him before and he has no idea what to do. I stood my ground this time and did not succumb to the force of his power. With Gaia backing me there is nothing he can do. He has lost. I stare hard at him. "I do not recognize your authority over me and you have no power or claim over me anymore. I formally renounce you as my father and I renounce any claim of authority you have over the Underworld. You are no longer our King. Olympus may choose to keep you, but we will no longer endure you as our ruler."

The wild whispers around us are more like a hissing wind than actual words. I prepare myself for retribution, but a hush falls over everyone as Hera moves towards us. She gives me a knowing smile before turning her full attention to her husband. He is red faced and huffing by this point, beyond angry. She glides her hand up his arm and stands next to his side, draping her regality and authority over her shoulders like a cloak.

"Husband, leave her be." I feel Great Mother Gaia ripple below us and see her faint power wrapping around Zeus. Hera's influence is powerful and he struggles against it, but he is weakened and does not have the strength to fight another battle. "I support Persephone's demand for emancipation." Zeus' shoulders heave and his red face contorts, but he does not negate her statement. He roars, dropping to his knees and splaying his hands out to the heavens. The sound vibrates the walls and leaves him breathless. There is an iron in the eyes of the Olympian Queen indicating her decision will not be overturned. Hades, Thanatos and Hermes take their place next to me. Zeus stares at us, furious, and looks back at the crowd that stands behind us in support. To deny us this now would lead us all into war.

"I also have a demand," Hermes pipes up. "I am no longer your mes-senger. I will be performing the duties of Psychopomp as my primary purpose." Hera grips her husband's shoulder firmly and he does not rise to challenge his son. We are free. The thought makes me dizzy.

"One more thing, a question that has yet to be answered." Everyone looks to me as I turn back to my mother. "I know why you and Zeus conspired in the famine, but why did Helios? How did you convince him?"

Mother looks nervous. She glances up towards the Sun and then back to me. "He is your father."

Everyone gapes at her. "What?!" Zeus and I shout the word at the same time.

Resigned, her shoulders droop and she spins the tale. "You are the daughter of Helios, not Zeus. I was already pregnant when Zeus assaulted me, but I thought if there was some outward symbol of his conquest he would leave me alone afterwards. He did and Helios never found out until you were taken."

My head spins at this news. We all stare up at the Sun. Helios is a Titan, one who fought for Olympus during the Titanomache. It is his power that allows me to grow whatever I please while my mother is limited primarily to crops. I have the ancient blood of the Titans and the power of Olympus inside of me. I understand why she never told Zeus or the rest of Olympus, but why did she never tell Helios? Why did she never tell me? He must be the reason she would disappear from Olympus all the time. Maybe she fabricated crop failures as an excuse to go and be with her lover. I would have understood, she never needed to hide him from me even without the knowledge of our connection. A new thought stems the tide of questions. He has known I was his daughter for centuries. He never once spoke to me, never acknowledged me in any way. I suppose there is no reason for me to expect one father to be better than the other, but it still hurts that neither of them wanted any kind of proper fatherly relationship with me.

I shake off the encroaching sorrow. I never needed them. I have all the family I need with Hades. The secrets and lies of Olympus and beyond are no longer my concern. "Thank you for finally telling me, Mother." I cast a firm look at Zeus. "This changes nothing. You will not take out your anger on her."

"Fine." He spits out the word like poison on his tongue. "Get them out of my sight."

My mother flees, fearful despite my command. Hera smiles at me and leaves her husband fuming on the floor. She is every inch a Queen, beautiful and strong. "I declare before all of Olympus that the Underworld is yours to rule, Persephone, alongside Hades. You are your own pantheon now, Gods unto yourselves, but I will always welcome you on Olympus, if you choose to visit."

I hug her, overwhelmed by everything. "May your eternal life be filled with many blessings. You are always welcome in our realm." I bow to her and kiss her on each cheek. The crowd wisely disperses after the announcement, fleeing from the repercussions of their king's anger. Hades slips his hand into mine and we evaporate on the wind, leaving Olympus far behind us.

As Hades and I return triumphant to the Underworld I slip my hand into his. "I almost forgot, a question I once asked you so long ago. What do you see when Elysium shows you paradise?"

He smiles and wraps his arms around my waist. "You. Since the first moment we met you have been my paradise."

A new feeling overwhelms me now, buoyant and miraculous. It is a feeling that was given to me by Hades, in what seems like eons ago. It is a feeling that I have finally given myself. Freedom.

EPILOGUE

HERA

Olympus recovered from the secession of the Underworld, Zeus' formidable fury draining away in the distraction of his next conquest. Persephone and Hades' freedom has, almost surprisingly, lasted until this very day. I ensured that Olympus retracted itself fully from the affairs of their realm and not even the Gods may interfere with the souls of the living once they have passed into the Underworld.

Persephone still returns to the mortal world each spring. The cycle of life and death became stable on Gaia's surface and none of us saw the need nor had the ability to undo something that Gaia had allowed to solidify. Persephone continues her duties by replenishing the earth and caring for the souls, free to live on her own terms.

I have made frequent visits into the depths of their world, something I am ashamed to admit I never did in all the years Hades was there alone. They showed it all to me, including the parts that brought them sadness. Persephone told me of the loss of her nymph, but in Elysium a lustrous white willow tree grows where she was buried, the last fragments of her soul creating a memorial to her existence. Persephone's world flourishes, filled with nymphs who live without fear and dæmons who happily serve their illustrious rulers.

The timid girl who I once rarely saw has blossomed into a Goddess sure of herself and her purpose, blessedly happy in her home and her love. Her visits to Olympus are short and infrequent. The animosity of my husband flares up when he sees her so I don't blame her for avoiding it. Unfortunately, her relationship with her mother was never truly repaired. Demeter is stubborn and erratic; considering their issues and the reprehensible actions taken I never expected them to be close. It has left a pleasant gap for me to fill and though I have my own children, there is a certain joy that fills me to see Persephone so happy.

Hades never stopped desiring a child, but the nature of his power and our previous removal of Dionysus contributed to their inability to conceive. Instead, they did as Prometheus once did when he created humankind. They fashioned a child out of clay and named her Thione. I blessed her myself when she was gifted with life and turned to flesh in her mother's arms. She is a fascinating child, possessing the magic of both her parents and a hand-crafted soul bound in gold thread from the loom of the Moiræ. She is a Goddess, albeit an unconventional one. She has an easy laugh and quiet temperament, but is easily recognizable as their daughter. Thione is beautiful, possessing the sleek, dark hair of her father and the sparkling green eyes of her mother. I watch over Thione's brother, the God of Wine, Dionysus. Persephone never asked me, but I wanted to. Gaia knows with only his father to guide him he will turn out poorly. He has never acknowledged or claimed Persephone as his mother, clinging instead to the mortal who bore him. So much was lost there, but they do not dwell on it and so I try not to either. I focus instead, as Persephone does, on Thione. Demeter has only met her granddaughter once and that occasion was a formality. My sister never grew to love the child, but that is her loss more than Thione's. The little Goddess has only ever known freedom and kindness. She has visited me on Olympus and in the Hesperides, but for the most part she prefers to stay close to home. She has adopted the role of Goddess of Souls and is a formal Guardian of the Underworld.

I am overjoyed that Persephone has the life she always dreamed of. Not all of us are so lucky. I try not to be bitter and mourn the things I have lost and the things I never had. Persephone's happiness mirrors back my own pain sometimes, but I love her and her family and wishing things were different will not make them so. My story does not have so happy a journey as hers.

Still, perhaps one day you will share the stories you have been told and open your mind to look past the versions recorded by history and forge deeper. There is more to us than you might assume; more to all our stories than what the myths and legends say. If you are patient enough to seek out the truth you may find yourself rewarded with a reality you never anticipated. For now, remember this story, of a girl who found herself and a man who found his heart.

CPSIA information can be obtained
at www.ICGtesting.com
Printed in the USA
LVHW032027220419
615089LV00002B/144